I0545497

CHRISTMAS PROMISES

ASPEN GOLD SERIES 21

CHERYL ST. JOHN   BERNADETTE JONES

LIZZIE STARR

Cover by Alexandrite Press

Cover image credit: Canva

Interior image credits: Depositphotos

Interior design by Cat & Doxie Author Services

The Baby Contract

Cheryl St.John

"Best enjoyed with a shrimp cocktail."
- Nick Miller, New Girl

THE BABY
CONTRACT-CHAPTER ONE

*M*eatloaf and mashed potatoes got heavy on the stoneware restaurant platters after several hours. They'd run out of the special early, so Marty Combs, who owned Pearl's Cafe with his wife, Edith, had sent Piper for fresh ground beef. Now she picked up tips and stacked used plates, more than ready for her own supper at home with Grandad.

Clearing tables gave her plenty of time to think, and all she'd thought about for months was having a baby. She imagined herself with a platinum-haired newborn in her arms, a chubby infant on her hip, a toddler whose bumped knees she'd kiss, an adorable cherub growing into a child she'd leave at school on the first day of kindergarten and cry all the way home.

The dream of a family was all she'd ever wanted. There was only one small hang-up. The only man in Piper Newcomb's life was her grandfather, and the last date she'd had was…well a long time ago. To be honest, what she'd focused her planning on in recent weeks was how she was going to get her baby.

"Piper, I hate to ask you this." Mary Beth Willett, the short-ish full-figured server came up beside her. "Darla came home from school with a fever, and I need to get her into Dr. Ewing's before he leaves for the day. Can you stay and fill in for an hour or two? I should be able to come back after her appointment."

Mary Beth was a dark-haired single mom who'd recently divorced a guy who never held a job. She'd barely had any help from him before, but now she was completely on her own. Piper considered it remarkable how cheerful and positive the sweet-faced young woman remained day in and day out.

"Yes, of course. You go take care of Darla and come back if you can. If not, I'll stay." She'd give Grandad a call and tell him to go ahead and eat the pork chops she'd left in the slow cooker. She'd take him a slice of apple pie.

"Thanks. You're the best. I owe you one."

Piper offered an encouraging smile and picked up plates from a booth where a young couple sat with their pig-tailed toddler and a baby in a car seat. "Can I bring you dessert?"

"Three slices of the apple pie to go, please," the young father answered.

She brought them a to-go bag and placed their ticket on the table. After settling the bill, he tugged a tiny pink jacket onto the little girl while the mom put a hat on the baby and covered him with a lightweight blanket. The husband held his wife's coat so she could slide her arms into the sleeves. It was still October, but by late afternoon, the air had a bite.

Piper stood holding the cash while they exited the café. Her chest felt as though there was a weight on it. She took a deep breath to relieve the uncomfortable sensation, but it didn't help. She'd made up her mind, and now she had to make her family happen.

She rang up the transaction, pocketing the tip, and bussed another couple of tables. There were only a few diners at the moment. Maybe she could take fifteen and grab a bite.

Kipp Hudson spotted an empty parking space on the street half a block from Pearl's, parked his truck and headed to the café. He'd probably missed Piper, though he wasn't sure about her schedule this week.

They'd hung out in high school, but had moved on to different colleges and other friends. Last summer, they'd reconnected during a volunteer search for a resident missing from the senior center, and since then had become good friends again. Occasionally they went to the Wild Card with a group or simply met up at someone's home. She was easy to talk to—and easy on the eyes.

It was all about friendship for her, so he'd been careful not to reveal his changed feelings. Maybe one day she'd see him differently, but for now, he wasn't spoiling what they had. A brisk wind caught the collar of his denim jacket and tousled his shoulder-length hair as he reached the door.

The diner was warm inside and smelled like beef and

gravy. His stomach rumbled. There were only a couple of customers, so he slid into his favorite booth.

Piper came from the kitchen, wearing her usual jeans and a long-sleeved blue pullover, her red apron wrinkled. She spotted him and her face lit up.

"You're working late," he said.

"Yeah. Filling in for Mary Beth for a couple of hours." She took her pad and pencil from her pocket and raised an eyebrow. "The meatloaf dinner, a side salad with balsamic vinegar, basket of bread and a glass of milk."

"You've got it."

"I'm going to grab myself a plate and eat with you. I'm starving."

"Glad for the company."

Ten minutes later, she placed both of their meals on the Formica tabletop and sat across from him.

He'd dated often enough to know most women weren't comfortable eating a real meal in front of a guy, and he appreciated Piper's lack of vanity around him. He pushed his breadbasket toward her and she buttered a slice for herself.

"Were you busy today?" he asked.

"Packed. Marty ran out of meatloaf and had to make more. How about you? Elk season or are people moose hunting or something?"

"Elk and moose are over in September. It's archery season for whitetail right now. I sold arrows all day. Several bows."

She raised an eyebrow. "If I was allowed to feed them, I might save a few."

"It's illegal to feed them for a good reason." He'd told her this more than once. "More than deer are drawn to the food, and besides that, concentrating deer in one place draws mountain lions to populated areas. Then Fish and Game has to come rehome or kill the lions."

She made a small swoop with her fork. "The circle of life and all that."

"When you draw the deer away from their feeding grounds, their habitat is in danger of being developed. Then where will they go?"

"You make it sound so logical."

He finished his meal and drank his milk. "It is logical."

Piper laid her fork on her plate and pushed it to the side. She met his eyes.

They had this discussion about once a week. She loved animals. He understood that. But a lot of money generated through hunting was used for conservation, and controlling healthy wildlife populations meant preserving their natural homes.

"I've made an important decision," she said.

"That we agree to disagree?"

"No. Well, sure, okay." She held his gaze. "I want to have a baby."

Kipp's thought process did a three-sixty, and his brain pedaled to catch up. "What?"

"I want a family. I've always wanted a family. So, I'm going to have a baby. Of my own."

He didn't know of anyone she'd been involved with. The news sucked air from his chest.

"I see the shock on your face," she said.

"Sorry. I'm still taking in your news. Are you seeing someone? Are...are you pregnant?"

"No, I'm not seeing anyone." She waved away that idea. "And no, I'm not pregnant. But I will be."

"Okay." He still wasn't sure what she was getting at. "You want to have a baby."

"I do. I visited a doctor in Denver. I'm healthy and fertile. I've started taking prenatal vitamins. All I need to do is monitor ovulation for the right time to get pregnant."

This seemed too personal of a conversation for friends, but maybe not. All of his friends were guys, so maybe this was what chicks talked about. "Well." He sure didn't want to say the wrong thing. "So, with a donor? Have you thought his through?"

"I've been thinking about it for a while. The doctor showed me a couple of sites online, and I looked. A lot of donors are graduate students—if they're telling the truth. Who knows? They're mostly between eighteen and thirty-nine. You can choose hair color, eye color, ethnicity, all that. They've been tested for health issues."

He was listening, but he wasn't comfortable with her plan. "Are there photos?"

"Some have pics, but not all. The thing is there are no tests for schizophrenia or criminal tendencies. I thought about it for weeks after the visit. I asked myself how can I know if this person is kind or generous or has a good heart? How much of that is genetic and how much is learned? The unknowns bugged me. Then I found a documentary about adults who have discovered they have fifty brothers and sisters, all from one sperm donor. One donor had fathered hundreds of babies."

Kipp leaned forward. "What?"

"Yeah, you'd have no way to know."

He tried to take it all in and wasn't sure what she

wanted him to say. "I guess not knowing the person would leave a lot to wonder about."

She nodded. "Too much for my comfort. Especially if there's a chance my child would discover dozens of siblings later in life. That's just weird. So, I want the donor to be someone I know."

He squirmed on the padded seat. Well, that was definitely another option, but he didn't know if he liked it any better. "Do you have someone in mind?"

Her intent blue gaze bored into his, and he reminded himself to breathe. "You," she said. "I'd like for it to be you."

Kipp's head buzzed for a full minute. Half a dozen images made his heart skip. He forced himself to hold her gaze. "But we're not...we're *friends*, Piper. Aren't we? Friends don't do—*that*."

"No, not like that. Yes, of course we're friends. It would be a procedure at the clinic."

The door opened and a group of six entered the café.

"I'll be right back." She got up as though they'd been chatting about the weather and handed the newcomers menus.

Had he heard what he thought he'd heard?

Piper came back to load up their dishes. "All I need is for you to donate." She tilted her head. "You know."

He did look away this time. Nothing about her wild suggestion fed into his secret longing. This wasn't exactly an ask to borrow a sweater or his truck. This was a favor that would last a lifetime. "You sprung this on me, and my head's spinning. I'm going to need time to think."

"Sure," she said. "Okay."

He handed her cash for his meal and picked up his jacket.

"I'll call you," she said after him.

He nodded and left to get some air and clear his head. Sitting in his truck, he started the engine, but didn't move out of the space. His friend had just asked him to father a child for her. Not the usual way. By means of a cup and a magazine. An impersonal contribution for the procreation of a person with his DNA, maybe with his eyes and hair and features…all very *personal* characteristics—what in blazes was she thinking?

Maybe she hadn't gone about asking him the best way. Piper chastised herself that night and all the next day. Maybe she should have presented her plan in a more private place, but she'd made up her mind, and that had been the first opportunity she'd had to bring it up. Of course, he needed time to think about it.

They were meeting friends at the VFW for a fish fry that evening, and she'd have a chance to talk to him again. Grandad and his friends had caught plenty of fresh trout for the event. She prepared an enormous container of coleslaw, knowing it always went fast, and drove to the VFW.

Dusty and Kendra Cavanaugh were there with their boy, along with Dusty's younger brother Crosby, their mom Liz and her friends. "Hey, Piper!" Liz called.

"Hey, Ms. Cavanaugh. Hello, Ian. You've grown a foot since I saw you last."

"I'm gonna be tall like my dad," he announced proudly.

Stephanie, one of Liz's twin daughters showed up and slid into the booth. "Hey, Piper. You're more than welcome to join us."

"Okay, thanks. I'm meeting friends, but I'll chat for a bit now." She'd always admired Liz, a loving mother and grandmother to a big family. Four sons and two adopted daughters, plus several grandchildren. Piper may never have that many children, but she was going to make her own family.

Fifteen minutes later, she headed to the kitchen. She helped Giorgio, the unofficial but always present cook at the VFW, by stirring a roaster full of au gratin potatoes. "Are you ready to serve?"

"Yep. Fish is ready."

She got out a stack of sturdy disposable plates and dished up servings. Loydelle Hendershot, Spencer's postmaster bustled about in a white apron, tossing an enormous bowl of salad and using tongs to place servings on the plates.

Another helper joined them, so Piper took a plate for herself and went out into the other room. Kipp was seated with Derek Wick, one of the deputies, Jenna, who worked at the lodge as a waitress, Bethel Tanner, who supervised childcare, also at the lodge, and Jordyn Schrader and Marissa Young who owned and ran Like New Reruns at the mall.

"Hey, Piper." Jordyn waved her over, and Derek pulled out a chair. She set down her supper and seated herself. Crosby Cavanaugh joined them, juggling five plastic cups of beer. He passed her one. Kipp took another.

"After we eat, does anyone want to check out The Altitude?" Marissa asked. "It's been open for a week or so, and I've been wanting to go. They have live music on the weekends."

"I'm game," Bethel answered.

"Do you want to go?" Kipp asked her.

"Might be fun," she answered. "But can we talk first?"

He nodded. "Sure."

"Let's stay warm in my truck." Kipp's suggestion would give them privacy. They ate, washed up and headed out.

Once inside, he pressed the starter and the engine idled.

"So, I guess you were pretty surprised the other day," she said.

"That's fair to say."

"I know," she said. "There was no way to ask except to come out with it."

"And you're still serious about this?" he asked.

"I've decided, and I'm going to make it happen."

He'd done nothing but think about her proposal and think of what to say and how to ask the things she needed to think about. "I have a lot of questions."

"Okay," she said.

"I feel like you haven't really thought this all the way through."

"Because I'd be a single mom? I've thought about that. Right now, I live with my grandfather. The house will always be mine. I have a home."

"But this is a child, Piper. For life."

"I know that. That's what I want."

"You're young. You're pretty. You have a lot of time and don't have to rush into something. You can wait for someone nice." *Well, hell no.* As soon as he said the words, he got a sick feeling in his gut and wanted to take them back. That wasn't what he wanted. He didn't want her waiting for someone else.

"Don't you think I'd do that if I thought there was the tiniest possibility it could work out?" she asked. "I'm not dreaming of a perfect fairy tale guy because I know there isn't one. If I married for the wrong reason, life would only get ugly later when things went bad."

He looked at her. "You're right. I'm sorry I said that."

She looked away and he studied her profile.

"Piper, if I did what you're asking, I'd be a parent too."

She didn't return her gaze to him. "I wouldn't ask any more of you."

He looked out at the vintage streetlamps lighting the paths in Brook Park. The trees were void of leaves, and the moon barely outlined the gazebo. "Well, that's a problem for me. You would have my kid, a son or a daughter, and I'd have no part of his—or her—life. I don't think that's the way I want to have a baby. I'd be a biological father, and I'd want to be a dad. My parents would be his grandparents. I have a whole family he'd be related to. Did you think about that?"

She looked out the windshield for several minutes. She hadn't worn her hair in its usual ponytail tonight, and the sleek blond tresses fell over her shoulder in waves. "I guess I didn't consider it like that," she admitted with a sigh.

"I get it. Wanting a baby is perfectly normal. But maybe you're looking at the baby with tunnel vision, seeing only that little bundle you want and not thinking about the other people involved."

"I told you I looked into selecting a donor. It's expensive, but it's not the cost that bothered me as much as not knowing the person. It seems more like a genetic crap shoot."

He thrummed his fingers against the steering wheel. "I've been thinking about it too. It is kind of a crap shoot, but so is every baby more or less. You can't be that specific about character traits."

She tilted her head in acknowledgement.

"I'm not discouraging you," he said.

"Are you saying no?"

He paused to form words. "I'm saying I need to think and make a decision based on what's best for everyone, me included."

"Okay." She smoothed her palms over her denim-clad knees. "I appreciate that."

He put the truck in gear and drove east on Highway 34. The Altitude had been constructed in proximity to the Grand Vista hotel. The club was easy to find off the highway, and he dropped her off at the door, parked and joined her. She already had money out to pay her own cover charge, so he paid his and guided her through the crowd with a hand on her lower back. The interior was dark, with laser lights flashing across the ceiling and loud pulsating music.

She turned and grinned. "It's definitely not the Wild Card," she shouted near his ear.

He shook his head and pulled out his phone to text Crosby. "They're over there," he said a minute later and located their friends at one of the waist-high pedestal tables. There were a few actual tables and chairs lining the walls, but for the most part, the only seats were at the bar.

Patrons who weren't dancing stood around the small pedestals.

"Where's Crosby?" he called. "He just answered my text."

While sipping her fruit-laden drink through a straw, Jordyn pointed to the crowd on the dancefloor. "Stella is here."

Stella Novak was a traveling nurse who had taken a fellowship at Edna Burnham Hospital ER.

"Who's going to dance with me?" Piper called over the music.

Derek stepped around Marissa to join her. "I'm ready."

Kipp ordered drinks. Once in a while he spotted Piper through the crowd.

Marissa tapped his arm. "You ready to try this?"

Piper and Marissa had showed him the simple steps for club dancing. The point was to not take up much room on the crowded floor. Nothing like two-stepping in a country bar, but he was willing. "I'm game."

He took her hand, and they found a space among the throng of dancers.

Marissa offered her most impressed expression. "You've got it, Kipp."

"Thanks. I haven't recognized a song yet."

"You're not an Iggy Azalea fan?" She laughed.

He glanced at the girl beside Marissa wearing faded jeans with suspenders over a bra.

"No, I am. Now." Kipp looked back at Marissa. "Big fan."

Derek and Piper showed up to switch partners for the next song, and after a couple more, Kipp danced with Stella.

"I'm ready to go whenever you are," Piper told him an hour later. "It was a long day."

"I'm ready." Somehow, they located their jackets.

The fresh cool air felt good on his face.

"Are you good to drive?" she asked.

"Yeah, I only had two beers."

She walked beside him through the lot. "That was fun. I guess I'd better get all my partying done before I'm a mom."

He used his key fob to locate the pickup in the dark. He unlocked it and they got in. "Would you miss doing that on Friday or Saturday nights?"

"I don't think so. I'll be able to take the baby to the VFW and get in a couple dances there." She buckled her seatbelt and laid her head against the headrest. "I'll be happy to stay home rocking him and reading him bedtime stories."

Kipp had been around his brother's kids. They barfed and got colds and went to the doctor and needed vaporizers in their rooms. There were bills to pay and groceries to buy and years of responsibilities. He didn't want to come across as a wet blanket, but there was more to the reality of parenthood than bedtime stories.

He pulled up in front of her house. "Your Grandad left a light on for you."

"He's done that since I went to football games with friends in high school." She looked toward the light behind the living room curtains.

"I remember," he said.

She probably considered the old man's mortality, thought about what her life would be like without him.

She doted on the guy. "'Night, Piper. We'll talk more after I've had time to think."

She got out and stood with one hand still holding the door handle. "I didn't bring this up, because it's not a big deal, and it's personal, but I had a bit of a health scare."

"Are you all right?"

"I'm perfectly fine. I had a little outpatient surgery on a benign cyst, but not knowing I was okay for a couple weeks convinced me of what I wanted. I'm not changing my mind."

He nodded. "Thanks for telling me."

She closed the door and a minute later let herself into the house. The porch light turned off.

He didn't want to change her mind. He just didn't know if he wanted to be a part of her plan the way she figured it. He'd always seen himself with someone he loved—someone who loved him—a relationship before a family. As of now, she was the only one he cared about in that way, and her plan didn't sound like the one he'd imagined. This uneasy feeling in his gut didn't give him peace about agreeing just yet. He had a lot more thinking to do.

CHAPTER TWO

*K*ipp had asked his mom to meet him at Maria's where they occasionally met for lunch. She managed a card and gift shop at Valley View Mall, but had assured him she was taking a long lunch. He'd asked his employee, Eddie, to handle his store while he was gone. He'd fastened up his nearly shoulder-length hair and left his camo cap in the truck.

Leslie Ann Hudson slid onto the bench seat where a marguerita was already waiting for her. "Are you trying to get me fired today?"

"You're the manager, Mom."

She grinned. "You're not joining me?"

"No one cares if you drop a card or a candle. I do have to handle ammunition and demonstrate compound bows."

With a laugh, she rolled her eyes. "Okay."

They ordered and Kipp took a deep breath. "I need to talk to you."

"Uh oh. Sounds serious."

"I want to get your thoughts on a decision I need to make."

"Is this about the business?"

"No. It's about myself and Piper."

She raised her eyebrows. Her expression showed interest and a hint of pleasure. "Is there finally something interesting going on between you two?"

"It's interesting, but not like you think. We're still good friends, but she's asked me to do something." He explained the conversations with Piper. "I'm looking at this long-term."

"Of course, you are. I really like that girl, but this is crazy," his mom said. She leaned toward him. "It takes a lot of nerve to ask you to be a sperm donor out of the blue."

"It's not out of the blue for her. She's been thinking about it for a long time."

"I watch tv and read books. People find donors anonymously all the time."

He nodded. "Have you read about the adults born from donors who are learning they have fifty or a hundred siblings they didn't know about?"

"What?"

He went on to explain Piper's list of concerns about not knowing the donor personally.

"Is that for real?"

"I looked it up and a young woman in New Jersey found out after DNA testing that she had fifty siblings. Her parents went to a cryo bank and picked a donor based on genetic qualities. Now she's afraid to date because she might find a brother she didn't know about.

Another fertility clinic in England used the same donor for twenty years."

Leslie Ann shook her head in disbelief as the information sunk in. "I sympathize, Kipp. I really do, and knowing about those incidents, it makes more sense that she'd want the person to be someone she knows. But you would be the child's parent for life. She couldn't expect you to sit back and watch from a distance while your child grows up without you. What about us? Your dad and I would be grandparents. Evelyn and Lillian would be his or her cousins."

"I know."

Their food arrived and Leslie Ann unfolded her napkin and picked up her fork. She poked her chicken enchilada distractedly. "Piper doesn't have parents, does she?"

He shook his head. "I know that's a primary reason why she wants a family. Since she was a kid, she's never had anyone except her grandfather."

"I sympathize," she said. "But expecting you to remain out of the picture isn't realistic. That's not who you are, is it?"

"No," he assured her.

"She might be able to take a few weeks off—maybe without pay—but she'd have to go back to work to support them. Who will care for the baby?"

"I didn't think to ask her that," he admitted.

"Does she have medical insurance?"

"I can only assume. I don't really know."

"If your name was on the birth certificate, you could add him to your insurance," she told Kipp. "Would she want you named as the father?"

"I don't know, but it might be part of the bargain."

"*Bargain*," she repeated scornfully. "Are you seriously considering this?"

"I'm taking her request seriously," he told his mom. "I don't want to dismiss it without really thinking it through, because I believe she deserves to be taken seriously."

Leslie Ann took a couple bites. "In order to be serious, an agreement would need to be legal. No room for questions or battles later on." She set down her fork and spread her hands in a gesture of dismay. "I can't believe I'm talking about this as though it might happen."

"I agree, Mom. I'd be the baby's father. You'd be his grandmother."

Her eyes were shiny with tears. "I'd love nothing more than a little one with your curly hair. But Kipp, you need assurance about the future."

"A custody arrangement is what I'm thinking," he said. "The child lives with her, but I'd have him for weekends, vacations, and share holidays."

Leslie Ann's expression saddened. "It sounds like a divorce without ever having a marriage. Or love."

He was hungry so he ate half of his meal, still thinking. He pushed the plate aside. "Well, about the love part..."

Her chin lifted. "What?"

"I think I'm in love with her. I probably was years ago, but we had our separate plans for college, and the future seemed a million years away. Back then there was no urgency to be tied to another person—not for either of us. But we've spent a lot of time together since last summer, and I feel differently. About everything. The future is now. Only she doesn't look at me like that."

"She must like you a lot to ask you to father a baby for her."

"I don't doubt she likes me." He drew a line down the condensation on his water glass. "I want someone who loves me."

She covered his hand with hers. "That's exactly what you deserve. I want what's best for you."

The ache of uncertainty in his chest was still there. "I don't want her to ask someone else."

There. A final admission of the certainty he'd been holding back, afraid to voice, afraid to recognize as truth.

"Then get a lawyer," she said. "If she wants it to be you badly enough, she'll agree to your terms."

He glanced away, hating thinking about the legalities, but he had to protect everyone involved. Which was the worst choice? Making something that should be created out of love into a legal bargain? Or having her find someone else to give her the baby she wanted?

"I need someone to talk to," Piper told her friend. It was her day off, and she'd asked Kendra to meet her at Seventh Star for lunch. "I need a little perspective from another viewpoint."

She'd been friends with Kendra Cavanaugh since the dancer had moved to Spencer. When they first met, Kendra had been alone, taking a break from her hectic career and living in the cabin she'd inherited from her aunt. Since then, Kendra had married her high-school sweetheart, Dusty, and become part of their big family and a mom to Dusty's son.

"Well, sure," Kendra told her. "I'll help however I can."

"You might think I'm foolish or crazy," Piper said.

"Everyone is foolish or crazy once in a while," her friend said with a smile.

Piper explained what she'd asked Kipp to do.

Kendra's eyes opened wide and she blinked. "It's not crazy...*exactly*. But it *is* surprising. "What did Kipp say?"

"He's thinking about it. His first thoughts were that he'd be the baby's father, and he couldn't neglect that responsibility. I respect him for that...and, I guess, knowing him like I do I should have known he'd feel that way. He told me I have tunnel vision."

"Do you?"

She shrugged. "I did. I'm seeing the bigger picture now." She paused while the server set glasses of iced tea in front of them. "It's just that there's no one I want to marry, and marrying someone for that reason alone would be wrong and end badly. My coworker Mary Beth was miserable in her marriage, and now the deadbeat she divorced is simply gone from the picture. I'm not setting up myself or my kid for something like that."

The other young woman nodded. "I'm sure no one ever thinks it will end like that. People in love always think the euphoria will last."

"I'll make sure it doesn't happen. And I know I can do this by myself."

Kendra took a sip from her glass. "Dusty was a single dad before we were married, but he had Liz and his sisters helping him." She held up a palm. "I'm not discouraging you. Not at all. I'm just pointing out that you'll need support. What about Kipp's family? I don't know the Hudsons well, but I know they're good people. Surely, they'll have something to say about this."

Piper hid her face in her hands for a long minute. Finally, she lifted her head and took a deep breath. "Yes. That's the thing, I guess. I've asked a guy with a family, so I'd better expect they're going to be a part of this. If Kipp says yes, anyway."

"You want him to."

He was a good man with admirable qualities. Piper nodded. "I really do."

The server took their orders for salads, and they talked until she placed them on the table. The two of them ate in silence for a few minutes.

"I only know that you live with grandfather," Kendra brought up. "But you've never said anything about your parents."

"I never knew my father," Piper told her. "He was my grandparent's only child. His name was Kelly, and he died in Desert Storm. We have photos of him, and Grandad tells me stories about him as a kid. He was handsome. I got my blond hair from him."

She took a few bites before speaking again. "Mom and I lived with my grandparents after he died and I was born. My grandma was alive then. My mom worked for a lawyer. I remember her, but I was four when she went on a skiing trip with friends. They said she lost control on a slope and hit a tree. She died instantly. Just a freak accident."

"I'm so sorry," Kendra said. "You were only a little bitty thing. Where were her parents?"

"They've lived in France for years. I think he was a

professor of something. I never met them. My father's parents raised me, so I never knew anything different, and they gave me all the love a kid ever needed. They came to school activities and took me to the fair and gave me the best life they knew how. But without other family, I always felt lonesome. Then about ten years ago my grandmother died. That was really hard for us both. Now it's just me and Grandad." She smiled. "He's the best."

A few minutes later Kendra said, "Having kids is a normal desire for plenty of people."

"You and Dusty have Ian," Piper said. "Do you want another child?"

Kendra had finished her salad and slid her plate aside. "We've talked about it. We have a few years before we have to decide. Right now, we're content. Dusty's older brother Joe and his wife Laurel have qualified for a foster child. That might be something to think about too. You know Dusty has two adopted sisters," she said. "Families come in all shapes and sizes."

Piper smiled. "I'm really happy for you and Dusty. I'm not counting on having something as amazing as what you two have. If it's only me and a child, I'll take that much and be happy."

Kendra reached to gently squeeze her hand. "Don't count anything out. Really, though. Love is pretty great."

"Oh, I'm not saying it's impossible. I'm only declaring I won't wait for something that might never happen. It was good for me to be able to talk about it. I know what I want, but I can see there are more things to think about and plan for. This has helped." She gave the other young woman a grateful smile. "You're a good friend."

"Thanks, Piper. When I got to Spencer, you were the

first person to reach out to me. You invited me to a fish fry, remember?"

Piper grinned. "I do."

"So anyway," Kendra said. "I don't know Kipp, except through you, and it would be good to get better acquainted. Will the two of you come for dinner one night?"

"That sounds really nice. I'll ask him."

"Good." Kendra picked up her bag. "We'll set a date. Meanwhile, keep me in the loop, will you?"

They hugged in the parking lot and Piper started her car and turned on the heat. The wind had picked up. She knew a lot of people in Spencer and could call many of them her friends, but there was something special about a friend she could tell an important secret.

She'd been thinking about clearing out the back bedroom next to hers, and this was a good day to get started. Her grandmother had used the area for a sewing room, but since she'd been gone, the space had collected boxes and extra clothing. There was a row of high windows that looked out over the backyard and a closet sufficient for a child. It would make a perfect nursery.

Piper had a plan—and nothing was getting in her way.

CHAPTER THREE

ipp hadn't liked doing it, but it had been necessary to find an attorney willing to take on their atypical agreement. He didn't want anyone in Spencer knowing their business, so he'd searched out a lawyer in Glen Haven. Bryce Keenan had to research to find and edit forms to meet their purpose.

"'There's a precedence for sperm donors that relieves them of financial and parental responsibility, but nothing that *assumes* those same obligations. Your situation is highly unique. You're not married, and you don't already have a child together. Plus, you want joint custody, so we have to build this contract from scratch,'" the lawyer had told him when he'd returned Kipp's call. After he'd received a retainer, they'd worked via email and phone calls to create first drafts.

There were mandatory financial disclosures, which seemed straightforward, but the parenting plans boggled his already burdened mind. Kipp read and reread the forms and then googled information, and the following week eventually had a folder to present to Piper.

She arrived on the scheduled evening. His English retriever Archie greeted her with a wagging tail, seemingly sure she'd be glad to see him, and she knelt to rub his ears and scratch his neck. Kipp took her coat and offered her something to drink. Archie padded along behind them and plopped on the hardwood floor.

"Archie, show Piper your skunk." Kipp gestured to the doorway. He changed his voice to sound excited when he asked, "Where's your skunk?"

The dog got up and dashed into the other room.

Piper sat at his small kitchen table while Kipp made her a mug of hot chocolate.

"It's the instant stuff," he apologized.

"It's fine," she said. "The wind is cold tonight so anything hot will be great." A manilla folder was the only thing on the surface. "Is that it?"

He nodded, nervous about showing her the paperwork. The red tape seemed overwhelming, but if his requirements put her off, he'd know he'd done the right thing.

Archie returned, his new prized toy dangling from his jaws.

"Good boy," Kipp told him. "Show Piper."

She gingerly took hold of the stuffed animal and Archie released and bit it repeatedly so the squeaker made noise, but didn't let loose. "That's a nice skunk you've got there." She stroked the dog's fur. "He sure is smart."

"He is," Kipp agreed. "Good boy, Archie. Go lay down."

The dog plopped on the floor a few feet away and laid his snout on the toy.

Kipp slid the folder in front of her. "This was new territory for the attorney I found, but he researched and consulted. I hope this is a plan we can work with. This is the first draft. We can still make adjustments, but I do have requirements."

She opened the folder to see what looked like a very official document and read the first page, explaining who the parenting partners were. Kipp's financial statement followed. She shot her gaze to his where he'd seated himself across from her. She'd been cold minutes ago, but her skin grew uncomfortably warm. "This is so...*personal.*"

His expression was earnest, his bright hazel eyes kind. She liked the way his hair fell in waves around his face, one side tucked behind his ear. "Well, this is a personal agreement."

He was remarkable. She'd always known that, always cared for him. She would never have considered asking him to do this if she didn't know him so well. In a flash of uncertainty, the possibility that this could be so much more pierced her confidence. She trusted him. She treasured everything about him, not only his character, but physical traits...his woodsy scent, the way his hair fell in waves. She immediately buried the thoughts deep. She wasn't counting on him ever having romantic feelings for her. "It feels wrong to look at your financial statements."

He grinned, that familiar handsome curve of lips creasing his cheeks. "If you're going to carry my baby inside you for nine months, I think you can look at my accounts and holdings."

Grasping that bare truth, she swallowed and read the pages. His outdoor goods building on Timberline Drive was more than half paid for. Hudson Outdoor Gear turned a nice profit, according to his tax statements. Besides this home, he owned a residential property west of the park that generated monthly income. He had insurance documentation, a truck title, bank accounts. "It's come to my attention that people underestimate you, Kipp Hudson."

"What do you mean?"

"You're all laid back and dress like the rest of us, wear your hair long and come off as a country boy with your dog and your pickup, but you're a businessman." She softened the statement with a smile. "You're a surprising man."

He shook his head and his eyes twinkled.

Experiencing a wave of panic, she sobered. "In fact… you're far more prepared to be a parent than I am."

Kipp covered her hand, his long warm fingers closing over hers. "You have the desire, Piper. You want a baby more than you want anything else. Isn't that right?"

She nodded and looked at him through a sheen of tears. "I do."

"You told me the house is yours."

"Grandad already gave it to me. Pearl's is my second job. I have a bachelors in accounting. I'm the treasurer for a tax-exempt company, and I do taxes. I have money in savings."

"You're probably making more with those jobs. How come you're waitressing?"

"I like working at Pearl's. I like people. I tried an office job for a realty company, but being stuck at a desk every day and following company regulations wasn't what I'd imagined. Once I secured a good account, I became self-employed. I stay at Pearl's because I like it. And the tips are okay."

"Well, you're a surprise, too. How come I didn't know that? I pay to have my taxes done. Do you take on business accounts?"

"I file for a couple of small businesses. I keep up to date."

He released her hand and moved papers so she could look at the parenting plan. "This is the section we might have to work out."

Piper removed the paper clip from at least eight pages and read the headings. *Parental Responsibility Concerning Parent and Co-Parent. Full Joint Parenting Plan.* Then *Allocation of Parenting Responsibilities and Decision-making.* The pages went on and on, listing education, medical and dental, religion, extracurricular, weekday and weekend schedules, transportation and drop off/pick up arrangements, a summer schedule when school is out, agreements for holidays and special occasions...even visitation for his parents.

Piper's heart fluttered. Christmas morning. Thanksgiving. Easter Sunday. Mother's Day, Father's Day. His or her birthday. They'd have to decide which of them had the child for every occasion. These decisions were overwhelming, especially when there was no child yet. This was evolving into a more complicated bargain than she'd ever imagined.

She read, "'Travel and vacation plans.' Does your family travel together?"

She didn't know much about what families did collectively, except by overhearing people's plans in the diner.

"We go camping. Ronnie and Delaney have taken the girls since they were babies."

"One of you has a boat, right?"

"It's my dad's. We all use it. The girls have had swimming lessons since they were babies and both wear life jackets."

"Did you cover swimming lessons in the education and activities section? I don't remember seeing it."

"Are you being sarcastic?"

"No. It's just...it's very thorough." She took of sip of her hot cocoa, which was barely warm now. "Maybe you're right about me having tunnel vision." She pointed to a page. "We even have to decide who claims this hypothetical child on their tax deductions."

She laid down the papers and, elbows on the table, supported her head on her hands.

Kipp pushed the hair from her face and tipped up her chin with a knuckle. "We're the best of friends, right?"

She willed her heart to be calm when he was this close and she was looking into his eyes. "Yes."

"We'll either figure it out or we won't. We won't let this discussion come between us or ruin our friendship. I won't let it."

Yes, this was a friendship. She took a deep breath and straightened, her fingers laced in front of her.

He dropped his hand to the tabletop.

"Okay." The holidays were probably the most troubling thought. She wanted her own child, so she'd have family on all the special days families spent together. Sharing a child wasn't her idea of the cheerful Christmases she'd imagined.

"You need time to think." He straightened the pages

and closed the folder. "Take these home and look over them. Come up with suggestions. Did you have supper?"

She nodded.

"Want to watch tv for a while? A movie maybe?"

She didn't want to think right now, so that sounded like a good idea. "Sure."

"Want a beer or anything?"

"No, I'm good." She stood while he grabbed a bottle from the refrigerator, and then he gestured her ahead of him into the cozy room at the back of the house. He'd refinished shelves around the fireplace and filled them with sports memorabilia among the books. The first time she'd seen the taxidermy deer head above the fireplace, she'd made him drape a sheet over it. She was used to it now, but still avoided looking right at its face. It was beautifully mounted at a head-and-shoulder side angle, as though the creature was looking toward the window. Her appreciation level was still low.

"You can control the remote." Was his offering meant to appease her?

"I've been watching *Bones* from the beginning," she said. "Can you watch a couple of those?"

"The forensic anthropologist lady and the special agent," he replied. "Sure."

"Have you watched it?"

"A couple episodes, but I liked the books better."

She looked at him. "Seriously?"

He grimaced. "What? You didn't think I could read? I graduated college."

"Of course, I knew you could read. I just never pictured you reading that type of book."

"Guess you figured me for a Batman comic guy." He

grinned. "Kathy Reichs is a crime writer who has the same job as her character. Was a professor somewhere south, North Carolina maybe. The books go into a lot more detail than the show."

Piper pulled up the app on his tv and found the next episode she wanted to watch. She took off her shoes and curled her legs under her. They'd sat this way many times, sometimes with the company of friends, sometimes only the two of them. Their relationship had always been easy.

Whatever came of this new development, she didn't want anything to happen to the ease between them. She was realizing more and more how far-reaching and complicated her idea had been.

Kipp chuckled at something on the show and sipped his beer. She glanced over, noting his long legs crossed and feet propped on the coffee table. If she agreed with his terms—if they could agree together and this happened, he would be the father of her child. Her original idea hadn't included a present father, not one who cared about the child's education and medical care. Not one who would take a son or daughter boating and fishing. Attend Christmas programs and sports events.

What a fortunate child she would have if that actually happened.

And as parents, their lives would be irrevocably entwined.

Parents.

He had thick healthy-looking chestnut hair, nicely shaped brows and a barely-there beard and mustache, and nice full lips that often slid into a smile. She allowed her attention to linger on those lips a minute too long. His corded forearms were lean, but muscled, and there didn't appear to be an extra pound on him anywhere, even with his penchant for mashed potatoes and gravy with his meatloaf, his love of cheeseburgers and root beer floats. If this plan happened, her child would have excellent genes.

In the background, Archie's toy squeaked incessantly. Kipp must have been used to the noise, because he seemed to pay no attention.

"What about the future, Kipp?"

He turned his gaze on her. "What do you mean?"

"I mean…" Thinking this made her heart hurt unexplainably. "What if you fall in love and want to get married, but your fiancé doesn't want our kid around?"

"That's harsh."

"Life is harsh. Unexpected things happen. What if in ten years I find someone I want to marry?"

His expression flickered, but he waited.

"How will that change things?" she asked. "You might not like him or think he's not a good influence."

"If you love him and trust him, then I doubt he'd be a bad influence. Unless you have a brain injury that changes your ability to make decisions."

She paused the show. "Crap, it might happen. Then what?"

"People don't plan their lives expecting something bad to happen."

"Sure, they do. They buy insurance."

"It's not the same thing. There's always a chance someone will have a disease or die, but that doesn't stop people from having kids."

"But we need a provision," she told him. "To cover what might change if one of us marries. Or if we both do. What would happen if one of us dies."

"The last is a will. But yes. Okay."

"I don't want him going to foster care because we didn't have a plan."

"That won't happen."

Somewhat assured, she nodded. "Okay." She resumed the show and a minute later paused it again. "Also, if while I'm pregnant I'm hit by a truck and am in a coma with no chance of regaining consciousness, I'd want you to make sure they keep me on life support until the baby is born."

Kipp's eyes widened. "Good grief!" He set down his beer on the low table and scooted closer to lay a hand on her knee. The warmth seeped through her jeans. "You're imagining some dark stuff."

"I saw it happen on a show, and the woman's husband and parents disagreed and fought over keeping her alive for the baby. I'd want my baby to be safe."

"That calls for a living will or an advance directive I think."

"What if you got married and then died? I wouldn't want your wife to share custody. She might fight me if she loves our kid."

"Bryce Keenan can help us with every imaginable outcome, so you feel better about every possibility—no matter how gruesome."

"Sorry."

He put his arm around her and hugged her shoulders against his chest. "Don't be sorry. If it's important to you, then we'll address it."

It felt really good to lay her head on his shoulder, feel his warmth and the touch of his hair against her cheek. He smelled great. Would their child have wavy brown hair and intense hazel eyes? Or be blond haired and blue eyed?

She hadn't studied genetics since high school. All she knew was that Kipp would be an awesome dad, something she'd never even considered in her plan.

She'd certainly never considered sharing this would-be child. Not with a sperm donor, though it was becoming more and more difficult to consider him that. Definitely not sharing the baby with grandparents or cousins. Her son or daughter would have more family than she did.

While the thought made her feel a little sick, she did want that for her child. She didn't want a lonely only child without grandparents or extended family. Feeling possessive was entirely selfish, she scolded herself.

She had a choice to make. An unknown donor whose contribution might bring unknown concerns in the future or this man she knew well who had pages of requirements and a family that would demand time with her baby.

How badly did she want this baby?

CHAPTER FOUR

*K*ipp's parents owned a home along Chickering Road that overlooked the Gold River. Piper had been there as a teen, but when Kipp pulled his truck up the drive, she noted the house had been repainted and a long garage had been added across the back of the lot.

"That's new," she remarked.

"Since you were here, I suppose," Kipp replied. "That holds the boat and dad's other toys."

"Toys?"

"A couple of four-wheelers, bicycles, all the camping gear. A camper, too."

Auggie Hudson exited one of the wide garage doors just then and rolled it closed behind him. Dressed in faded bib overalls and a flannel shirt, he was still a fit-looking fellow with steel-gray hair and a wide smile. She occasionally waited on him in Pearl's, and he was always friendly.

"Hey, Dad," Kipp said. "What are you working on?"

"Playing with that old Waterwitch," he said. "She starts now."

"That's an outboard motor," Kipp said to Piper. "Dad, you remember Piper."

"My favorite waitress," Auggie said with a grin. "She never forgets my hot sauce. Leslie Ann's got us a spread for lunch," he said. "Go on in."

Kipp opened the white-painted back door on the two-story house and gestured for Piper to go in ahead of him.

She stepped into the sun-filled kitchen with white cabinets and the same round oak pedestal table she remembered. A short vase of yellow chrysanthemums sat in the center, and four places were set with white Corelle© plates.

Kipp's mother turned from the refrigerator. She took off her apron and draped it on a hook.

"Mom, you remember, Piper."

"Yes, of course. Hello, Piper." Leslie Ann gestured to the table. "Please, be seated. Kipp, will you pour the iced tea?"

Piper and Kipp sat beside each other. The other two place settings were across from them. Apparently, Leslie Ann liked face-to-face conversations. Straight-forward like her son.

He picked up the glass pitcher and filled glasses that already held ice.

Auggie came in and washed his hands at the sink.

Kipp's mom took a tray filled with rounded scoops of chicken salad on lettuce leaves from the refrigerator and served them.

"This looks delicious," Piper told her. "It's always a

treat to have home cooking that someone else home cooks."

Leslie Ann seated herself and gestured to a bowl of diced fruit. "Please, help yourself."

She was being pleasant, but Piper was uncertain Leslie Ann truly welcomed her after what she'd asked of their son. She took a serving and passed the bowl to Kipp. He met her eyes with a reassuring smile.

They ate and Auggie asked Kipp if he wanted to try making an ice sculpture with him for the Winter Festival this year. "I've been watching YouTube videos on how to make them. Looks like fun."

"I'm no artist, but I can wield a chainsaw," Kipp replied.

"Hey, if it flops, we'll call it modern art. No one will know the difference."

Piper chuckled. Auggie was still a fun guy. She'd always liked Kipp's parents.

Once they'd finished their meal, Leslie Ann put on a pot of coffee and took mismatched mugs from the cupboard. "Do you take anything in your coffee, Piper?"

"A little sweetener, thanks."

Once everyone had a full mug, Kipp said to his folks, "Well, obviously we want to talk to you about our plan for me to father a child for Piper."

Piper paid attention to the fact that he hadn't used the term 'sperm donor' and wondered if that was intentional. Probably. Didn't seem Kipp did things by accident.

He gestured to her. "I think we should give Piper the opportunity to tell you why she prefers this idea to others."

"Prefers you to an anonymous donor, you mean." His

mother set down her coffee. "After Kipp told me about the incidents where adult children of donors learned they had hundreds of siblings, I did some research. Seems those incidents were quite a few years ago, and sperm banks have put limits on how many times someone can donate."

"That's true, some have. But there are no laws, unlike other countries. A recipient has to put complete trust in these strangers who may or may not be following their own regulations. I'm not that trusting."

"You're not that old," Leslie Ann said. "I can't help but think you'll meet a young man, fall in love, and want children with your husband."

"I'm afraid I'm not that optimistic. I know what I want. I'm not willing to wait until it's too late and I've missed my prime years to conceive."

"It's so...*unconventional*." Leslie Ann's voice held a note of dismay. "It's hard enough raising kids traditionally, let alone with someone you're not in a relationship with. What would you tell people?"

Kipp looked at Piper. "We haven't discussed what we'd say to others. Our lawyer is from Glen Haven, and it's a private agreement we're working out. We can tell people whatever we want." He appeared to think a moment. "I'll be sharing custody and taking the child for weekends and holidays, so it'll be pretty obvious that he's mine."

Piper studied Kipp's eyes a moment, thinking of the repercussions. "If we say it's our baby together, people might think we had a one-night stand or something. I don't like that."

"We'd need to direct the narrative," he replied, still looking at her. "What if others thought we were in a relationship that didn't work out? How would you feel about that?"

"Still not the best, but better."

His mother looked at Kipp. "What if you fall in love with someone in a year or two? She might want a conventional wedding and babies of her own. Not everyone wants to raise someone else's child."

Auggie's gaze raised to Kipp, somewhat sympathetic, yet as though he shared concern.

Piper's heart beat unnervingly fast and she willed herself to breathe evenly.

Kipp's fingers remained wrapped around his mug. "Maybe you're right. But if a woman didn't want to love my child, I wouldn't be marrying her."

That statement said so much about the man that Piper's chest ached. She wanted to lean over and hug him soundly. Was she robbing him of a chance at love? But he'd spoken the truth. He wouldn't love a woman who couldn't love his child. So her part in preventing him from a marriage might damage *their* relationship.

Leslie Ann's eyes misted and she blinked. "It's not that I don't like you, Piper or disapprove of you personally, please understand. It's just that having a baby together is a gift created in love. When a man and woman who love each other have their first child, they're connected in a way that transcends any other relationship. Every child should be that special and that welcomed. I realize that might sound idealistic in this crazy world." She waved dismissively before anyone spoke. "I know, single people adopt and those children are wanted too. But there are two of you. Agreeing to have a child without love or marriage. What do you tell him ten or fifteen years from now? We wanted you, but we didn't want each other?"

Kipp turned to meet Piper's eyes and they studied each other for a moment.

Piper gave him an uncertain smile and looked back at his mother. "You researched so you already know how many negative results are recorded. I'm not willing to risk those possibilities. I've studied this thoroughly. Each year thirty to sixty thousand children are born of artificial insemination and studies have been done. A large percent of children of anonymous donors say they spend their lives looking at others and wondering if they're related. How awful would that be?"

Leslie Ann folded her hands on the table. "I understand."

"We all look in a mirror and see resemblance to our families," Piper explained. "In ourselves we see our parents or grandparents or a cousin. Offspring of donors look into a mirror and wonder where they came from."

"That's awful," Auggie said. "They're missin' a part of their identity."

Leslie Ann cast her husband a sidelong glance.

"Statistically," Piper said. "These people are hurting more, feeling more confused, feeling isolated. Children from anonymous donors are twice as likely to have problems with the law before the age of twenty-five. And more than twice as likely to report substance abuse. I get it. Plenty of people do it, but that's them. The risks are too high for me."

"Surely not all of them are as unhappy as you make it sound," Leslie Ann said.

"Of course not. But what would I tell my child about

an anonymous donor? That his biological father was the seed donor or the Y guy? Everyone has a biological father, and everyone wants to know who that person is. It's part of who we are."

Leslie Ann shook her head. "You have no idea of the depth of parental love." She looked at Kipp. "What if after you've committed yourself and helped raised this child, Piper marries and you can't bear to see the new man in the place of her husband and as the new father figure? Legal rights don't affect emotional attachments."

Kipp looked at his hands on the mug.

Piper's heart dropped. Was his mother changing his mind? He'd told Piper if she agreed to his legal terms, he'd go through with it. But she didn't want to cause a rift in their family, and she didn't want him to do something that he wasn't as sure about as she was.

"I know situations like that happen for a lot of parents," Kipp said. "I have divorced friends who've gone through breakups. The way I figure it though, I'm avoiding the divorce. I'm willing to see what the future brings and work it out together."

Piper held back tears. "I can't have my desire to have a child be the cause of hurt or hard feelings in this family. I'm not willing to do that. I respect and care for Kipp too much. He's the kindest person I've ever known, and his friendship means everything to me."

He reached to squeeze her hand. "Back at ya."

"We'll support Kipp in any choice he makes," Auggie said. "He's a level-headed guy, and I trust his wisdom in this and everything else he does. He doesn't do anything without weighin' the outcome."

Leslie Ann got up and carried the carafe back. "More coffee?"

Auggie pushed his cup forward. Kipp and Piper declined.

She returned the glass pot and took her seat. "We only want to make sure you've looked at all the angles without emotion clouding your judgment. I know that's at odds with an emotional choice like a baby, but please make your decision is based on what's best for the child."

Later, as Kipp drove Piper home, she asked, "Are you having second thoughts?"

"I've had second and up-to-hundredth thoughts, Piper. This can still be a gift of love—and friendship that we give each other. We don't know what the future holds, but right now we can shape it any way we want. We can make choices based on our mutual commitment to this child—and to each other."

Sharing her baby wasn't a hundred percent what Piper had wanted or planned, but it was better than living her life alone after Grandad was gone. Kipp was making a huge concession; she could do the same. "Okay," she said. "Come in and we'll finish up the paperwork so you can get a final copy. We'll have the agreement signed and make our appointment."

"Okay." He pulled into the drive. "Now we tell your Grandad."

"Okay," Piper said as they sat in the doctor's office. "Our story is that we've decided being friends is better than being a couple. Right?"

"You said Kendra knows the truth," he mentioned.

"And your folks and Grandad," she concurred. "That's it."

"What about others you're close to, like Mary Beth, or Marty and Edith?" He mentioned others she worked with at Pearl's Café.

"They've seen us together, so it won't seem unlikely," she answered.

He nodded. "And our friends have seen us hanging out and know we're close. Might be a surprise, but not a shock."

"Right."

Her smile and the pleasure in her eyes were worth all the awkwardness he was going to experience during the next hour.

Forty minutes later, he sat in the waiting room with a *Sports Illustrated*, pretending to read for the fifteen minutes Piper had been instructed to remain lying down. When the door opened and she joined him, her face was flushed. She reached for his hand, and he squeezed hers. Once he'd helped her into her coat, she pulled her knitted hat from her pocket and pulled it on. He shrugged into his parka, and they walked to the truck.

"How do you feel?" he asked.

"I feel fine. Excited," she said breathlessly. "We'll know in about three to four weeks. They said it sometimes takes more than one insemination."

"And if this one didn't work?"

She looked up at him. "We'll do it again. Right?"

"Right." He hadn't relished the experience, but it wasn't the worst thing he'd ever done.

They climbed into his truck, and he turned up the heat. November had brought snow that melted during the warmth of the day, but without sun today the air was frigid. It had been five weeks since Piper had asked him to join her on this journey, though it seemed like a lot longer.

"Shall we celebrate?" she asked. "Seems anticlimactic to go straight home."

"Sure. Eddie is working for me this afternoon. I don't have to go in until later—or even until closing."

She glanced out the window. "What shall we do?"

"You call it."

She seemed to think a minute. "How long since you've been roller skating?"

"Seriously?"

"Come on. We used to go all the time when we were in junior high."

"Is it safe? You know, right now?"

"Sure. If roller skating prevented pregnancy, everyone would be doing it."

He agreed with a chuckle and turned right to take Brook Park Road southwest. "You called it."

Her laugh revealed her joy in this moment and what they'd done.

After renting lockers and skates, they stood on the carpet at the entrance to the rink. "Looks like we came on the right day," he remarked.

A dozen or more gray-haired men and women with knee pads skated in twos around the floor near the wall. Several gripped adult-size skate trainers that looked like triangular walkers on three wheels. *Senior day.* Over the loudspeakers The Everly Brothers sang *Wake Up Little Susie.*

Piper laughed out loud. "It is kind of perfect. Come on, gramps. Want me to rent you a trainer?"

"I'll do it without or die trying."

She took his hand and they rolled out onto the floor. His legs were a little unsteady at first, but he quickly remembered his balance and how to maneuver the floor so he could keep up with her. She took a band from her jeans pocket and pulled her hair back out of her face.

They took a break to sip colas at the snack counter. "This place is awesome," Piper said appreciatively. "I knew the Gonzales' bought it along with the arcade and fixed it up, but this is almost exactly how it looked when we were kids."

"It's pretty amazing," he said. "The neon signage alone must have cost a pretty penny to restore."

"The carpet is different," she noted about the bright planets and stars on the floor, "but the colors are the same." She studied him, wondering about the years they'd been apart. "Did you have a girlfriend at college?"

"Not really. I was working and studying. I didn't really have time for dating."

"What about when you came back to Spencer? Who did you see?"

"I saw LeAnn Abbott for a while."

"The mortuary girl?"

He chuckled. "Her dad was a funeral director. Her brothers run it now. I don't know what she does. I took Whitney Chandler to a concert in Denver."

"The outfitter's sister?"

"She lives somewhere else now. Don't remember where."

"Anyone more recent?"

"Recently? That would have been Marissa."

"Our Marissa? Marissa Bloom?"

"Yep."

"I think I remember that. What happened?"

"Nothing happened. We went out a few times. That's all. How about you?"

"I saw a guy named Eric who worked at the lodge for a year or so. It wasn't serious. Do you remember the bartender at the Wild Card who always wore band t-shirts? I went out with him a few times. He moved south, somewhere near Nashville."

"Was that serious?"

"Not at all."

"Seems like you only dated guys who were in Spencer short term. Was that deliberate?"

"Now that you bring it up, no, but it might have been subconscious. Or else I was just never invested in a guy."

Piper appeared fragile, maybe because she was slender and her hair so pale, but he knew her strength. Physically, she worked a demanding job, on her feet and dealing with customers. Emotionally, she'd risen above the loss of her parents and grandmother and had seen to the well-being of her grandfather. She had the iron constitution of a lumberjack. She'd known what she wanted and nothing would have stopped her from getting it. She'd been forthright about her wishes, and she'd come to him.

He wasn't kidding himself. There was more than friendship and congeniality on his part of their arrangement. He might be a friend to her, but he would have liked more. He'd had a thing for her since those junior high days.

He was thankful for this connection, thankful she trusted him. Hopefully one day she would feel something more.

"One more time, okay?"

She was standing in front of him, eager for another spin around the rink. The Monotones were singing *Who Wrote the Book of Love?*

"One more time," he agreed. Friends had a good time together.

CHAPTER FIVE

*I*t was a busy Saturday morning in Pearl's Café, a day many of the regulars didn't come by for coffee or breakfast because they were at home. The weekend crowd never generated the same energy with jovial conversation or calls to acquaintances, but the day held its own charm. Families filled corners booths while couples, some gray-haired, some young, occupied the tables.

Piper recognized the familiar faces of a father and son who often ordered breakfast on Saturday. Over time, she'd caught on that the young father had his son with him every other weekend. Today when she'd approached to take their orders, which she already knew by heart, the dad was explaining that the weekend of the Winter Festival wasn't his weekend for them to be together.

"But if you ask, Mom will say yes," the boy said in a pleading tone.

"She didn't, Pax. I talked to her about it last week. I'm sorry."

He leaned back and pouted. "She's gonna make me go to stinky ole Roger's house. I don't get to play games there even. It's boring."

The young dad's pained expression tore at Piper's heart. "Good morning, gentlemen." She offered the boy a smile. "Can I get you stack of blueberry pancakes and orange juice this morning?"

"I ain't hungry." The boy slumped in his seat.

"Mind your manners and sit up, Pax. Answer Miss Piper."

The boy sat up, but his expression didn't change. "Yes, please, Miss Piper."

"Okay," she said with a smile. "And does Dad want the Sunrise Benedict?"

"Yes, please, but I'll have my eggs over easy rather than scrambled."

"Got it. I'll be right back with your juice and coffee."

She clipped their order to the carousel and called to Kurtis Dorn, who was working the grill today. While she filled their drinks, she heard again the disappointment in the little boy's voice. Her hand trembled and the juice spilled over her fingers. She poured it into a clean glass and refilled it.

Had she thought of everything? Did Kipp's paperwork cover every possible scenario that might disappoint a child? She rinsed and dried her hands. Why couldn't that kid's mom just agree to let the dad take him to the festival? Piper hated to think the woman was a spiteful person, but there were people like that. Maybe she simply had something else planned. Or maybe the boy was going to sit bored at the boyfriend's house all weekend.

Piper cut off her thoughts midstream. She couldn't fix

the world's problems. All she could do was come up with a plan to avoid those kinds of difficulties in her life. Even though Kipp's tome of child rearing plans had seemed to match *War and Peace* for page length, she still got a little panicky wondering if they'd thought of everything.

The rest of the day she couldn't get the boy's disappointed expression and pleading eyes out of her mind. Pax. Probably short for Paxton. Nice name. She hadn't let herself think about names yet—and oddly enough naming the kid hadn't been in their agreement.

Well, there was *something* she could do herself.

Had Kipp deliberately left that decision to her?

Her shift ended at one when part-timer Dillon Stuckey arrived and clocked in. He was a tall slender college student in his early twenties. His form-fitting pullover sweaters and hundred-watt smile earned him lucrative tips from the supper crowd, which included divorcees and widows who'd figured out he was here on Saturday evenings. The Ladies Aid bridge club had even started eating early suppers here before moving to a member's house for games. Dillon was utilizing his advantages. More power to him.

Piper clocked out, pulled on her coat and hat, and trudged to her vehicle. It had started snowing. She took boots from the back of her car and put them on while her trusty old SUV warmed up.

Dressed in his red plaid sherpa-lined coat and hat with ear flaps, Harm Newport was shoveling when she parked at the end of the drive. Only a half inch or so had fallen, but he liked to keep up before the snow got heavier. She knew better than to suggest he wait for her or their nearby neighbor who usually brought a snowblower, because even at seventy-eight, her grandfather liked to take care of things himself.

She got out and helped him clear the driveway, then parked in the garage and bundled them both inside, where she checked on the chicken she'd left in the crockpot.

Grandad hung his coat and left his boots on the tiny back porch. "I'm gonna watch the Broncos' game."

"I'll join you later," she said. I have a few more boxes to move, and I'm going to tape so I can paint tomorrow."

"Still hard for me to think there'll be a little one around," Harm said. Harm was a Dutch name, short for Herman. No one except a telemarketer ever called him Herman. "He'll be cute. You were the cutest little tyke ever there was."

There was a knock at the back door, and he stepped out into the enclosed porch and motioned for whoever was on the other side of the window to come in. The door opened and his VFW pal Jeeter could be heard talking while stomping his boots clean.

"I didn't tell you Jeeter was comin'," her grandfather said. "And he's brought a six-pack and a bag o' chips."

"You two don't spoil your supper," she told them. "I'm fixing chicken enchiladas that should be ready at inter-mission."

Grandad and Jeeter exchanged a brief glance. Her grandfather gestured toward the other room.

Piper took the beer, handed them each a bottle and put the rest of the brew in the refrigerator. "Need help with the remote?"

"I got it on the channel before I went out to shovel," Grandad said. "There's pre-game shows."

The two men sauntered into the other room and made

themselves comfortable. Grandad wore hearing aids, but Jeeter claimed he didn't need them, so the volume was already blasting by the time Piper escaped to the back of the house.

The closet was full of her grandmother's totes of fabric and patterns. Her progress slowed when she found a box of old cards and letters and browsed through them. Piper had only finished packing and stacking totes in the hallway when the back doorbell rang.

The gentlemen riveted to the pre-game show either didn't hear it or ignored the sound, so Piper hurried to the kitchen. Through the window, she recognized Kipp's parka.

She yanked open the door to find him holding a stockpot with hot pads. She took it from him, so he could remove his boots and coat. Whatever was inside smelled savory. "What's this?"

"My deer chili. I didn't want to come empty-handed."

She frowned and made a face. "Surely, you don't expect me to eat Bambi."

His grin was crooked. "Harm said you had chicken too."

He took the pan from her and carried it to the stove. From a backpack over his shoulder, he took out shoes and sat to put them on.

Something was up, and Piper wasn't sure what. "Did Grandad call you?"

Kipp gave a sheepish grin. "I don't want to get him in trouble."

"What did he say?"

"That you might need a little help in the tykes room."

That sounded like Grandad. "How did he get your number?"

"Calls to the store come to my phone when they're not answered."

"Why aren't you at the store?"

"I was earlier, but it's snowing now and the game is about to start. Everyone's at home or at the Wild Card." He stood. "Show me what to do."

"I'm prepping for paint."

"Hey Harm. Hey Jeeter," Kipp said on the way past.

Grandad raised a hand in greeting but didn't look over his shoulder.

"Is this game a showdown or something?" she whispered.

"It's the Broncos playing at Mile High. Every game is a showdown."

"Well, here it is." She stood in the center of the room and looked around, seeing the space from his eyes. His home was completely remodeled inside. Inadequacy crept into her thoughts. "I can get a pretty rug."

She shut down her defensiveness. This baby was a hundred percent her idea. It didn't matter what he thought of the room she planned.

"Have you wiped the woodwork?" he asked.

She shook her head.

"Point me to the rags and I'll do it before we tape."

Not only did he have blue painter's tape protecting the window trim and floorboards, but he'd stirred the paint and trimmed around the same areas by the time the sounds from the television changed.

She put the lid on the paint can. "I think it's intermission."

He held in a laugh. "It's called halftime."

"Right. They used to show the marching band, now it's all talking heads. Time to eat."

"I remember. All that's left to do is the rolling." He asked for a plastic baggie to save his paintbrush.

She'd made the enchiladas and baked them while he'd still been painting.

He washed and dried his hands, then touched his pan gingerly. "You kept the chili hot."

She bent to remove her baking dish from the oven and carried it to the table. "I'm not eating it."

Kipp admired the curve of her flushed cheek, the sheen of her ponytail that swung forward, the way her painting jeans fit her curvy backside. He'd been here on several occasions, and he enjoyed watching her in her home environment. She was easy on the eyes at Pearl's too, but this was different. She was one with her surroundings in her home. He thought of wrapping his arms around her and burying his face in her neck and hair. That's what a normal couple trying to have a baby would do. She'd turn in his embrace, maybe smile, definitely kiss him.

Thinking of kissing her, thinking she may already be carrying his baby made his stomach dip. Only one thing could make a man and woman closer.

"I don't think we'll pull those two away from the statistics and clips of today's other games," she said. "Might as well make them trays."

"So…you're not into football?"

"I watch with him sometimes, but I look at my phone a lot. I guess I just don't understand what's going on. For example, it confuses me when those umpires throw rags on the ground."

Keeping a straight face took all his willpower. How had he never realized this about her before? "They're the referees, and those are flags. They throw them when there's a penalty for stripping or holding or pass inter-ference."

Her eyes widened. "Stripping?"

"Illegally taking the ball from an opposing player."

"Isn't taking the ball the whole point?"

"Yeah, but there are right ways and wrong ways to do it."

"It just seems like so much work, stopping and starting and trying to get that ball a few yards. They have to get frustrated with how many times they're stopped. I get frustrated watching."

Kipp took a deep breath. He appreciated so many things about Piper that her ignorance about football wasn't a big deal. It was actually somewhat charming.

Harm and Jeeter enjoyed bowls of his chili alongside their chicken enchiladas—which were delicious. Kipp washed down his dinner with a beer while the guys caught him up on the game.

Occasionally, Piper asked a question, and he did his best to answer. She asked, "There are eleven players on the field at a time, and extras over there on the bench. Why do their numbers go all the way to eighty-eight?"

Kipp briefly met Harm's eyes. He had a lot of work to do. "Numbers go to a hundred and are assigned according to their positions, like the quarterback's number is usually between one and nineteen."

"Why?"

"It's NFL rules. We'll look it up, okay?"

"Okay." She picked up everyone's dishes and carried them to the kitchen.

When Harm muted a commercial, Kipp spoke softly. "How does she know so little about football?"

Her grandfather shrugged. "She's never been interested."

"Well, I can see how this game is going to end, so I'm going to go paint walls."

"You're a good man," Harm replied.

The paint she'd chosen for this one wall was a light green color. The can said soft sage green. Kipp poured paint into the pan and rolled.

"Is it going to be too dark?" Piper asked.

"It will dry a little lighter. See the trim?"

"Oh, sure. I think I like it. The color for other walls is called alpaca blanket, a soft off-white. I have rattan shades I've been looking at and an off-white rug. I was thinking a small potted tree in the corner."

"A real one?"

"Yeah, is that bad?"

"He'll be crawling before you know it. We could put a gate across the corner."

She looked thoughtful. "No, you're right. Maybe a little wooden table and chair. Something more useful."

"What about a crib?"

"Grandad told me to pick one and he'd buy it."

"That's nice of him."

She paused in spreading old sheets along the other side of the floor. "You'll probably have a room at your house, too, won't you?"

"I guess I will."

She moved to stand behind him and watched him roll on the paint. "I hate to admit this to you now, but I'm a little scared."

He paused his task and turned to her. "About what? You were a hundred percent sure you wanted to do this."

"And I still am. A hundred percent." Her eyes filled with the sheen of tears. "But will I be good at it? Will I know what to do?"

"I expect every parent in the world wonders that. Every parent I know has had their doubts, even though they're great parents."

"Really?"

"Yes. I remember Ronnie panicking before Lillian was born. As soon as she was here, he figured it all out. He's a great dad."

Piper nodded. "I guess you're right. I've never even had a dog. Grandad is pretty independent, but I look out for him. The only one that depends solely on me is Luna."

"Where is that cat?"

"She hides when people are here. She's probably on my bed—or under it. After we're done in here and shut the door on the wet paint, I'll find her for you."

"It's so much easier to paint an empty room," he told her a couple hours later, as they stood back and admired the fresh walls.

"I can't wait to see it in the daylight tomorrow." She pounded the lid on the last paint can and picked up the brushes. "I'm glad I bought those disposable trays."

They washed brushes, hands and arms at the old kitchen sink. "You don't take those off?"

She'd indicated the narrow silver band, bead band and a woven one he always wore on his left wrist. "No. Lillian made me this one out of thread, and it's tied on. I'd have to cut it."

How sweet Kipp was. His love for his family was endearing. What would it feel like to have his devotion focused on her? The thought prompted heartwarming impossibilities she couldn't afford to think about. Brushes set to dry and hands clean, she motioned for him to follow. "I'll find Luna for you."

The fluffy cat was lying on her bed as she'd predicted. Piper thought she was beautiful, with her gray striped fur, white chin and chest and blue-grey eyes. Her tail was a darker gray than the rest of her. The cat raised her head and blinked at Piper, then looked at Kipp. Her tail flopped back and forth.

Piper sat on the edge of the bed and urged Kipp to join her.

"Come here, Luna," she crooned. "Come see our friend." She pulled the cat onto her lap, and Luna stretched out, waiting for a belly rub. "Go ahead. She'll let you pet her."

Kipp ruffled his fingers through the fur of her neck and rubbed her tummy. Luna purred.

"She likes you."

He grinned. "Kids and animals love me."

"Because you love them."

He lifted his gaze to hers. It was so unusual to have a man in her house. In her bedroom. She usually saw him in the diner, often hung out at his place, participated in joint activities with their friends. This two-of-them-alone thing felt different than it had before. She studied his hand in Luna's fur, let her gaze move across his wrist to his sinewed forearm, where his sleeve was still rolled back.

An unfamiliar sensation dipped and rolled in her belly. Her heart seemed to beat awkwardly. Were her nerves manifesting in this belated manner? No, Kipp had put her fears to rest earlier. This was different. Something... something about the shared intimacy of what they were doing and their close proximity.

She shouldn't like it, but she treasured the feelings.

Raising her gaze, she studied his familiar features, the arch of his dark brows, the close-cropped beard that covered his jaw...the curve of his smooth lips. And she imagined kissing him.

He lifted his dark gaze to hers.

Her stomach dropped.

They were friends. This was weird.

Her skin flushed and when his gaze darkened, she knew her blush was visible.

"My mom would like for you and Harm to join us for Thanksgiving," he said.

Her thoughts did a three-sixty and came into balance. "Oh. Thanksgiving."

"Is the diner open?"

"Only half a day, but Dillon and Aryal will be on the schedule."

"Mom said she'd call you. I'll be heading home now."

"Okay, great. About the call." She placed Luna back in her spot on the coverlet and walked him through the house. Jeeter had left and Kipp called a goodbye to Grandad.

"Thanks for your help," she said.

"My pleasure." He donned his coat and picked up his cooking pan before heading out the back door.

Piper leaned back against the counter. What in the world had that been about? She tried to remember if she'd ever had thoughts like those about Kipp before, if she'd ever been jealous of seeing him with another girl. If she had, the feelings had been buried deep.

And that's where they needed to stay. Piper turned and scrubbed the baking pan she'd left soaking. She and Kipp had a deal that didn't involve a complicated entanglement. She intended to keep it that way.

CHAPTER SIX

*I*t was black bear rifle season and Kipp had just finished filling out all the paperwork for a youth license. He was certified to teach the hunter's safety conclusion class, so he always enjoyed providing materials and encouraging the young people to study and take the online class first. They couldn't take the conclusion class unless they'd passed the online one. "You study and you can have your license in time for this season."

The boy and his dad were looking at rifles when Kipp's phone rang. He pulled it from his pocket and glanced at the screen. It was rare for Piper to call when she knew he was at work. She had to have been at work too. He touched the call button. "Hey, Piper. What's up?"

"I did a test."

"A test? Oh! A test!" Not a hunter's safety test. He'd purchased a dozen pregnancy tests and she'd told him she'd use one after a couple of weeks had passed.

"The smells of the food were making me sick all

morning. I threw up yesterday and today, so on my break I did a test."

His whole body tensed. "And?"

"It's positive."

Kipp's scalp tingled at the news. His skin prickled and his thoughts went blank for a moment.

"I'll do another one tomorrow."

"Do you think this one was accurate?" he asked.

"I think I've never felt so much like barfing in my life."

This could be the moment they'd anticipated. She could be pregnant. For real. "If you don't feel well, tell Marty you need to go home."

"I will if I don't feel better soon. I think I'll be okay. I ate a few saltines and sipped a little cola. I feel better. I just wanted to let you know. You have to be first to hear it."

"I don't know what to say. Are you happy or are you going to wait for confirmation to be excited?"

"I don't think I can keep from being happy. The doctor said it could take several tries, but I don't think this is my imagination." She paused a moment. "Can this really be happening?"

"I just don't want you to get your hopes up too much."

"I know. But this could be it. This could really be it."

He didn't know what to say. "We'll know soon," was all he could think.

He hung up and finished with his customers, forcing himself to be present and attend to business and safety. Once they'd left the store, he perched on the stool behind the knife counter and let his thoughts run wild. He'd handled every last detail of his financial and legal obligations as though their contract was an everyday business deal. But it wasn't. Their deal involved a new life. A child that was his and hers together.

The immense reality sunk its teeth in. Kipp didn't regret doing this, in fact he felt the opposite. He was thankful she'd asked him, grateful for this new human who would bind them to one another for the rest of their lives. For a fleeting second, he felt as though he'd taken advantage of her. However, she wanted this more than anything, trusted him. Neither of them had taken advantage of the other.

The following days she called him after performing more tests, all which also turned out positive. The following week she went to the doctor for urinalysis and a blood test and called him afterward.

Piper was pregnant. And Kipp was the father of her baby.

Their baby.

Piper had been nervous about Thanksgiving ever since Leslie Ann's call. Kipp's mother had been cordial on the phone, but not exactly warm.

"Kipp told me there's a baby coming," she said.

Piper stood in the bathroom with her phone to her ear. She'd been getting ready for work. "Yes, it's certain."

Piper waited uneasily for a scolding or congratulations. Neither came.

"That certainly happened quickly," the woman said.

"I'm really fortunate," Piper told her. "I was told it

could take several attempts, but one insemination worked."

"Yes," Leslie Ann said, probably uncomfortable with the topic. "We should probably get to know each other better. Our lives will be connected now. I don't want awkwardness between us to have an adverse effect."

Affect Leslie Ann or the baby, Piper wasn't sure. She'd signed up for this when she'd agreed to Kipp's terms. She tried to place herself in the woman's shoes and imagine what she was feeling or concerned about.

About her son having a baby with Piper Newport, the waitress, obviously. No one had voiced that, but Piper couldn't help but suspect they didn't think she was worthy of their son.

"We'd like for you and your grandfather to join us for Thanksgiving. We always have plenty, and it would be a good opportunity to spend time together."

Piper couldn't think of a single good reason to refuse, except that the idea of being an outsider in their family made her nervous. She and Grandad had no plans. "We'd love to join you. What can I bring?"

Leslie Ann had placed her in charge of two pies. Was it a test? Did she suspect Piper would bring pies from Pearl's and lose points as a capable person? She sure wanted to bring Edith's pies, but Edith made a distinctive pastry that was easily recognizable. Though she had to fight nausea at the sickeningly sweet smell of the baking fruit, Piper practiced and froze eight unattractive pies before she figured out how to make both crusts and fillings pretty as well as tasty. She and Grandad would have dessert for the next year.

The night before, she finished an apple and a pumpkin

pie. On Thanksgiving morning, she curled her hair and wore it down, then dressed in pants and a soft ivory sweater she'd ordered for the holiday. She remembered her mother's ruby earrings and necklace and wore them.

She and Grandad lived on an acreage to the north while the Hudsons lived south and west, right at Spencer's boundary, the Gold River. Their driveway had an incline, but her old Volkswagen hatchback had no trouble reaching the wide area in front of the garages where two other vehicles were parked.

Auggie came out to help carry in food. "What year is this VW?" he asked.

"Nineteen ninety," she replied.

"How did you come by it? I've only seen them at car shows. Isn't it European—a Golf Hatchback?"

"No one ever knows that," she said in surprise. "Grandad bought her at an auction years ago."

He reached for the pies in the back. "You've taken good care of her."

Kipp walked alongside Grandad, even though the drive had been plowed and the path to the door was level.

Delaney was the first to greet them. She'd been stacking golden dinner rolls in a basket and covered them with a tea towel.

Piper had taken deep breaths outside, praying none of the smells sent her running for the bathroom. Barfing wasn't the impression she wanted to make.

"It's nice to see you two," Delaney said with a smile.

Piper knew Ronnie's wife from occasionally bumping into her at a volunteer firefighter's Friday night barbeque in the park or seeing her with Ronnie at the Wildcard. She was a curvy brunette with pretty brown eyes, wearing jeans and a rust-colored cardigan sweater. Her smile was friendly, but Piper wondered what she was thinking. She felt like a germ under a microscope.

Leslie Ann came from the hallway and greeted them. "Mr. Newport, would you like something to drink?"

"I don't think so just yet. You call me Harm, like everybody else."

"Piper?" she questioned. "There's apple cider, tea or water."

"I'll wait until dinner, thanks."

Kipp gestured toward the doorway. "Ronnie is probably watching the Bills and Lions."

"Started at twelve-thirty," Grandad said.

"They'll bring us up to speed," Kipp told him.

Kipp turned to Piper. "Want to watch? You're welcome to join us."

"It's okay if you want to watch," Leslie Ann told her. "Or you can hang out in the kitchen, maybe finish setting the table with us."

"I'll say hi to your dad and Ronnie and then visit with your mom," she told Kipp.

Once she'd greeted the others and Kipp had introduced her to Lillian and Evelyn, who were playing with dolls on the floor, she returned to the kitchen.

"Your granddaughters are so sweet and pretty."

Leslie poured water over potatoes and set the pot on the stove. "They sure are. I never knew being a grandma was going to be one of the best things to ever happen to me. I just adore those girls."

Piper smiled. "I loved my grandma very much."

"I remember her," Leslie Ann said. "She was a kind and

generous woman. We organized a library fundraiser together once."

"I didn't know that."

"It was quite a few years ago. Kipp was in college at the time." She wiped her hands on a towel. "I didn't work until the boys were in high school. That's when children only seem to need you for locker fees, lunch money and keeping the refrigerator stocked. That's an exaggeration, but I was a little lost, so I plunged into a job and volunteer work."

Piper only nodded. She got the not-so-subtle message that a mom should be home with her children. Nice gig, but not realistic for everyone.

"The time goes by really fast," Leslie Ann said. "They're babies and then they're in school and then they have their own lives. I'm determined to enjoy every second with my granddaughters."

And hopefully this baby. "What can I do to help?"

"The tablecloth is on and Delaney is setting out the plates. You can ask her to show you the silverware and napkin drawer."

In the enormous dining room, Delaney showed her where to find the rest of the tableware. She gestured to the pies Kipp had placed on a sideboard along the wall. "Your pies look beautiful. You even made little leaf cut-outs on the crust. I'm not much of a baker, so I can't wait to taste them. They look like my granny's used to." She placed three sets of small silver-lidded salt and pepper shakers on the table. "How are you feeling?"

"Much better. My doctor gave me a prescription for the morning sickness. It helps, but occasionally I still feel nauseated. It was rough for a while there."

"Probably especially working at the diner where you see and smell food all day."

Leslie Ann carried the basket of dinner rolls to the sideboard. "I'm sorry to hear you've been so sick."

"Thanks. I'm better."

"Kipp says you work two jobs. I didn't realize that."

"Two part-time jobs," Piper clarified.

"Still, that's a lot of hours, especially on your feet at the diner and being around so many people all winter."

"I'm quite healthy, Mrs. Hudson. I rarely catch a bug."

Leslie Ann nodded. "Even so, I don't think you're prepared for how much time a newborn takes and how valuable your sleep becomes. Will you have maternity leave?"

"I'll be able to take a few weeks off from the diner, yes. Tax season won't be until March and April."

"And the baby is due in July?"

"Yes. And it's a desk job, so I'll be off my feet a lot."

"Which job pays the best?"

It was a personal question, but Piper acknowledged that sharing a child was personal. "My accounting business pays well. I pick and choose my clients. But it's solitary for the most part. I like working at the diner because I see friends and learn what's going on in Spencer. Marty and Edith are like family."

Leslie Ann stood with her hands on the back of a wooden chair and met Piper's gaze. "If you're going to do justice to being a mother, you're going to have to choose one or the other."

Piper wasn't sure if she should feel hurt or angry. Probably neither. She hadn't done this without adequate thought and preparation.

Kipp's mother went on, saying, "I realize you need a job to support yourself, even though Kipp will be helping financially, but a child takes a lot of time and nurturing. How much time will you have for your baby if you're devoted to two jobs?"

"Kipp will be taking him part of the time," Piper told her. "That wasn't my original idea, but it's the plan now. When the baby is with Kipp, I'll need to keep myself busy."

"I think you're kidding yourself about how much time and energy it takes to be a parent."

Delaney looked from her mother-in-law to Piper, obviously apprehensive. "Maybe this isn't the best time to talk about this."

"No, it's all right," Piper said kindly. "This is as good of a time as any." But she did feel sick now. Her stomach quivered and her heart thumped. She wanted to escape the room and the house altogether, but she couldn't. She was going to have to face the questions and doubts and scrutiny. Others outside this family would judge her choices as well. She might as well prepare. "I know you never liked the idea." Piper kept her voice steady as she spoke to Leslie Ann. "And I get it. But Kipp is all in, and I've made provisions for his requirements. If he didn't believe I was capable of taking care of a baby, I don't think he'd have given me his."

Leslie Ann's eyes filled with tears. "I already know I'm going to love your baby so much," she said. "That little child will have my heart, just like Lillian and Evelyn. I'm afraid for Kipp and for you and the baby. I don't know if I can trust you."

Her honesty pierced Piper. Leslie Ann was trying to protect herself as well as Kipp and the baby.

"You don't know me well enough to trust me, I guess. All I can do is show you in time. I can't promise to be the perfect mother. No one can do that. But I want this baby more than I've ever wanted anything. I can promise I'm going to give all of myself to loving him and making a home for him. Or *her*. Kipp required legal assurance that you'll be part of his life. I don't want to be sorry about that."

Leslie's Ann's expression flattened. She pursed her lips and looked from Piper to Delaney and back. "I don't want any of us to be sorry."

Delaney stepped closer, took Piper's hand and squeezed it. "Let's finish the table."

Leslie Ann nodded. "When you're finished, Piper, will you mash the potatoes?"

Piper acknowledged that Kipp's mother was including her. The woman had a right to voice her concerns. She hadn't been rude or vindictive. Kipp had probably learned his forthright honesty from her. Piper didn't like being confronted, but she appreciated that Leslie Ann spoke her fears directly. Her questions were unnerving, but maybe Piper did need to keep her plans realistic.

She was surprisingly hungry when they sat down to eat, and the food was delicious. Grandad sat beside her and patted her hand from time to time. They'd been alone for quite a few years. Sometimes they ate holiday dinners at the diner and a few times they'd had Jeeter and Jonas Finch over. Once the Tanners had invited them to their ranch for Thanksgiving dinner. Those were all nice days, but none compared to holidays when Gran had been alive. She knew Grandad missed her every day, but most on days like this.

On her other side, Kipp was his usual unpretentious self, he and Ronnie telling stories of camping trips and times they'd gotten into trouble as kids.

Lillian, age five and Evelyn, age four, were adorable with wavy dark hair. Evelyn's eyes were brown like Delaney's, but Lillian's were the same bright hazel as Kipp's. Curious, Piper noted the others' and discovered Auggie was the one with the hazel eyes. Maybe her baby would have those same eyes. She looked at Lillian again, appreciating her sweet features and her charming dimples when she smiled.

A rush of emotion overcame Piper and brought tears to her eyes. She'd wanted a child for so long, and her deepest wish was coming true.

Delaney said something softly to Evelyn, and the little girl smiled up at her, then ate the carrots on her plate. Children had to be reminded to eat their vegetables, of course. Piper probably needed to read a few books.

When time came for dessert, Delaney's strawberry pretzel gelatin seemed to be a family favorite. Piper asked for half a slice of Leslie Ann's apple crisp cheesecake, and Kipp took her other half. Leslie Ann sliced Piper's pies and dished them up. This morning she'd whipped cream. Auggie took a generous dollop from the plastic container and plopped it on his slice of pumpkin pie. "You didn't buy the frozen kind?"

"She made it," Grandad said.

Auggie tasted a white-laden bite of pie and rolled his eyes skyward. "Heavenly."

"If you couldn't tell, this family likes to eat," Ronnie said.

"Everything was delicious," Piper said. "I like Marty's

stuffing at the diner, but this was even better." She gave Leslie Ann a hesitant smile. "You'll have to teach me how."

"I'd be happy to," the older woman replied with an easy smile

After the food was cleared away, Kipp and Auggie took over cleanup. In the family room, where a muted football game played in the background, the coffee table and side tables held board games and a checkerboard.

Piper wasn't sure how Grandad would react to not hearing the television, but he quickly became absorbed in a checkers match with Ronnie.

Delaney and Lillian asked Piper to join them playing Clue™. She was surprised to see the new character tokens were tiny replicas of the suspects. "These were plastic playing pieces when I was a kid."

"They were wooden when I was small," Leslie Ann added.

Evelyn lay on the floor with a coloring book and a plastic container of crayons, happily coloring a dalmatian pup wearing a red fireman's hat.

After the second game, Piper excused herself and went into the kitchen where Kipp and his father were seated at the breakfast nook watching a video on an iPad.

Kipp slid over. "Come sit."

She scooted in beside him. "What are you two fellas up to?"

He'd paused the video on a still shot of a man with protective eyewear. "Planning our project for the competition at the Winter Festival. We're watching how ice sculptures are made."

He started the video and shards of ice flew as the creator used a chainsaw to whittle away at an enormous block of ice. "This is how the basic shape is formed," Auggie said. "Add ons are done by gluing them with water. You use small chisels and even a blow torch to refine shapes. We did some practicing last winter."

Kipp opened his phone and scrolled through photos. He showed Piper a dolphin and a wagon with wheels. "We're not planning to win," he said with a grin. "Most of these guys have been doing this for years. We're going to do it for the experience."

"And fun." Auggie had a twinkle in his eyes. Kipp seemed to have inherited his adventurous spirit from his dad.

"What are you going to make?" she asked.

Auggie unrolled paper she hadn't noticed. The drawing depicted a brick wishing well with a bucket and beside it a boy in a wheelchair. "Larger than life size," Auggie said. "About twelve feet high."

"I talked with someone from Dream Weavers for Kids," Kipp told her. "They love our idea and plan to come take shots of us sculpting. They'll be on site Saturday and Sunday to accept donations."

Piper's heart swelled and she got tears in her eyes. "What a wonderful thing you're doing."

"It won't be easy," Auggie told her. "We've convinced Ronnie to join us. Hopefully, we find another person who's done this before to be on our team. Kipp will need help at the store. The sculpting will take thirty-four hours straight."

"I'll do what I can," she said. "I have no idea how to work at your store, but I can balance your daily income and make the bank deposits. I can provide your team with meals and hot drinks."

Kipp rested a hand on her arm, a casual touch, but she liked his warm touch through the sleeve of her sweater. She read the excitement in his eyes. "That would be great. We just called to reserve a space in the fairgrounds lot for the camper. The hotels filled up quickly for this entire weekend, and we want to be on site. If you're serious, you can bring us Pearl's takeout or you can heat up food or cook in the camper."

She grinned. "All of those. Whatever you need. I'll bring you meatloaf for sure."

Kipp wrapped an arm around her shoulders, and she leaned into him, resting her head. She'd never known anyone as easy to be around, besides her Grandad. Kipp soothed her misgivings and bolstered her confidence.

Why had they grown apart after high school? They'd both been focused on college, and she'd earned a scholarship to the community college. She'd been really proud of that, and she'd been first in her family to earn a degree. In the years that followed she'd been content until she realized she and Grandad were alone and she didn't want to be alone for all the years to come.

Piper wanted what she'd seen others have, a family… love. After that she'd been determined to make her own family. And she admitted she'd been a little short-sighted and starry-eyed. But asking Kipp to fulfil her dream hadn't been a mistake. He was everything she wanted and needed. When she was with him, her heart was full and her fears subsided.

They'd grown familiar with one another, and that was a good thing for two people who would share a child soon.

Kipp was the father of her baby…and her best friend.

But this unexpected attraction was concerning her more than Leslie Ann's mistrust. Piper feared she was in more deeply than she'd planned...there was nothing impersonal about how she felt about this man. If she was completely honest with herself, her feelings would run away with her, and all the careful planning would be for naught.

CHAPTER SEVEN

It snowed the first week of December, covering the streets and drifting. As predicted, motels and hotels were filled with artists and visitors arriving for the Winter Festival. The guys had been wise to rent a space at the fairgrounds for the Hudson's camper. She'd imagined the old pop-up, not realizing they owned an RV with a well-equipped kitchen and sleeping space for six.

Seeing Kipp and Ronnie side by side in their parkas on Thursday, it was obvious the Hudson brothers were no lightweights, so adequate space was a requirement. Auggie told her when the boys were in high school, he and Leslie Ann had purchased their first RV.

She joined them at the fairgrounds as the carvers checked in and set up their areas. The ice sculptors had been designated places within a huge fenced off-section not far from where food vendors who would set up booths and tents. Family and artists had to show ID tags to enter. Tall, slender Tony Burnham had joined their team. She'd watched him build incredible treehouses on his HGTV show, so his artist's eye and gifts would be a benefit.

Sculpting was scheduled to begin at eight a.m. the next morning. She'd brought provisions, so while they set up, she found a cubby in the RV for her clothing and a few hair things, since she planned to stay overnight while they carved. Tonight, they would all go home for a good night's sleep and be back early.

Tension was high among those gathered in assigned areas the following morning as they waited for starting time. The men were fresh and eager to begin.

"I stayed in the RV overnight," Auggie told her. "What are the streets like?"

"They're good right now," she said. "I stopped at Pearl's on my way. The plows have been running, but there's more snow predicted. The locals are helping out the street crews because of all the visitors and the festival starting. Are you guys going to be okay out here all day in the cold and snow?"

"The cold is the perfect environment for this," Kipp answered. "Some of the artists told us they've competed at times when the temperatures melted their projects."

"Okay, well, food will be hot when you get hungry and there will be coffee and hot chocolate at the ready."

A bullhorn announced starting time. All the competitors jumped into action, and it wasn't long before the sound of chainsaws filled the air. Piper watched them for a few minutes, then walked between the cordoned off areas, curious about everyone's beginning process. After half an hour, she strolled the center aisle where the vendors were set up and bought herself a funnel cake and a cup of apple cider. Eventually, she became too cold and headed to the RV.

Marty had baked her two meatloaves. She unwrapped one, sliced it and placed the slices in a covered dish. She boiled and mashed potatoes and kept a generous serving of gravy warm for the first person who came.

She'd brought her phone charger and a couple of books. The RV had all the comforts of home, so she read for a couple hours. Not having seen anyone for a while, she dressed in her warm clothing and ventured out to see their progress. The sculpture had already begun to take shape, the brick well emerging as Kipp and Tony used blow torches to smooth the ice. She wondered why they hadn't simply used blocks of ice for the structure, but then after checking out some of the other competitors, understood they wanted their piece authentic with a degree of difficulty.

"This is the easy part," Kipp told her. "The rope and the boy will be our challenge."

Piper was glad she'd worn layers and covered her head and face. Snow was blowing from the north. "Where do the blocks of ice come from? They're so clear."

"It's machine made by a company in Loveland," he told her. "Each team gets fifteen three-hundred-pound blocks and thirty-four hours to complete their sculpture. We won't use all of ours unless we make a lot of mistakes, but we'll need every minute of the time allotment."

They had to be finished by six p.m. the following evening. "And you'll be up all night tonight?"

"We will," Auggie said. "We're fresh today, but tonight will be more challenging. I'm recommending power naps."

Ronnie called over. "We have dry clothing ready. If you

could throw our wet stuff in the dryer when we change, that would be great. Only one thing fits into the machine at a time, and the coats are a challenge, so that will be helpful."

It was amazing there was even a clothes dryer in the RV. She acknowledged him with a with a nod, happy to be helpful. "Will do."

Around one, her first diner was Ronnie, his face and nose red, his lips chapped. She took a jar of salve from her bag and set on the counter. "Use this before you go back out."

He changed into dry clothes in the back room, stuffed his coat into the dryer, and sat to eat. "You don't know how much this helps, Piper. I'm used to the cold, but dang, this is more than I expected. Delaney thinks we're crazy. She's bringin' the girls later."

She served his hot meal. "It's pretty exciting. I've never been part of anything like this before."

"We appreciate your help, but you should rest whenever you can," he told her. "Delaney was exhausted all the time those first months. Takes a whole lot outta ya to grow a baby."

She appreciated his thoughtfulness as well as his mention of the baby. "I'll be here reading. It's so warm and comfortable, you might have to wake me up next time."

She wasn't asleep, but her eyelids were heavy when Kipp showed up. He used the bathroom, changed and gulped a cup of coffee before sliding onto the bench seat at the small table. She served him, then stuffed his coat into the dryer, glad she'd hung up Ronnie's before resting. "How's it going?"

He took out his phone and showed her photos.

"The well is beautiful! The rope looks realistic, and the wood you've made look grainy on this slab of roof is going to be incredible."

"Dad's starting the bucket. Ronnie and I have laid out blocks for the wheelchair. We'll work on the roof together." His face was reddened, but his voice conveyed the joy of accomplishing something he'd never tried before. "I have to grab more propane bottles for the torch."

"You thought of everything."

"I hope so. I don't want to waste time running out." He glanced up. "How are you?"

"I'm fine. I'm in here where it's warm, reading."

"Sometime we'll have to take the camper out together."

Spend nights in here with no one else around—except a baby? Her imagination conjured up images she'd been trying to avoid. "You think that's a good idea?"

"Sure, go fishing. Spend a couple nights relaxing by a fire. Or then again, we could pitch a tent instead."

"No, this comfy abode suits me just fine."

He laughed and stood. "Well, enjoy your comfy abode." As he put on clean coveralls and zipped into a dry parka, he told her, "The Dream Weaver cameraman and an associate are here now. They've been taking pictures and video. You want to come check out our progress so you can see them."

"Sounds good. I'll go back with you."

She bundled in her warm clothing and joined him at their site where in every direction dozens of sculptors worked on their projects. The buzz of conversation and the sounds of saws and blow torches seemed an odd accompaniment to the steady snow that fell in huge flakes, blanketing the ground and the nearby tents. The ground around the well was a trampled ten-foot circle in the white layer. Tony was sweeping snow from where their tools were arranged on a tarp.

"It's really beautiful so far," Piper told the team. Tony was carving what she supposed was the boy's head, and Ronnie and Auggie were making slender spokes for the wheels of the chair. "You're doing an amazing job. I didn't imagine it would be this stunning."

"Oh, ye of little faith," Auggie called to her. He wore a ski mask, but his eyes were clearly sparkling.

"We're ahead of where I expected to be," Kipp told his dad. "If we get a jump on these pieces and the roof, we could add more features, like grass around the base, a bird on the roof, whatever."

"We could," Auggie replied. "Let's see how this little boy comes along overnight."

Piper had brought ingredients for a hearty beef stew, so she simmered that and baked biscuits in the small oven. Over the course of the day, the men ate and changed in shifts, sometimes napping in the rear bedroom for half an hour.

By eleven that night, they knew they would be finished in plenty of time, and all came into the camper to warm up and talk. They ate the rest of the stew, and then she made them sausages and oatmeal. They talked about other pieces in the competition, about the sculptors they'd met, about the vendors and what they planned to go eat when they were finished. Tony wanted a cupcake from Cookie's bakery.

"I think we have all the kinks ironed out for next time," Ronnie mentioned.

Conversation stopped and the men looked at each other, then glanced over at Piper.

"Are you going to do this again?" she asked.

Kipp's hair stood in rumpled waves after removing his stocking hat and letting his hair loose. He'd washed up and donned a clean shirt, which he wore with the sleeves rolled back. His face was still red, his lips and nose chapped, but he was still the most handsome man she'd ever seen. Her heart swelled at the sight of him looking so happy. He was focused on her.

Was he looking for a reaction? Approval?

She only raised her brows to affirm her question.

"I'd do it again," Kipp said. "I'd like to do it again, now that we've got the hang of working with the ice. We're not pros by any means—some of those guys have done this for twenty plus years, but we have the drive and ambition."

Auggie nodded. "I think we've learned a lot this time."

"Let's talk about it after this one is behind us," Ronnie suggested.

"I'd be game," Tony added. "I saw some really impressive stuff, and now that we've learned techniques, we might do something more advanced."

"Like maybe a treehouse?" Piper asked excitedly. "Like a house on an enormous branch or something? That would be awesome."

"I do know something about treehouses," Tony answered with a chuckle.

After a long night of carving in the winter cold, the guys cleaned up again, ate, and by that afternoon, they knew they would be finished in plenty of time. Before six that evening, the tools were packed and snow cleared from the sculpture.

The Dream Weavers' representatives had placed a large sign near their sculpture that read:

Dream Weavers for Kids
MAKING WISHES COME TRUE
Your donation today will weave a dream
for a child with a critical illness
Give from the heart
Give generously

The parking lot was still full, and visitors stood around the ice sculptures as the judges visited each display and scored the entrants. They would convene somewhere warm, and winners would be announced at noon the following day.

The guys all congratulated each other before going to inspect the other entrants' displays. Leslie Ann, Delaney and the girls had arrived and joined them.

"I've taken the girls to play games and eat cupcakes already," Delaney said to her husband. "You ready to go home?"

"Boy am I. I'll meet you at the house."

Wearing a white cable knit hat and gray coat, Leslie Ann said to Auggie, "You bringing the RV home now?"

Her husband nodded.

"I'll help you get it hitched," Kipp said.

"Are you fellas starving?" Leslie Ann asked.

Auggie shook his head. "Heck no. Piper kept us well fed. Hot meals and drinks."

Leslie Ann gave Piper an appreciative smile. "I have a feeling this won't be the last time they do this."

"I have a feeling you're right."

"Thanks, Piper," Kipp said as they walked back to the camper. He grabbed a shovel and broom from an outside compartment on the RV, cleared off her car and shoveled around the door. "Toss me your keys."

Minutes later, her vehicle was warm.

"You're welcome to come over and chill with me," he said. "I'll be on the couch, under a blanket the rest of the evening."

Being warm and cozy inside with Kipp sounded pretty good. "I'll check on Grandad and be over."

Grandad had company when she got home. He and Jeeter were playing chess with a recorded football game on in the background. "What are you watching?"

"We're not really watching. It's the 1991 divisional playoff with the Oilers. The game with Elway's fifteen-point comeback."

"I guess that's a good one?" She had no clue where they found this stuff to watch, but didn't ask. "Did you guys eat?"

"I brought a tuna casserole Mrs. Harper gave me." The woman he mentioned was his neighbor who kept him stocked with baked goods and casseroles.

"She's sweet on you, you know," Piper told him. "You need to invite her to stay and eat with you."

"What's a lady like her need with an old geezer like me?" Jeeter said.

Grandad glanced up at Piper and grinned.

"A friend?" she replied.

"Nah," he said. "She's got lots of friends. They're always over making quilts."

"Those are *girl*friends."

Jeeter waved her off, and she laughed. She showered quickly, rinsed their dishes and loaded the dishwasher, then told Grandad she wouldn't be too late.

By the time she arrived, Kipp had showered too, his hair dried into waves. He wore a faded red plaid flannel shirt with gray sweat pants, and she loved that he was his own unpretentious self around her.

"I have water on to make you a cup of tea." He went into the kitchen, Archie's nails tapping on the wood floor as he followed.

She settled on his couch and glanced at an oversized postcard on the table where he'd dropped his mail. "'Storybook Holiday in Evergreen, Colorado,'" she read aloud.

"I get a postcard every year." He set a steaming mug on the table.

"Have you ever gone?"

"Nope. I think it's geared toward kids. You?"

"I haven't." She pointed to the small print. "They have ice sculptures you could check out. It's next weekend."

"Might be fun to see how they compare to the ice

sculptures at Winter Festival. Let's make a day of it. Dinner somewhere nice before we drive home."

The dog had returned and now settled at her feet with a soft grunt.

She glanced over as Kipp seated himself on the other end of the couch. His suggestion almost sounded like a date. Her stomach dipped. "That might be fun."

He switched on the television. "What are you in the mood for? Detectives? Aliens?" He looked over at her. "A western?" He turned his attention back to the movie selections. "Romance?"

Piper's heart fluttered. She picked up the mug of tea and blew across the top, then took a sip. Was he flirting or had her hormonal imagination gone wacky? She was still thinking about the question, when Kipp set down the remote and picked up his iPad.

"Wait, would you mind helping me choose presents for the girls?" He turned on the tablet and it opened to the shopping app. "I have their lists." He fished a piece of paper from under the mail. "But I get confused when I look at all the stuff. I've been scrolling through pink and purple toys for over a week."

"Might be iffy finding something last minute. There are still a couple weeks, I guess." After putting the mug back on the table, she scooted over beside him to look at the screen. "Be prepared for popular items to be sold out."

With a look of concern, Kipp showed her the list, written in childish scrawl. "Lillian wrote these."

"Glamour Guinea pigs?" She opened an app on her own phone. "Oh, they're *adorable*."

"No, you are," he said.

"No, you are." With a grin, she glanced over. He was

looking at her like he wanted to say something else. "What?"

He went back to studying the tablet.

"A mama and three babies," she said. "And each one has a glowing light heart. They come with a hutch for them to sleep in. It's available."

He leaned close to see her phone. "It is?"

He smelled really good. Her insides turned to liquid. She tapped the screen. "Delivery in two days."

"Tell me exactly what it's called." He found it on his app and ordered it before it was gone. "Oh my gosh, thanks. Now this."

"'Fruits and vegetables to cut,'" she read and gave him a curious look.

"Yeah, carrot and beet halves with Velcro® that holds the slices together. Kids cut it with a play knife. Evelyn has a little kitchen."

She took the iPad and located what he wanted. "These, I think?"

"Perfect. I'll get two different sets."

Would they be sharing shopping lists for their baby next year? Was it too soon? She lifted her gaze to his profile. "Should we get something for the baby?"

His attention shifted to her. "Your first ultrasound is at eighteen weeks."

"Too soon, I guess."

"No, no it's not. We could get one of those dangly things for the crib—"

"A mobile?"

"Yeah," he agreed. "And a stuffed animal maybe. A nightlight. And every kid needs a special blanket."

They put their heads together over Kipp's iPad and

murmured comments when he followed a suggested link to something else. "Look at these striped socks with little rattles on the toes," he said. "Let's get these."

He poured over items, and Piper snuggled closer to see better. Never would she have imagined they'd be shopping for their baby. *Their baby.* The words felt like a foreign language. But they felt so right. And she was experiencing a joy she'd never before known. She was hopeful...and happy.

She studied the wave of his hair falling over his cheek, his lashes and dark defined brows, the curve of his lips.

As though feeling her scrutiny, he faced her and lowered the tablet to the cushion.

"I never in a million years thought we'd be doing this." Her voice came out thicker than she'd intended. Almost quavering.

"I know. I wanted a family someday," he said softly. "I didn't imagine it would happen like this." He reached to run his fingertips along her cheek and across her jaw, the touch sending tingles across her skin.

More than once, she'd imagined kissing him, wondered what it would feel like, if it would be awkward or enticing. The thought alone was exhilarating. She wanted to discover once and for all exactly what it felt like. If it was a mistake, she'd know—they'd know.

CHAPTER EIGHT

She leaned closer, raising her face to his. Kipp encircled her in his arms and their lips met in a warm dance of discovery. Butterflies fluttered in her stomach; her body tingled with exhilaration.

She wrapped an arm around his neck and clung. He kissed her cheek, her chin, her neck and returned to her mouth. He stroked her ribs and back through her shirt and framed her face with both hands.

If this kiss was a mistake, it was a glorious one. A mistake she didn't regret. She wouldn't take it back for a million dollars. With his arms around her, the world settled into place, and she felt as though she'd found something that had been out of reach her whole life.

"I keep waiting for you to jump up and run," he said, bracketing her face in his palms.

"I'm not running," she replied. "I'm wondering if I'll wake up and find this was a dream."

He kissed her again, an indulgent deep-drawn kiss that

said this was very real. When he slowly drew away, she was breathless.

"I've wanted to do that for a very long time." His voice was gruff.

"Why didn't you?"

"I didn't want to spoil our friendship."

"Is it spoiled now?"

He relaxed his hold but didn't release her, remaining only inches away. "What do you think?"

"Honestly. I'm terrified, but not enough to cut and run. Not enough to not do that again. In fact…"

"What?" he asked.

"Now I want to know if it's as good the second time."

Their second kiss was even better.

Eventually, Kipp turned on the movie, but neither of them watched much of it. Holding each other, looking at the other through the lens of discovery was all consuming.

"If I'd known this was my magic shirt, I'd have worn it for you a long time ago," he teased.

"If I'd known you had that shirt, I probably would have used it for a paint rag," she teased back.

He laughed.

"I know what to get you for Christmas."

He raised his brows. "A new shirt?"

"A matching one for me? Red flannel pajamas?"

Perhaps feeling left out, Archie put his head on her knee and gave her a pitiful look until she petted him. The dog queried with both front paws on the sofa, tail wagging.

Piper looked at Kipp. "Can he come up?"

He grinned. "Can't say no to either one of you."

She patted the sofa beside her and Archie leaped up and, with a soft groan, made himself comfortable.

Piper and Kipp exchanged an amused glance, and he wrapped his arm around her shoulders. Safe and contented, she snuggled against him.

She didn't sleep much that night, remembering their kisses, remembering the way he'd walked her to the vehicle he'd already warmed up, then sat inside, holding her for a long giddy moment until finally getting out, saying, "Text me when you get home."

She felt as though a light had come on—a light that been right there all along, but she'd missed its illuminating abilities. Now she couldn't bear to turn it off. Her world and everything in it had changed colors, was brighter, the edges defined.

She texted him that she was home safe and sound.

He replied: 'I can't wait to see you again.'

She sent a smiley face with hearts. Doubts didn't crowd into her spellbound consciousness until she'd slept a few hours and woke to prepare for work. It was Sunday, a day like all the other Sundays that had come before it... except...now she realized she was wholly, hopelessly, transcendently in love with Kipp Hudson.

Monday morning Kipp perched on a stool behind the glass knife counter in his store. He'd been pulling boxes from the cabinet underneath, checking identifying codes and keeping a list on the laptop. The first of the year would be here in a couple weeks, and he'd need to have inventory finished. His attention hadn't been on the task, however.

He'd been looking at his phone lying on the counter, willing it to ring, wondering if Piper regretted what had happened night before last. He'd called her yesterday to tell her their ice sculpture had received an honorable mention. She'd sounded excited. She'd congratulated him. He'd thanked her for her part in their accomplishment. They'd both avoided mentioning the monumental personal development or their feelings about it. Was she sorry? She hadn't seemed sorry. Did she feel as elated as he did? Impossible. He'd glimpsed the possibility of his dream coming true.

"You've counted that same stack three times," Eddie said. "You must still be tired."

He was tired, but not resulting from all the hours sculpting in the cold. He'd barely slept the past two nights. He needed to say something to her. They had to talk. But what would he say? They couldn't pretend it hadn't happened. Those kisses were life-changing.

At least for him.

"I'm going to get a bite to eat," he told Eddie. "What would you like from Pearl's?"

The front windows of the café were painted with enchanting figures of elves and gingerbread houses when he parked in front. Each year the high school art class offered to paint windows along Silverville and Brook Park Roads, accepting donations to fund class trips to The Denver Art Museum. Inside a small, decorated tree sat by the register, and Edith's ceramic Santa and reindeer adorned the top of the bakery case.

Mouthwatering sweet and spicy aromas notified him

it was chili and cinnamon roll day. He spotted Piper behind the counter where only a handful of customers sat on the chrome pedestal stools. He hung his coat, and she spotted him as he found a seat.

Her cheeks blushed a becoming pink and she gave him a hesitant smile that plucked at his already vibrating heartstrings. "Hey, Kipp."

He leaned on the counter. "How are you?"

"Good."

He glanced to see if anyone could overhear them. "I didn't ask if you'd told anyone about the—you know who —yet."

"Only Marty and Edith. They needed to know."

He nodded. "Planning ahead."

"What will you have?"

He met her eyes. "Are we okay? I don't want it to be weird between us."

"Is it weird?" she asked.

"I hope not." He glanced aside. "Maybe a little right now."

She turned and spotted the other server. "Mary Beth, I'll be back in ten."

The dark-haired woman simply nodded.

Piper motioned for Kipp to join her and led him into a tiny office area opposite the restrooms. Among the clutter was a desk holding a computer, racks of papers and mail, and two mismatched straight-back chairs. She stood facing him, but not close enough to touch. "I don't like not knowing what you're thinking."

"Same," he replied. "It's driving me crazy."

She opened her mouth, but faltered, obviously struggling to form words. Her hesitancy made his gut ache.

"I'm afraid to say what I feel. As afraid as I was to feel anything in the first place."

"Because?"

"Because I don't want to hope for something impossible. I don't want to…feel what I feel and then lose it."

"What do you feel?" he was pushing her, but he wanted to know. Had to know.

She glanced at the wall behind him for burning seconds before meeting his gaze. Muted music filtered in from the café: Bing Crosby singing *White Christmas*.

She placed her hand over her belly.

"Is something wrong? Does something hurt?"

"No," she said quickly. "My stomach is full of nerves." She clasped her hands in from of her. "You know how badly I want a family. I was afraid before. Afraid of being left alone. This makes me afraid again."

"What is scaring you?" he asked and gently held her upper arms. "Is it me? Is it something I've done or didn't do?"

"No." She shook her head. "No, I don't know." She looked him in the eyes and took a deep breath. "This, you and me, Kipp—this feels like family. To be honest, I've buried these feelings for a long time, and the last few weeks have peeled away the denial until I'm bare and raw."

Her words soothed all the aching places inside, and his hope burst into reality. This. This was what he'd only dared dream of, having her return his feelings. "You and I feel like a family to me, too," he said. "I kept my distance because you wanted to be friends, but I've probably been in love with you since high school. I considered it a crush and figured I'd get over it and move on. But when we started hanging out last summer, the same emotions hit me like a tidal wave and didn't let up. I love everything about you, Piper Newport." He allowed his gaze to caress her hair, her wide blue eyes, the soft curve of her cheek. "I love your voice, the way you smile, how you love animals, the way you love people, how you give of yourself so generously. I love that you don't know beans about football. I love you."

Her eyes filled with tears and her lips trembled. She grasped his forearms, and he slid his hands to her shoulders.

"I don't ever want you to feel afraid again," he said. "There's nothing more that I could ever want besides you and our baby." He thought a second and grinned. "Except maybe another baby."

She smiled tremulously and he used his thumbs to wipe her tears.

"I love you, Kipp. I want to be with you and make a home and have our baby together."

She loved him. He kissed her, drawing her into his arms.

"You love me," he said against her hair.

"I do."

"This is going to be the best Christmas ever," he said. "I was happy before, but now…you love me? Our baby will be the frosting on the cake."

Christmas Eve at the Hudsons was an event. Leslie Ann's enormous, decorated tree held candy canes and cookies with see-through candy centers, which the adults pretended not to see the girls sneaking to eat.

Delaney's parents joined them, and her mother had made a kettle of oyster stew. Leslie Ann had prepared what was apparently her traditional lasagna. Delaney made her strawberry pretzel dessert and Piper baked herb and cheddar rolls and a pie. After they'd eaten and were settling around the tree in the family room to open presents, Kipp spoke up. "Piper and I have an announcement."

"Another one?" Ronnie asked. "Is it twins?"

"No," Kipp replied. "At least I don't think so." He and Piper exchanged a glance before he settled beside Piper and took her hand.

Leslie Ann's eyes widened, and the other family members sat like statues, all except Lillian and Evelyn, who continued to peruse packages under the tree. Piper locked gazes with her grandfather, whose eyes crinkled at the corners. They'd already told him. He gave her a comforting nod.

"Piper and I are going to get married," Kipp announced.

No one spoke for a full thirty seconds, and then Auggie said to Piper, "You said it would be wrong to marry only to have a child."

"It would be." She gave a shy nod. "But that's not the reason we want to get married. We could have parented the child apart." She laid her other hand over Kipp's and looked at him. "We're getting married because we're in love. I mean crazy happy, all-in in love."

Her soon-to-be husband wrapped his arm around her

shoulders and drew her close, giving her a sweet kiss. "Crazy happy," he echoed.

"Oh, my goodness!"

"That's wonderful!"

"Oh, Kipp!"

"I knew it!"

The voices combined to rejoice over their news, and rounds of hugs and tears followed. Leslie Ann slid onto the sofa next to Piper. "Kipp told me weeks ago how he felt about you." She reached for Piper's hand and squeezed it. "I can tell you truly love him back."

"I do. I didn't let myself think it or admit it. Fear of being abandoned or rejected kept me frozen from letting myself feel. Thanks goodness everything aligned the way it did or I'd still be hiding from myself."

"You were brave to tell him how you feel."

Piper grinned and glanced at Kipp, who was listening. "We were both holding back saying what we wanted to say. Now I can't even remember how it all came out."

"You said what we have together feels like family," he reminded her.

"Yes." She smiled. "It very much feels like family."

"I guess that contract is null and void," Ronnie commented from across the room.

"I guess it is," Kipp replied. "We'll have a new contract in February. Our wedding vows."

"February?" Leslie Ann nearly squealed. "A Valentine wedding?"

"Whatever Piper wants," Kipp replied. "Lillian, Evelyn, there's a small red package under the tree with Piper's name on it. Her name starts with P. Can you find it?"

Evelyn found it first and darted forward. The girls sat at Piper's feet. "Are we opening presents now?"

"After Piper opens hers," Delaney answered.

Piper took the small square package and easily untied the gold ribbon to reveal a blue velvet ring box. Her heart stuttered, but it was a deliriously happy feeling. She glanced up.

His bright hazel eyes conveyed his adoration and the promise he was making.

She opened the box. Rose gold vines surrounded a square diamond in a vintage-style engagement ring with tiny diamonds entangled in the vines. Granted she'd never looked at engagement rings much, but she'd never seen anything as beautiful as this.

"Do you like it?" he asked.

"I love it," she answered breathlessly.

He took the ring from its velvet cushion and motioned for his nieces to stand on either side. In an unexpected gesture, he knelt on one knee and held out the ring.

"Oh my." Piper's heart swelled at his romantic behavior. She glanced at the expressions of those watching. Grandad was grinning from ear to ear, and Leslie Ann had her fingers over her mouth in anticipation. Auggie reached to guide his wife from her sitting position and wrapped an arm around her shoulders.

They'd already decided they wanted to be together forever, but she adored Kipp's formal and very public gesture.

"Piper," he said. "I've loved you for a long time. I only dreamed you would love me back someday. Our love is a dream come true. I would have waited for you, but I'm sure glad I don't have to. We'll be combining our families into one. We'll be having at least one baby together, maybe more. But from now on, we'll be planning life together. Will you marry me?"

She hadn't stopped smiling since she'd opened the gift. Her heart had never been this full. "I will be very proud— and very happy to marry you."

She offered her hand. He slid the ring along her finger, over her knuckle and nestled it into place. Through a sheen of tears, she admired the sparkling gem, her heart beating in a joyous rhythm.

Still holding her hand, he stood, urging her to stand before him, and she raised her gaze, in awe of the love in his eyes. "I love you," she whispered.

Sighs and a few sniffles from the others accompanied his responding, "I love you."

She'd begun this journey with the single-minded goal of having herself a baby, so she could have a family. Well, she was having a baby. But not alone. She and Kipp were having a baby together and, along with the others cele-brating this moment with them, they'd be a family. It had come in the most unexpected way, but Piper had the family she'd always yearned for.

Eve
Before Christmas

Bernadette Jones

EVE BEFORE
CHRISTMAS-CHAPTER ONE

"What do you mean you can't fix it? You're a plumber," Mitch asked, looking at the split pipe the man was showing him. Mitch had already been up for over twenty-four hours. There'd been an emergency at the hospital due to a bus accident and he'd been called in early. When he'd returned home, he'd heard water running and found the basement of the house he'd purchased less than thirty days ago filled with a foot of water.

"I'm sorry man, that snowstorm hit hard and along with the freezing temperatures there's been considerable destruction. A lot of people are experiencing busted pipes," the plumber sympathized. "Honestly, you got off lucky. Once the parts come in, we can fix yours in a day or so. Since you haven't done any finish work down here the cleanup shouldn't be too bad.

"Dalgleish Construction doesn't normally do work in this housing edition because Keane doesn't like fixing the other contractors' messes. But I guess you're a friend.

"I guarantee your plumbing will be done correctly so this won't happen again. It will take us about an hour to pump out the rest of the water. Then we'll hook up the dehumidifiers. You'll be without water for a few days, so you might want to find a place to stay. I'd start calling places now. A lot of the hotels are booked with the storm and Winter Festival."

Shit. Mitch glanced at his watch. He had to be back in the ER in a few hours. He nodded and thanked the man. If it hadn't been for Doc Gage Ewing and his friendship with Dagleish Construction, Mitch would still be waiting for a plumber and watching the water continue to rise.

Going back upstairs he pulled up the numbers for the local hotels. He got lucky on the eighth call. Between the snowstorm, breaking water pipes, and the upcoming holidays, most rooms had been booked. The Prospector Inn on Burnham and Chickering Road was the first place with an unoccupied room, so he grabbed it.

An hour later, he pulled into the motel's packed parking lot. He studied the slightly rundown exterior. Maybe there was a reason this place had a room. He stepped from his Jeep and shook his head. It didn't matter. He'd take what he could get.

Since it was after eleven p.m., he followed the posted instructions on the lobby door and rang the bell for entrance. A young woman behind the desk glanced up. When the latch released, he walked into the small lobby. The slight woman slid from her stool, placing her book on the counter as he approached.

She smiled. "Welcome to Prospectors Inn. Do you have a reservation, sir?"

Damn, was he dreaming? Deep blue eyes, blonde hair,

and an angelic face. The woman was gorgeous. But the smile, the 'welcome home' smile, was what made his heart speed up.

"Sir, if you give me your name I can check for your reservation."

Her soft voice finally registered and he gave himself a mental shake. "Sorry. Yes, it's Mitch Smith. I called about an hour ago."

"Oh yes, I remember. You mentioned you'd like a quiet room. It's next to last on the short side of the building. There's someone on the end, but they're quiet and work nights so they shouldn't bother you. The guest on the other side is one of the artists at the festival, and he'll be gone most of the time."

"Thank you." He leaned forward to read her name tag and noticed her sweet baby bump. "Norma."

She placed a form on the counter. "Check out is ten in the morning. If you'll sign and give me your credit card, I'll get your key."

He pulled his card from his wallet and hesitated. "I might need to stay longer than tonight. Do you have openings for the rest of the week? Should I book now?"

She hesitated before leaning closer. "Normally we're never full, but it's the Winter Festival and with the snowstorm we've had more guests needing last-minute accommodations. Your room was the last one open. If you think you may need to stay longer, you probably should reserve it now."

"Okay, book me through next Wednesday."

She gave him a quizzical glance. "You aren't traveling through town?"

"No. I live in Spencer. I work at the hospital. The

water pipes broke in my house and they won't be able to get the parts for a few days."

He leaned his hip against the counter and waited as she checked him in. He glanced at the two library books beside the computer. One on early childhood development and the other on baby-led weaning. "How long have you lived in Spencer?"

"A little over four months," she answered.

"You're not from Spencer?"

"No, I moved here looking for a fresh start. It's beautiful and so peaceful near the mountains."

The doctor in him rose and he studied her face more intently, noting the slight shadows under her eyes and her pale cheeks. She moved sluggishly, deliberately. Everything about her screamed over tired. Pregnancy had that effect on most women. She was slender, only about five foot five. Was she taking good enough care of herself? Why the hell was her husband letting her work nights?

He glanced at her hands as she typed in his information. She didn't wear a wedding band. It was none of his business, but he couldn't seem to stop himself. "What's your husband do?"

"Oh, I'm not married." As if realizing what she'd admitted, she handed him his card and placed her left palm on her belly. Her shoulders stiffened defensively. "Lots of women have babies on their own."

"Yes, they do, and they do a great job of it. I have a good friend who's a single mom and she's fantastic. I'm sure you will be, too."

Her shoulders relaxed. "I'm going to be. I've been reading all the books at the library."

"What about family nearby to help out?"

Slipping his room key in a card envelope, she wrote his room number on top and shook her head. "No, I lived with my aunt and uncle until I was old enough to get a job. They already had too many kids and didn't need another mouth to feed."

The automatic way she repeated the phrase, he suspected she'd been told it more than once. "How long did you live with them?"

"Mom left when I was twelve and I got my first job when I was sixteen." She frowned, laying her palm on her bump. "I never knew my dad. He didn't want kids. My baby's father doesn't want kids either and not knowing my ex is probably a good thing."

She met his gaze, giving him a self-reliant smile. "But we'll be okay."

He nodded in agreement. She'll be better off without an asshole who wouldn't support his child. "Are you having a boy or a girl?"

"I don't know."

"Your doctor couldn't tell from the ultrasound?"

She glanced away. "I haven't had an ultrasound. I don't have insurance. The closest free clinic is Boulder. My car died, which is partly why I stayed here in Spencer."

Concerned, Mitch straightened. "When was the last time you saw your physician?"

"When I first found out I was pregnant. There was a free clinic in Denver."

"You said you've been here four months." He looked at her, quickly doing the math. She's too small for being five months pregnant. "How far along are you?"

"The doctor in Denver told me to expect the baby in late January. I think I found a midwife here in Spencer.

She sounded nice on the phone. She told me all the things I'd need to buy, so I've been trying to get a few items each week. Oh geez. Listen to me blab on." She blushed. "Comes with working the night shift alone."

Seven months! He choked down his frustration and concern. What if something went wrong? He looked at her weary eyes. What if something was already wrong? "You know, there may be local groups to help. Let me do some checking and I'll get back to you."

"Oh no, you don't need to do that." Her eyes opened wide. "Oh, I forgot you said you work at the hospital. What do you do?"

"I'm an ER doctor."

"That must be exciting. All those people you get to help."

And all those he lost, like the young man he'd tried to save earlier that evening. The exhaustion and sorrow of the last few hours washed over him, a not-so-subtle reminder he had to be back at the ER soon. "I'll check for social services groups tomorrow. When's your next shift?"

"I run the desk from eleven at night to six in the morning," Norma responded with a smile. "And my cleaning hours start around eleven in the morning."

"That's a lot of hours for a woman carrying a child." No wonder she looked exhausted. "Why so many?"

"I didn't have much savings when I left Denver. When I got here the manager offered to let me have a room really cheap if I worked the night desk and did some of the cleaning. It's worked out well for me, especially since I don't have transportation. I'm saving for the things I'll need when the baby comes."

"Good for you," he automatically encouraged. Mitch

stooped and lifted his duffel bag, stopping to wave as he went out the door to locate his room.

She worked two jobs seven days a week? What a deal the manager was giving her. Fucking asshole. Mitch shook his head in disgust. Tomorrow, he'd add asking around about the owner of this little fleabag motel to his list.

CHAPTER TWO

*N*orma watched the handsome man exit before sitting on her stool. She pulled a package of peanut butter crackers from her pocket and nibbled the corner of one. Wow! Now she understood what the romance novels meant when they said, 'her heart was aflutter'.

She couldn't remember ever meeting such a handsome man. Coal black hair, dark lashes and blue-gray eyes. He was younger than any doctor she'd ever met. The doctor at the clinic who'd told her she was pregnant was old, balding and pudgy. Mitch was probably only mid-thirties and built more like a football player. His white button-down shirt had been tight across his chest and biceps.

His musky aftershave lingered in the air and she inhaled deeply. The scent was a welcome relief from the lobby's irritating disinfectant smell. The memory of his smile brought one to her lips.

When he looked at her, she felt special, as though she had all his attention. Someday she wanted someone to look at her that way and mean it. She ran her palm over her bump. Someone who would want and love her and her baby.

She gave her head a shake. She'd make sure her child knew how much they were wanted and loved. As if her little one knew her thoughts, it gave a kick then pushed up under her ribcage.

Sliding off the stool, Norma walked around the lobby, straightening cushions and giving the baby room to stretch. Living at the motel was not the ideal situation to raise a child, and she didn't know what she'd do after the baby was born. She didn't make enough money to afford childcare. Somehow, she had to convince her boss she could still cover the desk and get the cleaning done with the baby at her side. She'd read newborns slept a lot.

Once the snow melted and she wasn't so tired, she'd walk to the library and use the computer to check the neighborhood. Maybe she could find someone willing to barter for child care.

The next morning, as Mitch was leaving, he saw Norma entering the room next to his. The last room on his wing, the one she'd said was occupied by someone who worked nights. And days. He fumed at the disparity of the working class need and lack of support. He was a firm believer that women should have free medical care for pregnancy and children should be provided free care until eighteen. He'd been raised to believe taking care of each other was a responsibility, not an arbitrary choice.

Dr. Gage Ewing walked into the ER a little before the end of Mitch's shift. "How's it going, Smitty? Did they fix your pipes?"

Already annoyed with the day, Mitch glanced up. Damn, he hated that nickname. It was his own fault that people called him Smitty.

Spencer, Colorado, was his first venture away from his family and old classmates. Burnham Hospital had been his career-starting residency and now he held a permanent position. At his first staff meeting four years ago, they'd asked him what he wanted to be called privately. He could have dumped the nickname then, but out of habit he'd responded with the dreaded moniker that had been his through high school, college and med school.

"Why the hell doesn't Spencer have a free clinic for women?" His frustration added an extra snap to his words. "Why do they have to go all the way to Boulder? What if they don't have transportation?"

Gage leaned against the counter, arms folded over his chest and studied him for a long moment. "I don't know the answer to that, but you and I can check into it. Is there a particular reason this is a concern today? A patient?"

Mitch looked away. Gage wasn't that much older, but those years had been hard lived before he'd come to Spencer. His experience in high crime ERs along with a danger filled life of his own had to have been an advanced class in emergency medicine.

Coming from sheltered roots, Mitch had learned more about the real world from his friend. Gage had actually saved his life when he'd been given a drug overdose by a psychotic killer. Gage was the best mentor a guy could ask for.

Mitch scrubbed a hand over his face and exhaled a heavy breath. "The plumber came, but so many houses in that division had problems they're out of parts. It's going to be a few days. No real damage, just inconvenience." He reviewed and signed a progress note from his shift, then cued another.

"Between the festival and snow, the only room I could find was at Prospectors Inn. The place is a step up from a rent-by-the-hour. Well, maybe a step up. The night clerk is a young pregnant woman. We talked a bit and I found out she hasn't seen a physician since she learned she was pregnant. The asshole who got her pregnant didn't want her or the baby. She's on her own with no family nearby."

"That's tough," Gage agreed.

"She's about five-foot-five, willowy, with this cute little baby bump. Beautiful honey-blonde hair and the bluest eyes you've ever seen, with long dark lashes. She's gorgeous and sweet. And so excited to have this baby, a family of her own. I could hear it in her voice." He signed the next report and glanced up.

Gage arched his brow and grinned. "So, she's hot?"

Mitch cleared his throat. Shit, was he that obvious? Gage was a good friend and Mitch could talk to him about anything. But he wasn't sure this was the place to discuss his love life—or more importantly, lack of. Besides, he'd just met her and she had a lot on her plate without him making a move on her.

"She's due at the end of January. Her eyes are shadowed and she's too thin. I'm not sure she's even taking vitamins due to her financial situation. I'm concerned. Professionally."

Gage nodded. "I'm back in my office on Monday. Get her schedule and let me know. I'll work her in."

"She'll balk. I don't think she can pay."

"You've got a great bedside manner. Convince her. You'll think of a way to talk her into coming." Gage glanced at his beeper and headed for the door.

Mitch grabbed his last file to review. Yeah, convince her. But how?

It was close to one-thirty before Mitch pulled into the inn's parking lot. He'd stopped at the all-night quick shop to grab a few things, at his house to check on the basement, then made sandwiches and grabbed fruit, chips and yogurt. He realized he was making assumptions, but he couldn't help but suspect she didn't eat enough.

When he pushed through the doors, Norma smiled. "Good evening, Dr. Smith."

"Call me, Mitch. May I call you Norma?"

"Sure of course. Did you need something?"

"No. I got off late and grabbed a snack. I thought maybe you'd share a sandwich with me and keep me company. There's not a lot of people up at this time of night—actually early morning—to talk to."

Norma nodded. "I understand. With the no vacancy sign flashing, no one is stopping to even price a room. Typically, it's pretty quiet after midnight, anyway." She grinned. "I've started singing and dancing to the radio for company. Thank heavens no one can hear or see me or they'd think I was possessed."

She slid from her wooden bar stool, opened the cupboard door behind her and grabbed a second stool. Before she could lift it, Mitch had rounded the corner and taken it from her. He placed it on the opposite side of the counter. Shrugging out of his jacket, he laid it over one of the guest chairs in the lobby behind him before taking his seat. Placing a large bag on the counter, he pulled out two bottles of juice.

"Apple or orange?"

"Mitch, I can't take your food. But I'll keep you company."

"My mother would say it's bad manners to eat in front of you, and since I grabbed plenty there's no reason for either of us to go without." He raised an eyebrow. "Apple or orange?"

"Apple."

Next, he pulled out paper plates, napkins, two bags of chips, and three twelve-inch hoagie sandwiches, followed by two huge oatmeal raisin cookies.

Eyes wide at the spread before her, Norma gasped. "Do you always get this much food?"

"Most of the time I'm lucky if I get to grab a cup of coffee while I'm at work. I've pretty much learned to wait until I'm off to eat. As a medical professional, I do not recommend this lifestyle to my patients. But…." He shrugged. "I have, however, become the sandwich connoisseur. We have ham and Swiss cheese, or turkey and gouda with slivers of fresh apple. Last option is avocado, fresh mozzarella and tomato." He held up a sharp knife. "If you can't decide, I came prepared to give you a sample of each."

"They all sound wonderful." She met his gaze. "I'd like the sampler plate, chef."

Norma studied him in amazement as he devoured half of each sandwich and a man-size handful of baked sweet potato chips.

He'd given her a fourth of each sandwich and she struggled to finish the second. She hadn't eaten properly the last couple of weeks. Her energy was down and so were her spirits. After talking to the midwife and realizing the cost, she'd tried to save extra money where she could. She still needed more diapers, blankets and clothes for the baby. Her options were clothing for the baby or food for herself.

Consumed with her financial issues, she hadn't paid attention to the weather forecast. When the storm hit, she'd been low on the cereal and boxed milk that were her staples, and she'd been out of bread, peanut butter and canned tuna for over a week. Lately, she'd been so worn out, she couldn't even come up with the energy to walk to the store, let alone worry about food.

With this latest snowfall hitting during the Winter Festival, the motel was full for the first time since she'd been hired. She had to clean all sixteen rooms and the lobby. Working and sleep were all she could handle right now. It would be better in a couple of days. Only desperate people tended to stay at Prospectors Inn.

When she'd first come to town, her old Chevy Impala barely made it into the motel's parking lot before gasping its last breath. She'd had enough money for three nights lodging. She'd asked the manager, Bobby Weiss, where she could get a job.

Once he understood her circumstances, he'd offered her a deal. If she worked the night shift on the desk, it would pay for her room. Then he offered to let her clean the rooms, which would give her cash for food and baby supplies. The agreement had seemed like a godsend at the time. Now, further along in her pregnancy, working so many hours was more physically taxing.

Her minimum wage salary didn't give her much money after taxes. She'd been on her own for several years and knew how to look for bargains, but she'd made more money in Denver, and there'd been bargain places to shop. Even though she'd been doing pretty well, the medical expenses were going to be high. Somehow, she had to convince Bobby to let her have the baby with her while she worked.

Denver also had more charities and shelters, but the baby's father was there. He'd already attacked her once trying to make her lose the baby. She couldn't take a chance he'd find her. Somehow, she had to find a way to stay in Spencer. She felt safe here.

"So do you?"

Mitch's voice interrupted her thoughts. Norma gave her head a shake and smiled. "I'm sorry, I think I zoned out for a minute. What did you ask?"

He held out a mint tin. "Would you like one?"

She nodded and took one. He'd bagged up the food and stood at the counter. "You have one of the mini refrigerators in your room, right?"

"Yes."

"Why don't you take the leftovers? By the time I would get back to them they wouldn't be good, and it gives you something different. You can run them down to your room now."

"What if someone comes?"

"I'll watch the desk. I doubt anyone one will stop anyway. If someone does, I'll tell them you took a bathroom break and I'm watching the door till you return."

She looked at the bag. It didn't seem right to take his food, but the sandwiches would get her by for several days and save her trudging through the snow. Maybe she could even get a little extra sleep tomorrow.

Norma nodded and showed him where to hit the button to unlatch the door. "I'll be right back."

"Wait." Mitch grabbed his jacket and draped it over her shoulders. "It's cold out there, even if it is a short walk."

CHAPTER THREE

*W*hen she returned, Mitch studied Norma with a professional eye. She was dead on her feet. He waited until she took her seat across the counter from him. "Do you do all the cleaning?"

"Yes. It's usually not this much. I don't think I've ever had more than eight rooms before. The snow has made it difficult for people to make day trips to Spencer for the festival, so they're staying overnight."

"Your boss doesn't have anyone to help you when the motel is full?"

"No. There are two parttime desk clerks during the day. But no one else cleans. Besides, I need the money."

"He doesn't have back-up in case you're sick?"

"I don't know." Norma shrugged. "I've never been so sick I couldn't work."

"Does your boss pay you overtime?"

She shook her head. "No. Bobby says that I'm technically working two separate jobs. Same as if I worked here and at the hotel down the street."

"What time will you be done on Monday?"

"Probably close to four. Most of our guests will be checking out Sunday and Monday because the events will be over. Tuesday we only have five guests pre-registered." She tilted her head. "Why do you ask?"

"My friend has a family practice and does free wellness exams when he can. He wants to see you on Monday. There's no charge."

"Why? What did you tell him?" She clasped her hands on the counter.

He noticed her white knuckles and the anxious note in her tone. He only wanted to help, not frighten her.

He placed his hand over hers. "It's okay. I told him you hadn't seen a doctor since you got pregnant. I explained you're a little over tired. From what you just told me you're working too much. But it could also be a vitamin deficiency. Let him see you, Norma, for the baby's sake and yours. I'm off the next three days and I can take you."

She jerked her hand away and crossed her arms over her belly. "Why? Why do you care? Why me?"

"Because pregnancy screenings are important, both for the mother and child. I see how fatigued you are. Helping people, getting people help, is what I do. You'll like Gage. He's a great guy."

Her face paled and her voice cracked. "You think something is wrong with my baby, don't you?"

"No. I'm saying it's time to get a checkup to make sure you have the right vitamins and care to keep you both healthy. Based on what you've told me, you're around thirty to thirty-one weeks, the stage when the baby should start gaining weight. It's an important time in your pregnancy. Norma, this is a blessing. Accept it."

"You're sure he understands I don't have insurance or money right now? I could make payments later."

"Yes, he understands, but this wellness check is free." He held her gaze, willing her to accept.

"Could we go after my cleaning shift? I can start early and have time to get showered."

"Perfect." Relieved she'd agreed, he hesitated. "Now I have one more favor. I'd like you to lay on the couch and take a nap. I'll stay and if anyone pulls into the parking lot, I'll have plenty of time to wake you before they get to the door."

"Oh no. I couldn't do that. It would be wrong to sleep on the job."

He reached across the counter and covered her hands with his. A pleasurable jolt shot through him. He glanced down to where they touched. She was so soft, so delicate and fragile.

She seemed innocent and trusting. Her asshole boss was taking advantage of her and she was defending his explanation. She thought because she felt well that all would be okay with the baby. He had a feeling she probably hadn't received much medical care growing up.

He fought the urge to cross behind the counter, lift her into his arms and take her away. All day his attention had wandered, turning to ways he could watch over and protect her and the baby. To take her away from this manipulative environment without hurting her pride. He'd even called the shelters in Boulder, but they were all full.

He'd also made a few calls about her boss, Bobby. Although the man managed a number of properties for someone who had disappeared suspiciously, Bobby wasn't blatantly crooked. But he did bend legal boundaries to his advantage.

"What's wrong, sweetheart, is that your boss is working you more hours than allowed without paying you overtime. A split shift is not working two jobs. What he's doing is illegal."

She sighed and her eyes glistened with tears. "I know what he's doing. But Mitch, I need this job so I have a place to live. No one wants to hire a pregnant woman who's almost due."

Mitch firmed his lips. He'd be damned if he gave in on this. She would start taking better care of herself. "I won't say anything. For now. But I need you to take a nap. The baby's health, and yours are what's important."

After a moment, she surrendered. "Just a little while. So, I can catch my second wind."

"Just a little while," he assured her. Once she was curled-up on the couch in the lobby, he covered her with his coat. She was sound asleep in five minutes. He sat, simply watching her breathe for almost three hours.

He'd always had a soft spot for the exploited, but Norma was determined not to be a victim. Her conviction to succeed for both herself and her baby inspired him. Now he wanted to show her that accepting help wasn't a weakness or failure.

Later, after Mitch had caught a few hours of sleep, he reached out to Gage. "Will Monday around four-fifteen work?"

"Yes. Is there any way you can get her to the hospital today for an ultrasound?" Gage asked.

"She works till four. We could be there around four-thirty? Earlier if I can swing it."

"Great. I've called in a couple favors and made special arrangements to have the results rushed to me. I'll let the technicians know you're bringing her in today."

After disconnecting, Mitch went in search of Norma. He knocked on the open door of the room she was cleaning. She glanced across the bed from where she'd been tucking in a sheet and smiled the breathtaking smile he looked forward to. "Hi."

"Hi. How many rooms do you have left?"

"Three, then the laundry."

"Doc Ewing has an ultrasound scheduled for you this afternoon. If you show me the laundry, I could work on it while you finish the rooms."

"Mitch, I—"

"I've got nothing else to do. They're still working on my house. Besides, I'm excited to learn if the baby's a boy or girl."

"I—"

"It will help Doc Ewing if he has the reports before he sees you. When you're done with the rooms you can come help with the laundry. We'll get it done faster and then you'll have time to get ready."

As they pulled into the hospital parking lot, Norma glanced nervously at the man who'd been doing so much for her. "Are you going in with me?"

"I'd like to if you want me to."

"I've never been to a hospital before. I—I don't know where to go or what to do. I'm a little anxious."

He smiled and covered her hand with his warm palm. "This is the easiest, most exciting exam you will ever have. The images show up on a screen like a computer monitor. You'll be able to watch, see your child and hear the heartbeat. When they're done, you'll get a still-shot printout of the ultrasound imaging. Your first baby picture. This is nothing painful. It's all joy."

Her baby's father hadn't wanted a child and he'd ranted about not paying child support. Two days before she'd run away, he'd grabbed her by the arms and shaken her, then slapped her hard and pushed her down the stairs at the apartment. Although she'd bruised her elbows and knees, she'd thought she'd protected the baby. What if she hadn't?

What if something was wrong? Was it better to know now?

"Mitch, there's something I need to tell you before we go in. My baby's father pushed me down the stairs, hoping I'd have a miscarriage. But it was early on and I protected my belly when I fell. I wasn't even hurt. It was only six stairs. I… Do you think…?"

Mitch clenched a fist on the steering wheel, but kept his gaze for her warm and reassuring. "I'm sure everything is fine, but that's one more reason this ultrasound is important."

Once out of the vehicle, Mitch rested his hand against her back and she relaxed. He led her to radiology and waited with her, holding her hand in his. Excitement and dread wared within her.

Today she was finally going to see and hear her child for the first time. She'd get a picture and find out the gender. Over the last couple months, she'd experienced the changes in her body and the baby moving. Today she would see.

Mitch stroked the back of her hand with his thumb. If only… If only he was more than a friend. She'd lain awake the last couple of nights wondering what it would feel like to lie next to him. Have him hold her and snuggle. Have him make love to her.

She tried not to let her daydreams take over, but Mitch was the perfect man. Kind, considerate, thoughtful, and so damn hot. She knew there was more to sex than her ex's slam-bang approach.

What would it be like to have a thoughtful lover? To have someone want her? She longed for real love. A love like this feeling growing in her heart for Mitch.

She'd seen the concern on Mitch's face the night she told him she'd only seen a doctor once. He already cared more for her and her child than anyone ever had. He was here, holding her hand and supporting her. If only…

A woman in scrubs walked into the waiting room and called her name. When Norma and Mitch stood, the woman introduced herself. "I'm Sue, your technician today."

The tech glanced at Norma, then shot a bewildered look at their clasped hands. "Dr. Smith, are you coming back with Ms. Brown?"

Norma looked up at him. He leaned forward and whispered, "That's your choice, Norma. If you want me to be with you, I can and I will. I want to be here for as long as you need me. Even after the baby is born."

Relieved, she turned to the technician. "Yes, Mitch is coming with me."

The room with all the machines made her nervous.

After reading the pregnancy pamphlets she'd received at the first free clinic visit in Denver, she'd stopped drinking caffeinated beverages. She'd never smoked or done drugs and didn't miss the occasional alcoholic drink. The generic vitamins from the drugstore were supposed to be just as good as the brand names.

She'd done everything she could afford to do. What if she'd still done something wrong and there was a problem with her baby? Suddenly, she was afraid. What if she'd failed the little one depending on her?

Since the room was small, Mitch waited in the hall until Norma was on the exam table and ready for the procedure. Once he sat next to her and took her hand, her nerves settled. When she heard the baby's heartbeat, she cried out in joy. "Mitch, listen. That's so awesome! That's my baby."

"Yes, it is." Eyes fixed on the monitor, he grinned. "That's a great little heartbeat. Strong, like momma."

Norma scrutinized the screen as the technician pointed out arms and legs, the head, face and little ears. Love like she'd never imagined filled her chest. My baby. So perfect. Wonder and amazement swept over her and she glanced at Mitch. The expression on his face mirrored her feelings of excitement. She wondered if he got this excited for all his patients. Or maybe he felt a little of the same connection she had for him.

Sue spent several minutes trying to get the baby to roll over or shift. "This little one is being a stinker, keeping the butt and back turned to us. I can't get a shot of the genitals to tell the sex. Looks like your baby is already stubborn and independent."

She tried a few more times and finally shook her head.

"I guess you're just going to have to wait and see. I'll get these reports to Dr. Ewing before I leave for the day. He also wants you to stop and give a urine sample and get blood drawn on the way out."

Once she was dressed, Norma walked into the hall to join Mitch. He handed her the black and white ultrasound image. His smile and the joy in his gaze sent little sparks of awareness dancing up her spine. "This feels so much more real now. After hearing the heartbeat and seeing that little body, and now having something tangible to hold on to."

Lost in his tender blue gaze his voice called her back.

"Do you have a baby book to put that picture in?"

She shook her head.

"The phlebotomist will only take a few minutes, then we could stop at the hospital gift shop and get you one. After that I'd like to take you to dinner at Pearl's. You should still be able to get a couple hours of sleep before you have to be at the front desk."

CHAPTER FOUR

*M*itch sat across the booth from Norma at the café. Her gaze kept shifting to the seat beside her where she'd laid the new 'First Year Memory' baby book. She'd chosen a white one with an insert on the cover to slip in the ultrasound picture and a special pen to record all the milestones.

Her blush of excitement magnified her natural beauty. With a little more rest and a few extra meals, her color and fatigue seemed to be improving. He looked up and caught three different guys watching her, interest plainly evident in the intensity of their stares. No way, assholes. She's mine.

Mine. He stared at his unfinished pie. Mine. He wasn't sure where the conviction came from, but it felt right. True.

At the age of fifteen, he'd decided he would be a doctor. His father had smiled, but then told him it was possible he'd change his mind a dozen times before he graduated high school. Mitch hadn't. During his second semester of med school, he'd known he was going to be an ER doctor. After his first interview with Ursula Quimby, the Burnham Hospital Administrator, he'd known he'd be moving to Spencer and making the town his home.

That same peace and certainty filled him as he studied the quiet woman across from him. He'd found his dream girl, and together they'd make a home for the child he already loved as his own.

Norma met his gaze, tilted her head and frowned. "What's up? What's that silly grin about? You kind of look like the cat that swallowed the canary."

Similar to telling his father about his career plans as a teenager, he knew this was too soon to tell Norma his plans for the family they'd build together. He needed to give her time to get to know and trust him.

"I'm content. Dinner was delicious, the company outstanding, and I'm glad we were able to get the medical tests done today so Gage will have the results Monday. It's been a good day." He flagged down the waitress, asking for a box for Norma's leftovers and the bill.

For the next couple of hours Mitch stayed with Norma while she managed the desk. They talked about preferred movies, best and worst books and favorite foods. He learned she loved action movies, hated horror books and films, and her favorite pie was lemon meringue. But her favorite dessert was tiramisu. She'd also beaten him ten out of fifteen games of poker. It was the most enjoyable evening he could remember.

Doctor Gage Ewing was not what Norma expected. He wore blue jeans and a black T-shirt under his red and gray plaid flannel shirt. His sleeves were rolled up, displaying the tattoos covering his arms. He looked more like a biker or bodybuilder than a physician. His gaze was intense but kind.

"Hello, Norma. You're Smitty's friend, right?"

"Smitty?" she questioned.

"Dr. Smith. He referred you."

"Oh, you mean Mitch. Yes, he said he talked to you. He's been helping me a lot. He's so nice. I bet he's a great doctor."

Gage smiled. "Yes, he's excellent and a good friend. He tells me you're a little behind on appointments, so today we're going to get caught up. After I do the exam, we'll talk and go over the results of the tests you did this weekend."

Thirty minutes later, after she was redressed, Dr. Ewing came back into her room. "Norma, you've authorized me to talk to Mitch about your health care. Are you sure?"

"I don't have anyone else, and I don't know many people in Spencer. Mitch already knows all about my situation and what is going on in my life. If something were to happen to me or the baby, I need someone I can trust. He said he wants to be there for us."

"What about the baby's father?"

"He doesn't want the baby. He told me to get rid of it. He… he tried to make me miscarry in the beginning by pushing me down the stairs."

"Have you told Mitch this?"

"Yes. I got scared before the ultrasound."

"Did you file a restraining order against your ex?"

"No. I just left Denver as soon as I could."

"Do you think he'd come after you again?"

She noticed the way Gage's jaw firmed and his hand clenched the edge of the computer cart. The care and concern these strangers showed her was more than she ever expected.

She thought about Dennis, her ex, and how selfish he was. "I don't think so. I promised not to ask for child support, and I didn't tell him I was leaving or where I went."

"Do you have any mutual friends who know where you are?"

"Just one girlfriend, but I haven't talked to her in months."

Gage nodded. "I'd like you to consider filing a restraining order just as a precaution." He held her gaze. "I'm sorry you haven't had any support. But that changes now. Since you listed Smit—Mitch, do you want him to join us to discuss your exam?"

"Yes, please." Relieved, she relaxed as Doc Ewing left the room. Mitch could always explain the medical terms she might not understand.

Mitch came in and sat in the chair beside her. A flare of disappointment rose when he didn't take her hand. She told herself she was being silly. Mitch was a friend. A helpful friend. Nothing more.

Dr. Ewing stood next to his portable computer cart. "There's nothing overly concerning. But there are some adjustments I want you to make. You're a little anemic, and I'd like you and the baby to both put on more weight. Before you leave, stop at the desk and see Carmela. She's got some new vitamin samples I want you to take. She'll also have a list of meats and vegetables as well as food combinations I suggest you increase.

"You need to get more rest. I understand that can be difficult with your current situation. But try. Mitch says he's willing to help, so let him. These last few months are important for you and the baby. Otherwise, everything is progressing normally. I want to see you again in three weeks. Any questions?"

Norma shook her head and tuned out when Mitch asked questions about blood counts and numbers. How was she going to eat better? She had a microwave and a mini fridge that barely held her milk for cereal. If she walked to a restaurant for meals, she'd lose sleep. Besides, she didn't have enough money to eat out all the time.

Mitch squeezed her hand, pulling her from contemplation and rising panic.

"Norma," Dr. Ewing said. "It's all going to work out. You're doing great. Now you have friends to help when you need it. I'm confident everything is going to be fine."

After getting the bag of vitamins from Carmela, Mitch led her to his Jeep and helped her in. He paused, holding the door open. "Gage is right. Everything's going to be fine. Before I take you to the motel, we're going to dinner. You should still be able to get about three and a half hours of sleep before your shift."

"Mitch you should—"

"Burger and fries with a shake at Itza Burger or we can go back to Pearl's. I think tonight is meatloaf night at the café."

She didn't try to hold back a wistful tone. "Oh, I haven't had a burger in forever."

"Then burgers it is. Buckle up."

Once Mitch got Norma settled back at the motel, he called Owen and asked him to meet at the home improvement store with his truck.

"What's up?" Owen asked when he arrived at the store.

"I need a dorm-sized refrigerator with a freezer section, and it won't fit in my Jeep."

"I thought your new place came with one of those industrial size double door units?"

"This is for a friend."

Owen smirks. "The cute little lady friend you've been taking to dinner?"

"How do you know?"

"The guys at the body shop are worse than women with their gossip. One was pissed because he said you gave him the hands-off glare at Pearl's the other night. They all want to know where you found her, because they had never seen her before."

Mitch arrowed his gaze. "Tell all of them to stay away from her. I'm taking care of her."

Owen chuckled. He pushed open the door to the mega hardware store and hummed, 'and another one bites the dust'.

After picking out a stainless-steel mini refrigerator, Mitch noticed a portable induction cooktop like he'd used in college. Considering the layout in his room, he decided she'd have enough square footage for a narrow kitchen cart to hold a toaster and the cooker, as well as shelving for storage. He also grabbed a small fry pan and saucepan combo to use on the cooktop, plates, bowls and silverware for two.

They loaded everything into Owen's truck, and Mitch led the way to the motel and directed his friend where to park. He'd seen Norma at the front desk as he drove past the lobby. The display on his dash read nine p.m. Damn it, she was supposed to be sleeping.

He pulled open the lobby door and waited impatiently as she checked in a new guest. Once the guy left, Mitch approached the registration desk.

"Why are you working? You should be sleeping," he snapped.

She looked at him in surprise and studied his face. "It's okay, Mitch. Don't worry. The other clerk had an emergency and had to leave. I've only been here a little while. I'll be all right. There are only eight rooms to clean tomorrow."

Damn it, this had to stop. She shouldn't be working this much. He had a plan but if he pushed her too hard, too soon, she'd refuse. He slowly let out his breath. Maybe this would be easier in the long run.

"I did some shopping and grabbed a couple things for you. Can I have your key and I'll put them in your room? I have to run to check my place, then I'll stop in and visit when I come back."

"Sure. But you've got to stop feeding me, Mitch. This is the last time."

He took her key card and impulsively leaned across the counter to kiss her cheek. "We'll talk later."

Mitch pushed open the door to her unit. The blinds were closed, and the bed made. The area smelled like the disinfectant she used in all the rooms. There were two packages of cloth diapers, ten to a pack, and a package of diaper covers on the dresser. Next to them was a bag from Like New Reruns, a used clothing store. He frowned and glanced around. There was so much she'd need.

"Where do you want the refrigerator?" Owen asked as he walked in behind him.

Together they set up and plugged in the refrigerator, put together the portable shelving unit, and arranged the countertop burner, toaster and dishes.

Then Mitch went to the store and picked up the groceries Gage had recommended Norma add to her diet. Stopping at his home, he placed the perishable items in his refrigerator. The mini fridge wouldn't be cooled to the appropriate temperature until two in the morning. His shift tomorrow started at noon. If he slept for a couple hours now, he could go back to the motel with the rest of the food and watch over her so she could grab some sleep. And still have time to get more rest for himself.

He grabbed his phone to call her and realized he didn't have her cell number. Pulling up the motel number, he dialed the reception desk.

"Good evening, this is Prospectors Inn, how may I help you?"

Mitch smiled. "Hearing your voice has already brightened my night."

"Mitch, is everything okay?"

"Yeah, I realized I don't have your cell number." Her pause told him the answer before she spoke.

"I don't have a phone," Norma responded. "I was on the same plan as my ex and he took it from me when he kicked me out of our apartment. Before I left Denver, I contacted the apartment manager and had him remove me from the lease. I canceled the phone and utilities that were registered in my name. I lost all my deposits, but I thought that was smarter than letting him run up bills in my name."

"Good move on your part." He didn't have to ask; he knew she couldn't afford a phone now. What pissed him off was that she drove all the way from Denver in a piece-of-shit car with no way to call for help. "Look, Babe, my work schedule starts back up tomorrow. So, I'm going to grab a couple hours of sleep here at my house and then bring you your room card around two. Is that okay?"

"I'll be here. Sleep as long as you can. What time does your shift start?"

"The next three days I'm scheduled from noon to midnight."

"Then sleep. I can always make a second card if you aren't here when I get off. How is your house coming along?"

He glanced at the email on his laptop. The parts were in, and he could move back home on Saturday. But he couldn't leave her alone. If he moved out of the motel, she'd argue with him when he still came back to take care of her. It was too soon to tell her how he felt. He didn't want to lie to her, but he needed to be with her. "Still no water. Maybe soon. Not a big deal."

"Oh Mitch, I'm so sorry. I know how expensive it's been for you."

He held back his snort. He'd spent more in Denver for a weekend sports trip with the guys than this motel cost for the week. "Don't worry, Norma. I can afford it. Have you eaten your leftovers or the yogurt? Remember Gage suggested you eat small meals every couple of hours."

"Yes, Dr. Smith. I ate one of the yogurts and plan on another snack in a little bit."

He heard the teasing smile in her voice and visualized her beautiful face and how her eyes lit with humor.

"Was there anything else you wanted?" Norma asked. "You need to get to bed."

He wanted her in his bed. He wanted to see hunger in her gaze when she looked at him, the same hunger he felt every time he was with her. Her pregnancy did nothing to diminish his desire. He wanted her in every way.

The need to taste her sweet lips was fast becoming more than he could resist. He already used every excuse possible to touch her. He longed to run his hand through her hair, brush his lips over her forehead and kiss a path down her neck until she shivered with need.

At night he lay awake imagining how to please her. He longed to hold her in his embrace, feel her breasts against his chest, rest in the cradle of her hips, so she'd feel every inch of his need and craving.

Dreams of making love with her filled every down moment. How her moans of desire as he suckled her perfect breasts and trailed a path to her core filled his mind. His name would slip from her lips as he brought her to climax after climax. He would satisfy her in every way so she'd never think of anyone else. He needed her to know his feelings weren't fleeting, but the forever kind.

But what if her asshole ex had left her in doubt of all men and their motives? If he could just get his hands on the bastard for pushing her down the stairs...

"Mitch, is everything okay?"

He cleared his throat. "Yeah. My turn to zone out for a minute. Keep the door locked, eat your snack and I'll see you in a couple hours. Write my number down in case you need anything. If I don't pick up, keep calling."

Mitch pulled into the motel lot at two in the morning, went into Norma's unit and unpacked the food. The new refrigerator hummed at the perfect temperature. He glanced around the room. There was so much more she needed, more that he wanted to do for her, give her. Patience, he reminded himself. Patience.

He walked to the lobby, his extra blanket over his shoulder. She glanced up when he pressed the bell. Her welcoming smile was genuine, but the physical evidence of her weariness continued to worry him.

*N*orma hit the unlock button, slid from the stool and plastered a cheery smile on her face. Mitch was too observant. He'd see how beat she was if she didn't hide it. She was troubled by all the hours he'd spent with her the last few days when he should have been catching up on his own sleep.

After he crossed into the lobby, she waited for his approach. Instead of stopping on the other side of the counter, he came around the corner and wrapped her in his arms for a hug. "How're you doing, Babe?"

She shouldn't get so attached, but she sank into his embrace, his warmth, and let him hold her. She wasn't classy enough for a man like him, and this fantasy of having him for herself couldn't last. So, she'd savor the comfort and caring while she could and store the memories of a love she almost had for the years to come.

He was a doctor, an educated man with friends, a home, and an important career at the hospital. She'd finished high school and one semester of community college. Her crowning achievements were a history of waitressing and cleaning jobs, getting her own apartment, feeding herself, and paying her bills—mostly on time.

Mitch had a kind, caring heart that drove him to take care of others. She was probably one of a hundred charity cases for him. He was so out of her league. She sighed and pulled back.

"What is it, Babe?"

Babe. How the endearment warmed her, made her feel special and wanted. As much as she'd like to be more, have more together, she had to remember she was just another patient.

She looked up and smiled. "You smell nice. Did you rest?"

"Actually, I slept like a rock. One of the first things I learned from Gage was how to shut everything off and sleep when I get the chance. I swear I've seen him take a twenty-minute power nap and work a whole second shift."

"Can you teach me how to do that?"

"Someday, but right now I can let you sleep. Come on, cuddle up on the couch and I'll watch things."

"No, Mitch. You have a shift tomorrow."

"Remember, I slept like a log. And when I leave you in a couple hours, I'll grab more sleep. Come on, baby needs you to take care of yourself."

She observed his earnest expression. Take the attention while you can, her inner self warned. He'll be gone in a few days.

He woke her at five-fifteen. "Oh Mitch, what have you done? Now you won't get much sleep."

"I'm fine. I would have let you rest longer, but I saw a guy on the camera screen loading his car."

As if on cue, the guest approached the door. After Norma finalized the bill and the gentleman left, she turned to Mitch and settled into his welcoming embrace. "Thank you."

She basked in his arms. Too soon, he cleared his throat and stepped away. He reached into his pocket, retrieved her key and handed it to her. "I should go."

Norma sighed. "Yes, go to bed."

"One taste," he whispered.

Before she realized his intent, he pulled her into his arms and kissed her. His lips were warm, his breath sweet, the flavor of the mints he was so fond of.

The kiss was more than a brush of flesh on flesh, yet less than a possession. He teased her senses with the sweep of his tongue over her lips and the gentle tug on her lower lip. Shifting, he pecked a path up her cheek and pressed a longer kiss to her forehead. "Be safe and get to bed as soon as you can. I'll stop back on my way to the hospital."

"Thank you, Mitch, for caring. For being a friend."

He met her gaze, and something she didn't understand flickered in his expression. He kissed her temple. "I care, Norma. I care a lot."

She watched him walk out the door. In such a short time he'd become the best friend she'd ever had. Melancholy washed over her. Someday he was going to make some lucky woman the perfect husband.

At the end of her shift, Norma entered her room and stopped in her tracks. The bed had been shifted a couple feet to accommodate a refrigerator and small shelving unit placed against the wall. Hesitant, she moved closer to investigate. A toaster and some kind of a countertop burner filled the top shelf. Her favorite cereal, bread, peanut butter, a variety of soups and other foods lined the second. Kitchenware and pots were on the lower level.

Opening the refrigerator, she discovered almost all the foods Doc Ewing had instructed her to start eating. A note was affixed to the milk.

These last months are important for your health and the baby's.

Let me do this for the two of you. I treasure our friendship.

Mitch

Could she hope? Did she dare? Was he starting to have the same feelings for her she already had for him?

Norma was in the middle of cleaning the second room of the eight she had for the day when Mitch walked in.

"Hey, Babe."

She turned at his greeting, placing her hands on her hips. "Mitch Smith, what do you think you're doing?"

A breathtaking smile tilted his lips. "Helping?"

"Mitch, it isn't right. You bought a refrigerator."

"It's a small one. No big deal. When you're done with it, I'll put it in my garage for beer. What's important is that you and the baby have what you need right now."

"It's a big deal to me, Mitch. Something I couldn't have gotten for myself."

His face softened and he cupped her face with one

hand. "You work so hard. I wanted you to have it." He pulled a phone from his pocket. "Speaking of needs, I'm worried about you not having a phone in case of an emergency."

"Mitch!"

"Hear me out. What if you're walking to the store and fall? Or go into labor? This is a safety concern for the two of you. This is an old phone I don't use anymore. Reactivating it didn't cost anything. You'll have unlimited minutes, so if you want to load a couple games to play late at night go ahead. I programmed my number, Gage's, and the hospital's. Now if you need me, you can text. Keep it in your pocket."

He tried to hand her the phone, but she took a step back and held up her hands to keep him from coming closer. "Phones aren't free. At minimum you're paying for the second line. I can't take this."

"I understand how you feel."

"Do you? How would you feel being a charity case?" Somehow she kept herself from shouting in frustration.

"You aren't a charity case. You're mine," he snapped.

Stunned, she could barely get out the words. "What did you say?"

"I didn't mean to blurt that out." He ran a hand through his hair. "That's not how I wanted to start this conversation."

"Okay, then let's start over. What's going on here, Mitch?" A slight hitch in her voice made her wince. She didn't like being helpless.

"I really like you, Norma. I want to date you. I want us to see if we can have a relationship together."

"You realize I'm pregnant. I'm a package deal."

He laughed. "Yeah, I got that. It doesn't change anything. You could have five kids and I'd care about each and every one, like I care about you. If we work as a couple, we'll make everything else work. I wanted time to court you. To let you get to know me better. But safety is our biggest concern for the next few months, and I can't ignore some of the things you need. I would feel better if you had a phone."

He wanted her. She couldn't have heard him right. No one wanted her. Not even her mom. Was it even possible her dream could come true? That the man she wanted really could want her?

She glanced at the phone in his hand and met his gaze tentatively. "You want to date me?"

"Yes." He took a step closer.

"Be my boyfriend?"

"Your boyfriend, your lover, your biggest supporter."

He wants me? "Why?"

"Because I like you. I like your laugh, your kindness, your determination. I think you're beautiful. And sexy as hell."

She fanned herself with an open palm. "Wow."

A crooked smile lit his face. "So can I finally kiss you like I've really wanted to kiss you?"

She smiled back. "Um, yes."

He closed the distance between them and cupped her face in his palms and slowly lowered his mouth to hers. At first, he simply rested his lips against hers, then he slid the tip of his tongue over the seam of her lips, seeking entrance. He teased and taunted her senses. The heat melted her against his solid body. Never had she been kissed with such all-consuming hunger.

Keeping one hand lightly against the back of her neck, he slid the other down her side and cupped her butt cheek with his palm, urging her tightly against the cradle of his hips. The obvious bulge of his desire pressed against her as he deepened the kiss. When he finally ended the kiss, they were both gasping.

He pressed his forehead to hers and spoke. "Do you understand where I'm coming from now?"

"Yes," she gasped.

"Good." He straightened. Kissing her forehead, he pulled back and found the phone on the floor where he'd dropped it. "The password is the date we met, but you can change it if you'd like."

She typed in the numbers, the screen lit up, and she went to contacts, hitting 'Mitch'.

His phone rang and he grinned, delighted their first meeting held a special memory for her too. Pulling his phone from his pocket, he answered. "Well, hello beautiful. I thought you'd never call. Can I see you again later tonight?"

She beamed. "I'm looking forward to it."

*N*orma glanced at the phone one more time. After texting her on and off all day, she hadn't heard from Mitch since eleven-thirty when his message said he'd see her soon. It was now three in the morning, and she was worried. She'd texted him at one-thirty with no response.

With a heavy heart, she shut off the phone and tossed it on the counter. Her ex-boyfriend lied to her all the time, making promises he'd never keep. When she worked the late shift at the diner, he'd cheat on her every chance he got. He'd lie and say he was going out to the bar with friends, then pick up any woman who'd take him home.

He'd been handsome, although not as good looking as Mitch. She should have known he wasn't interested in plain old Norma. He'd even hated her name and called her Mouse. He did like her paycheck and living in her apartment without ever contributing to the rent.

She'd hoped Mitch was different. That he really cared for her. She scoffed at herself. What was she thinking? He didn't need a pregnant, destitute nobody. He was a physician and could have any woman he wanted. His compassion seemed genuine, and his desire when he'd kissed her earlier had felt real. Oh hell, she was probably just one in a long string of women. His good deed for the month. Let the little mouse feel special for a day.

Lost in her thoughts, she jumped when the door buzzer went off. Mitch stood outside, his face pale. He had the spare blanket he always brought at night slung over his shoulder. Letting him in, she waited for the door to close and rounded the reception counter. "What's wrong?"

Mitch wrapped his arms around her, pressing his cheek to the top of her head.

"Are you sick?" she asked.

He cleared his throat. "No, just a long day. I need to hold you for a minute."

She slid her arms under his coat and around his waist. When she rested her head against his chest, the escalated beat of his heart pounded against her ear. After several minutes, the tempo slowed.

He needed comforting, yet the way he held her told her he needed her too. Relieved, the self-doubts she'd had earlier dimmed. He did care.

He pulled back and brushed the hair from her face. "Did you eat your snack?"

"Yes. Did you eat anything?"

He shook his head. "Not hungry."

"What happened, Mitch?"

"Right after I texted you, we were hit with several emergencies all at once. I couldn't leave. We even had to call Gage in." He pulled the blanket off his shoulder and slipped out of his coat, tossing it on the stool she'd vacated. Taking her hand, he led her to the couch.

"Doc Ewing works in the ER too?"

"He started out in the ER and doesn't want to lose his edge. He works two weekends a month and is on call for nights like tonight. We're a small hospital and we all pitch in when needed."

He sat in the corner of the couch and pulled her across his lap. Kissing her forehead, he leaned his head back on the cushion and closed his bloodshot eyes.

Gently, she stroked her hand over his chest. "Do you want to talk about it?"

When he didn't answer for several minutes, she thought perhaps he'd fallen asleep. Not wanting to wake him, she stayed on his lap where she could still see if someone came to the door. As tired as she was, this time she'd stay awake to watch over him.

"Some guy shot himself cleaning his gun. Damn fool was drunk," Mitch began. "He'll be okay, but it was a mess. Two cars full of teenagers decided it would be fun to play chicken in the parking lot of the theatre. Six of the eight had injuries. Two broken arms, bruised ribs, broken nose, concussion and head stitches, miscellaneous bruising." After a pause and a single harsh chuckle, he said, "And from the sound of their parents some long-term driving restrictions."

Shifting them both sideways on the couch, he stretched out his legs and settled her with her back against his chest. He wrapped his arm over her, resting his broad palm over her baby bump. "How's the baby been tonight? Active? Or sleepy?"

"Mitch, talk to me. I can tell you're hurting. You've helped me. Let me help you."

After another long pause, his voice was low and filled with pain. "We lost a teenage boy from one of the outlying towns to suicide. He overdosed on aspirin."

"Aspirin? I didn't know that was possible."

"It's one of the leading causes of adolescent deaths. Easy access. We tried, but it was already too late by the time they found him and got him to the hospital. In the end all we could do was make it...gentle."

"Oh Mitch. I'm so sorry. I—" Her baby pushed up against where his hand rested as if sensing his pain.

He stroked her belly. "Aww, little one, thank you. Thank you both." He kissed her neck below her ear. "Holding the two of you has already calmed me. Let me stay like this for a couple more minutes, then I'll get up and watch while you rest."

An hour later, Norma slipped from his embrace and let him sleep. She couldn't even imagine the pain the parents of the teenager were going through. Cradling her own baby, she studied Mitch's face. He'd be a good husband and father. Losing a patient would never be easy for him, yet he chose to care, to put himself out there every day.

Although she saw him each of the next two days, due to his schedule their time was limited to a meal and her sleeping. She quickly realized his twelve-hour shifts were rarely twelve hours.

Every day he found happy things to text her and checked on her several times throughout his time at work. He gave her a hug every night, but he hadn't kissed her again. She wondered why.

Had he changed his mind about her? Was he rethinking taking on a woman with a baby? Had his kindness sent him rashly into declaring a relationship before he'd really thought it out?

Mitch pulled into the motel parking lot Saturday evening at eight. Earlier in the day he'd helped her clean, then asked her to nap so he could take her to dinner. Afterward he'd bring her back and keep her company.

The repair work at his house was done, but he wasn't ready to return to his empty home. Norma still needed him. He was off the next few days, but when his shifts started again, he'd be working midnight to noon. The hardest set of hours for him to be able to help her. Her color was better and her eyes less shadowed. Thankfully she'd put on a little weight, but he worried that she'd slide back into her old habits when he couldn't be there.

He was scheduled to work Christmas Eve and day, but those hours would be midnight to noon. He'd been wracking his brain for ways to get her out of this situation. He knew what he wanted. He wanted her in his home but was afraid to spring it on her too soon.

With a sigh, he climbed from his Jeep and knocked on her room door. When she stood in the open doorway, his breath stalled in his chest. Stunning. She was absolutely stunning. She'd dressed in a royal blue dress that accented her blonde hair and heightened the color of her eyes. The simple outfit hugged her shoulders and breasts, then flowed loosely to her knees. Did she have any idea how beautiful she was?

"Hi, Babe."

"Hi, you." She smiled, then ushered him in. "You didn't say where we were going. This is the only dress I have. Is it okay?"

"No. You'll have to change, or I'll be fighting off all the single guys in town all night."

Her soft laugh went straight to his heart.

She ran a hand over her bump. "I doubt that. But thank you."

He helped her slip on her coat. "How's baby?"

She glanced back at him over her shoulder. "A little restless tonight. I think it's doing push-ups against my belly."

"May I feel?"

"If you want to."

He curved his palm over her abdomen and immediately felt the push of a little foot. He laughed.

"Look mister, you wouldn't think it was funny if it was you having your insides rearranged," Norma teased.

Slowly, he smoothed his hand back and forth cradling her baby belly. "Listen to me, little one, I want to take Momma on a date. I need you to cooperate so we can relax. Will you be good for me for a little while? When we come back, I'll give you a massage. Deal?"

As if the child understood Mitch's voice vibration or his warm touch, it eased it acrobatics.

"How do you do that? I swear you settle the baby just by talking."

"It's my bedside manner. Most patients respond well."

He looked at her pointedly. "I wish mom wasn't so stubborn and would accept help and comfort as easily."

"Baby's mom is getting better. I'm trying. I've been on my own for a long time. It's hard to... let go."

He knew she'd wanted to say trust. "I know, Babe."

He took her to Marie's Mexican Restaurant. "You mentioned you were craving a Taco Salad."

She laughed. "Since being on those vitamins, I'm craving everything."

While they waited in the lobby for their table the door opened and Doc Ewing came in with a blonde. They both wore leather jackets and heavy boots. Gage had on jeans, the woman camouflage cargo pants.

Gage strode toward them, while the woman went to talk to the host. He bro-hugged Mitch. "Who let you two out?"

"She's got a craving." Mitch smiled.

Gage rolled his eyes. "Ivy had one the whole time she was pregnant. I thought once the baby was born, it would let up. But no, we're here or ordering a minimum of twice a week. I don't have a clue how many times she stops in for lunch."

Norma studied the slight woman with the long ponytail. "How old is your baby?"

"Niall will be three months on the twenty-second." He glanced at the woman when she joined them. "Uh-oh! That look does not bode well for me. What's wrong, Ivy?"

"No tables for an hour and a half. I can place a takeout order or we could go somewhere else."

Norma recognized the disappointment on the other woman's face. She turned to Mitch. "Why don't we see if our table would seat four." She looked at Doc Ewing. "If that would work for you?"

He and Ivy both nodded and Mitch went to talk to the host.

The blonde held out her hand. "I'm Ivy Vaughn."

"I'm Norma Brown."

"You're the night clerk at Prospectors Inn, right?"

Norma glanced at Gage, before answering. "Yes."

Ivy smiled. "I'm with the Spencer Police Department, and I've noticed you in the office when I'm making rounds."

Mitch and the host joined them. "We're all set and our table is ready."

Once seated and their orders placed, Mitch rested his arm over the back of Norma's chair. Tension tightened her shoulders. Ivy must have picked up on it too, because she glanced from Norma to Gage.

"Norma, he's not a doctor tonight," Ivy said. "He's just a guy. In the same way I'm not on duty so I'm just a regular person. It's a little hard in a town this size. Neither of us talk shop at home. But a lot of people know who we are and they get self-conscious."

Norma released a breath and smiled. "I think I remember you now. My first week at the inn, a drunk pulled the fire alarm after he set his bed on fire. You were one of the officers who responded. Actually, I think you were the one who restrained him. You were pregnant then?"

"That was me. The guy who started the fire is a regular. He likes to set fires, but has enough of a conscience to call it in or put it out himself. He acts like he's putting up a fuss, but he's really easy to handle. He spends some time in jail, gets out and behaves himself for a while, then does it again. Compared to other arsonists I've seen, he's pretty harmless. So far."

The rest of dinner was filled with silly stories of innocent mishaps around town or at the hospital. Then talk turned to the winter festival and the winner of the ice sculptures contest.

"Oh, I saw the pictures in the newspaper. It must have been lovely," Norma commented.

Mitch covered her hand with his. "Next year will be different. We'll be going and taking the baby to the kid's events."

Norma missed the look exchanged between Ivy and Gage. But Mitch didn't. He nodded to his friend.

Mitch took Norma back to her room and followed her in. "Thank you for inviting them to dinner with us. Gage is great. Ivy is usually pretty quiet so I was glad to see how easily she got on with you. But then you're always easy to be with."

"I've never been on a couple's date before. It was fun."

"It was a great night. You'll meet more of my friends soon. This is a good town to put down roots and raise a family."

He pulled her into his arms. One taste. One little taste to celebrate what was growing between them. To stave off the need. He lowered his lips to hers. The kiss went from gentle teasing to all-out possession in seconds. He was hard almost immediately and filled with a hunger like he'd never experienced. Norma was his other half, his life, and he was having a hard time being patient. Easing back, he placed his forehead against hers. "Get some rest, Babe."

CHAPTER SEVEN

*M*itch lay spread out on the bed in his room at the inn, staring at the ceiling. Norma was in her room resting before her night shift.

He wanted her to move in with him, now. She wasn't ready. They'd only known each other a few weeks and he couldn't risk scaring her off. She already had trust issues. In the meantime, there were things he needed to be doing at his house. Furniture to be rearranged, new furniture for the spare bedroom, and one more major purchase.

His room at the motel was reserved for the next three days. He'd keep going back and forth to his house like he'd been doing. Today he hoped to get Norma to look at nursery items online.

He wanted her to be at least living in his house before the baby came, but it was probably too much to think he could get her home before the holidays. Once the baby was born, he didn't want her to come back to this abusive labor situation. Somehow, he'd convince her she belonged with him. That their future was together. He'd never been so sure of anything before. Or so scared.

Later that night Mitch stood next to her and opened his computer pulling up pictures from a furniture store. "I need a bedroom set for my spare room. What do you think of this layout?"

"What's your house like?" she asked.

"The realtor called it a two-story ranch, which is definitely an oxymoron. Most of the living is on the main level with a large master bedroom and a good-sized private bath. There are two smaller bedrooms with a shared bathroom. A family room, kitchen and eating area. The laundry is off the garage entrance."

"How do you plan to use these rooms?"

"Eventually, the main level will be kids' rooms, but for now I want one guest room, the other could be for a child or a nursery.

"The lower level hasn't been finished. The original plan has a game room, storage area, and the potential for two more bedrooms. There's also a large bank of windows with a patio and fire pit. A full bathroom is already roughed out, but I'm thinking I want it different from the original plan. What do you think of making two bathrooms? If there are two kids downstairs and we are entertaining, I think it would be more practical."

"Sounds like you're planning on a large family."

He shrugged. "I like kids. I grew up with two sisters and a brother."

"Are you the oldest?"

"I was third. Boy, girl, boy, girl. They all have families and still live close to our parents in Denver."

"How many nieces and nephews?"

"Seven. Four boys, three girls. Mom says we need another girl to even things out."

"Sounds like you're all very close."

"Yeah. We had the normal sibling rivalries, but for the most part we got along. Still do."

"Did they all go into medicine?"

He laughed. "My dad was an over-the-road truck driver, now he's semi-retired and drives a school bus. Mom is a teacher. My oldest brother and sister are teachers. One college literature, one high school music. My youngest sister is a financial whiz. She works at a major financial firm and manages all of our investment portfolios. Hell, she's the reason most of us have one."

"It sounds like you have a nice family."

"I do. What about you? You mentioned your mom left?"

"She didn't want kids. I was an accident. I spent a lot of time with teenage babysitters. When mom finally had enough, she dropped me off at her sister's and never came back. The only reason my aunt's husband let me stay was so I could help watch their kids so he didn't have to be bothered."

"Sounds kind of lonely."

"Their kids were young and easy to entertain. I liked being with them, we'd play and read, and I helped with homework. We were close. When they went to sleep, I could go to my room in the basement and be alone. My years with them made me want to get a degree in early childhood development or education. One of the things I like about Spencer is the community college offers those programs. I had started before I met my boyfriend, but had to drop out at mid-term.

"I liked school, but mom wasn't good at taking me when I was young so I was always playing catch up. Once I could walk or take the bus, I never missed a day. Some of the teachers were great about helping me with the things I'd missed. Especially the librarian.

"Spencer has a good library. On nice days I can walk there to use their computers and check out books. I haven't gone in a while. I've been reading books people leave behind here when they check out."

"I'll take you soon," Mitch offered, then changed the subject. "Do you have a preference for the baby's gender?"

"No. Although it would have been kind of nice to see during the ultrasound so I could settle on a name."

"Do you have names picked out?"

"A million, but I can't decide. One of the books said to wait until the baby is born and the decision is easier."

"There's some truth in that. I've heard a lot of parents change their minds after the baby is born." He studied her for a moment. "Are you into pinks or blues?"

"No! Definitely yellows and greens. Maybe a little purple."

He chuckled. "Duly noted."

"I'm using cloth diapers because they're better for the environment and cheaper in the long run. I'm hoping I can wash them in the motel laundry. Marissa, at Like New Reruns, is holding a portable crib for me. I've been paying her a little each week. If she gets something cheaper, she promised to let me know."

"Sounds like you've got a plan."

"I'm focusing on the must haves right now. I'm hoping in the spring people will have garage sales for baby clothes."

"I'll remind Gage and Ivy to save their stuff. I have other friends who have children, I'll let them know you're looking."

Norma glanced at the clock. Today was Christmas Eve and for the first time in longer than she could remember she was excited for the holiday. Mitch should be off or getting off soon. He told her he had plans for the two of them so he wanted her to rest if she could after the cleaning.

Norma finished scrubbing the bathroom in unit six. She was thankful there'd been so few lodgers. Most guests were okay, but the motel hosted more than their fair share of drunks who got sick. Cleaning those bathrooms didn't settle well with her pregnancy.

Mitch brought her a jar of menthol gel to dab under her nose to mask the smells. He'd also started cleaning the bathrooms for her when he could help. She hated taking advantage of him. Honestly, if he wasn't helping her, she wasn't sure how much longer she could keep working both parts of her job.

Bobby had left a message saying he needed to talk to her, and she'd almost had a panic attack. Worried he'd found out she'd been taking naps while Mitch watched the desk at night, she'd stalled calling him. She'd thought herself lucky that he never stopped by, but now wondered if he had other ways of watching what went on at the motel.

When he'd called back, she was relieved to learn he

was letting her know he'd forgotten to place the order for the cleaning supplies and she could take money from the till to go buy some if she needed.

She'd started looking for a different job in the newspaper and online with the computer in the office, but there didn't seem to be a huge employment turnaround in Spencer. She'd been lucky to get this one.

The librarian had told her there would be more jobs in the spring and summer because of the tourist trade. If she could hold out that long maybe something would break. She tugged on her lower lip as she dusted. She'd had to find something soon. The clock was ticking and panic was setting in. The midwife had agreed to discount her services, but she wanted cash at the time of birth. Norma hadn't been able to set aside the money.

Pulling the sheets from the bed, she dumped them by the door with the towels. She'd tried to talk to Bobby about paying her overtime for work over eight hours but he said it was cheaper for him to hire a second person rather than pay her more. She couldn't afford to lose what she had.

After making the bed she ran the vacuum. All the tension and fear were getting to her, and she was having a hard time eating or sleeping when Mitch wasn't watching over her. Three more rooms to go, then she could take a nap and maybe try to choke down some food.

She could do this. She would do this for her baby. Grabbing the sheets and towels from the floor, she stepped into the doorway to dump them in the laundry basket. A noise caught her attention and she glanced up.

Oh, god.

Her ex.

Mitch slowed to turn onto Chickering Road and leaned forward staring through his windshield in disbelief.

He watched in horror as a burly man pulled Norma from the doorway of a room and threw her against the stone wall. The back of her head crashed against the hard surface.

Without thinking of possible consequences, Mitch floored the gas pedal, speeding the remaining distance to the motel.

He hit the call button on his steering wheel. "Call 911."

He jumped the curb into the parking area.

"911, what is your emergency?"

"Personal assault in progress at Prospectors Inn, Burnham Drive and Chickering Road. Send police and rescue squad. This is Dr. Mitch Smith."

He slammed on the brakes, threw the Jeep into park, and sprang into action. Before he reached Norma, the man smashed a fist into her abdomen.

As the man drew back for another punch, Mitch caught his wrist and spun him aside. He struck the man's nose with his other fist and shoved him against the wall. Shifting his weight, Mitch leaned into the punch as Owen had taught him, crashing into the brute's jaw with full force. The man slumped to the ground.

Mitch registered sirens in the background as he turned to where Norma lay motionless on the sidewalk.

"I'm here, Babe. I'm here now," he spoke quietly. Checking for a pulse, then the back of her head for blood, he gently placed a palm over the baby.

A firm hand on his shoulder drew his attention. He glanced up at Dan Rivers the EMT.

"Mitch, you need to step aside and let me get to her."

"She needs to go to the hospital."

"I know. And I know she's your girl. Let me do what I need to do so we can get her to the hospital." Dan's voice sharpened at Mitch's hesitancy, "Move over and give me a report, Doctor."

At the snap of authority, Mitch slid into professional mode, giving pulse and the details he'd witnessed. As they loaded Norma into the ambulance, he looked at the police officer who'd come to stand behind him as he'd related the events to Dan.

Ivy's gaze was filled with concern. "I need your statement, but you can give it to me at the hospital. You're not up to driving so you're riding with me."

At the hospital, Mitch bolted toward the emergency room, only to be blocked by Gage's hand against his chest. "You can't go back there, Mitch."

"I need to be with her. She'll be scared."

"I'll let you go to her as soon as I can. But not yet. I've already called in the neonatal team. The OBGYN specialist, Dr. Lisa Emmett is with her now."

"But I—"

"You need to give your statement to Ivy. I've talked to Ursula and you're off duty until things settle down. I will personally keep you posted on what's going on. Norma has you listed as her medical contact with my office. Nothing is going to happen without you knowing. Right now, we have to find out the extent of the injuries. I'll be back as soon as I have an update."

Mitch's head knew everything Gage said was true. But

his heart was dying. He couldn't lose them, either of them. Norma and the baby were his life now. He needed to do something.

"Mitch, give Ivy the information she needs to put this asshole away," Gage instructed.

Dan walked up with his bag and glanced at Gage. "Okay if I take him to one of the rooms to clean up his hand?"

Mitch glanced at his scraped and bruised knuckles. Dried blood covered the back of his hand and between his fingers.

"Sure. Ivy needs privacy to get his statement anyway." He rested his hand on Mitch's shoulder. "I'll be back with an update as soon as I can. I'll watch over the two of them for you."

Minutes turned into an hour. Mitch knew what was happening took time. But not being with them was killing him. He'd just finished with Dan and Ivy, when Owen appeared in the doorway to the waiting room.

"Thought I'd sit with you for a while." He glanced at Mitch's swollen and bruised hand. "Probably should put some more ice on that. Heard you clocked the guy good. Your first KO."

Mitch glanced up. But it hadn't been enough. He hadn't been in time to keep Norma from harm. "I need you to teach me more."

"You can't teach timing. But I hear you got there when they needed you."

"You know more than I do," Mitch growled. Leaning forward, elbows on his knees, he let his head hang.

"I know they're both alive and here in this hospital

getting the best medical attention possible. Because you got there when you did and took action."

Mitch glanced sideways at his friend. "I got off work around noon and headed over to help her with the cleaning so she could get some sleep before her night shift. I turned off First onto Chickering which gave me a view of the motel. If I'd been just a few minutes earlier…"

"Or a whole different story if you'd been a few minutes later. I'm telling you man, you have to let go of the guilt. The I-should-have-been-there-sooner shit. Focus on what has to be done now. And going forward."

Mitch rubbed a hand over his face and sat back in the chair. "She's not fucking going back to that place. Ever."

"Then what's our game plan?"

"I ordered bedroom furniture for the spare room, and it's set up. I have the stuff for the baby's room but I was going to let her choose the paint color. She likes green or yellow. At this point I want it painted yellow. She can always change it later. Then the crib and changing table need to be put together. I was trying to ease her gently into moving in with me. But I'm done. At least if she's staying with me, I'll know she's safe. And I can make sure she takes care of herself."

"You get me a set of keys, and the guys and I can get all that handled while you're here with her."

"Shit, I left my keys in the Jeep." It didn't matter. Without Norma nothing mattered.

Owen chuckled. "Wondered when you'd think of that. I parked it at the motel and have the keys in my pocket. I'll get the Jeep here and bring you the house keys later."

"Keep the house keys. I'll use the remote. Leave the door from the garage unlocked."

CHAPTER EIGHT

*M*itch leaned his head back against the wall and watched the clock slowly tick forward. One hour, eighteen minutes and twenty-nine seconds. Thirty, thirty-one, thirty-two… His mind raced through every worse-case scenario he could imagine.

He'd had such high hopes for their first Christmas Eve. He'd planned on taking Norma to his house for the first time tonight. A decorating service had put up a tree while he shopped for gifts for Norma and the baby. Today, he was going to tell her the truth of his feelings, share his hopes and dreams, and where he wanted their relationship to go. Today was supposed to be the beginning of the rest of their lives.

Gage walked in and led him to an empty consulting room. "Norma is conscious."

"Let's go." Mitch turned.

Gage stopped him. "Listen up. Norma is a little sluggish and foggy. Dizzy. We did a scan to rule out a bleed. Fortunately, she only has a mild concussion.

"She had back and abdominal pain as well as some vaginal bleeding. Dr. Emmett ordered an ultrasound. Mitch, Norma has a partial placental abruption."

Mitch sucked in a breath and leaned against the closed door. After the shock waned, Mitch the doctor's thought process kicked into gear. "Baby's heartbeat?"

"Steady and strong," Gage replied.

"She's about thirty-four weeks. What are they guessing the baby's weight to be?" Mitch asked.

"Around five pounds, maybe a little more."

"It's safer to take the baby now, than have it detach completely. Neonatal is on site?"

"Yes. They agree with Dr. Emmett's care plan."

"Baby was already in cephalic presentation. Induce and be prepared for cesarean?" Mitch continued.

"Yes, that's the plan."

"Have they talked to her?"

Gage grinned. "Well, they were coming to talk with you first, but since you've added it all up, we can skip that step. I'll text them to head to Norma's room instead."

Mitch nodded, and followed Gage. Medically speaking this could be handled. Norma and the baby were in good hands. So why was his hand shaking? He stuffed it in his pocket and continued to put one foot in front of the other.

His head knew there was a danger he could still lose one or both of them. His heart constricted. He hadn't told her that he loved her. She didn't know she was his life. They were his life.

Soft footsteps and gentle voices drew Norma from the pounding in her head. She sensed someone enter the room and forced her eyes open. Mitch walked to her bedside and rested his hand over hers. "How's my girl?"

"Mitch. Mitch, I'm so glad you're here."

He leaned down and kissed her softly.

"They said you rescued me. I don't remember anything other than Dennis grabbing me. I don't know how he found me."

"Dennis told the Spencer Police when you emailed your old landlord to see if you could get your deposit back, he kept your address. He and Dennis were friends so he gave him the information."

"I needed the money for the baby," she said tearfully.

"It doesn't matter. You're safe now."

"What's happening? Why do I have to stay on my side?"

"How do you feel right now?"

"I have a headache and was a little dizzy at first. My back hurts some. I'm sure I'll be fine after I rest. Bobby will be upset I'm not at work. I need to call him."

"Babe, the job can wait. Right now, this is about you and the baby. Everything is going to be fine, but there's a complication with the placenta. To protect you and the baby, the doctors are going to induce labor so that you have the baby safely now."

"No! No, it's too early." She glanced up as the female doctor she met earlier entered the room.

"The placenta is pulling away from the uterus," Mitch continued. "That means the baby may not get enough oxygen and nutrients. Baby is a good size and with the special care of the neonatal team will have a better chance. This is the safest thing for both of you. Can you trust me?"

"He did this." Tears slid down her cheeks. "He tried to make me lose my baby before. He tried to kill my baby. I told him I wouldn't go after him for child support. I promised."

"He's in jail and won't be coming anywhere near you again. It's you and me now and we're going to take care of the baby. Dr. Emmett is going to induce, and I will be right here with you the whole time."

Clutching his hand to her chest, she whispered, "I'm scared, Mitch."

"I know, but you aren't alone. It's going to be okay."

Hours later, Norma breathed through the latest contraction squeezing Mitch's hand.

Dr. Emmett sat at the end of the bed and smiled. "Okay Norma, baby has crowned so when I tell you, I want you to push. You're almost done."

A few minutes later the wail of her child brought tears to Norma's eyes.

"Good job, momma. Give us a minute to clean her up and I'll let you hold her."

Norma turned her eyes to Mitch. "It's a girl? Is she okay?"

"She's perfect," he assured her.

The doctor returned and laid the baby on her chest. With shaky fingers Norma skimmed the blond fuzz on the tiny head, traced her pale eyebrows and soft pink lips.

"Ten fingers, ten toes, and the cutest button nose," Dr. Emmett commented. "She's five pounds, four ounces, and seventeen inches. You get to cuddle her for a couple more minutes, but soon we'll take her to the neonatal ward.

She'll need a little extra care for a while. As soon as possible, we'll get you down there. Do you have a name for this precious little one?"

Norma looked at Mitch. The relief and joy on his face warmed her. "Is it still Christmas Eve?"

He glanced at the clock on the wall and nodded.

"What do you think of Eve Noël?"

He held her gaze and smiled. "I think it's beautiful and full of joy. A perfect name for our little one."

Our little one.

Two days later Mitch's comment still occupied her mind. He'd stayed the first forty-eight hours, sleeping in the chair next to her bed. Today, he was working a shift, but promised to stop in when he could.

She glanced toward the corner of the room. Two-dozen yellow and white roses sat on the table. He'd had them waiting for her the first time she woke.

He'd supported and encouraged her when the breast feeding wasn't going well, explaining it was always harder for the premature babies and that at this stage the skin-to-skin time was just as important. When Eve finally suckled for two minutes he was as excited as if his team had won the Superbowl.

Doc Ewing, Gage, as he insisted she call him, came in to check on her and to ease her mind on how much the birth of her daughter and their stay in the hospital was going to cost. He told her most would be covered by the hospital's benevolent funds he'd applied for on her behalf.

Still, she worried. Even if the hospital was taken care of, there were so many things she needed for Eve. Would she even have a job when they released her?

Ivy entered, interrupting her panicked thoughts and

helped her fill out the paperwork to file assault charges against Dennis. The police had secured a video of the attack from the hotel cameras and the judge had refused bail.

Norma checked the clock. Soon they'd let her see Eve again. Her concerns faded. All she wanted was to hold her daughter.

Mitch entered Norma's room carrying two food trays. Her eyes were red and puffy. She'd been crying. Placing the trays on the portable table, he sat beside her on the bed. "What's wrong?"

"They're releasing me tomorrow morning, but Eve has to stay. I've been pumping milk, but it's not enough and I have to work and already I'm a terrible mother—"

Her sobs broke his heart. He took her in his arms and rocked her. "Shush Babe, we'll figure it out." He allowed her time to get the fear and frustration out before he pulled back. "That's why I'm here, so we can talk."

He waited for her to wipe her eyes and use a tissue. "Norma, I have a plan. Do you trust me?"

She eyed him skeptically.

"Let me rephrase that. Will you trust me? You can't go back to the motel. Not with the baby. Not with her here and the hours he expects you to work." Tears poured down her cheeks and he rushed on. "I have this big house and with my hours always changing, I can't, and don't, want to have to clean it. If you were my live-in house-keeper, you could do that for me and make sure I know about any future plumbing issues. I don't use three bedrooms. You and the baby can have the spare bedrooms and bathroom."

"Mitch, I can't. You've already done so much."

"Hear me out. You'll have a job. I'll pay you to do the normal housekeeper stuff like cleaning, laundry, running errands and cooking. If you don't want to cook for me, you'd still have the kitchen to use for you and Eve. You'd be doing all the things I don't have time for. I've always known eventually I'd hire someone to come in and manage the house. Having you would be perfect."

Mitch watched her face carefully. Her furrowed brow worried him. Was she going to refuse him? She was always so resistant to his help. She didn't want to feel like a charity case. He understood she was used to being on her own. The support of others was foreign to her. And he'd messed up by not telling her that he loved her before she was attacked. He'd thought he had more time.

He hadn't wanted to rush her when she already had a baby on the way. He'd planned on gently easing her into their relationship. Earning her trust and letting her get to know him.

"You can gradually move into the job and we can figure everything out as we go. For the next week, maybe two, you'll need to be at the hospital a lot to be with the baby. I have a car you can use. Once Eve is home, you'll have the car with the car seat to go to the grocery store, for doctor appointments, whatever you need.

"This way you and Eve have a safe place to live, you have a job that will pay an equitable wage for normal hours, and I get someone I trust to take care of the house. It's a win-win for both of us."

Norma stared at him, slowly shaking her head.

Mitch rushed on to keep her from saying the words he dreaded to hear. "I know this is a lot to spring on you, but I've done some research on these positions and they're common. I have a friend who's drafting a contract so you can read it and feel comfortable that I'm not taking advantage of you." He hesitated. "And of course, you can quit anytime you want. You don't have to make a decision right now. Stay with me while Eve is in NICU. Give yourself time to think, to rest. I've got a laptop you can use to do your own research on the position. Regardless, you'll have access to the car so you can come and go to the hospital to see our girl."

"Mitch, you keep giving and giving to me. I feel like I'm taking advantage of your kindness. I—I don't know what to say."

"Say you'll give it a try. It's a perfect solution for both of us. I can get all of your things moved to the house. Then I'll take you home in the morning after my shift and show you around. What do you say?"

Norma worried her lip and his hope dipped. "Okay," she whispered.

"Is that a yes?"

"Yes." She nodded then smiled.

He started to punch the air, but pulled back his arm and settled for a grin and a quick kiss to her forehead. Baby steps, he reminded himself.

The next morning, after she'd spent time with Eve cuddling and nursing., Mitch led Norma to the car. "When do they want you to come back?"

"The nurse said three hours. Oh, Mitch, Eve and I did so much better today. She's gained almost two ounces."

Since he was dropping into the NICU every chance he got, he'd already heard all the reports. Seeing the excitement on Norma's face felt good.

He stopped in front of the steel gray SUV he'd purchased for her and opened the back door. "I checked all the recommendations, and this car seat has the safest ranking. It also serves as the seat for the stroller and as a carrier. If you don't like it, I can still send it back. But it's the same one Gage got for Niall. Oh, and before I forget, here's your set of car and house keys."

"Mitch, I—"

"Nope. You agreed to give it a chance. Do you want to drive now or wait until we come back to the hospital?"

"Since I don't know where your house is and I've not driven much around town yet, you drive. I'll practice on the way back."

The closer Mitch got to his home the more his nerves had him doubting his choices. What if she wanted green paint in the baby's room? Or maybe she wouldn't like the baby furniture? He'd gotten the same rocker his mother had used for all her kids and grandkids. He needed everything to be perfect. He needed Norma to stay. She was his future.

Hoping she'd like the house, he pulled into the driveway.

"Oh Mitch, I love the wrap around porch. Your view of the mountains is spectacular."

"Come on, we'll do a quick walk around the outside before we go in."

He told her about his plans for a pool in the backyard and a fenced play area along with where he wanted to plant a garden before leading her inside.

"Your room will be next to mine. Eve's room will be on the other side of you. But I put a bassinet in your room for now. There are baby monitors in your room, mine, the kitchen and a portable one you can carry with you throughout the house."

He stopped in the first doorway, inviting her to enter the room before him. He paused behind her when she hesitated three feet into the room. Doubt filled his chest. "Is the yellow okay? We can repaint if you want."

It had felt wrong leaving her baby in the hospital. In all the scenarios of how life would be after the birth, this hadn't been one of them. She'd never imagined going home alone.

Norma swallowed hard and tried to take in everything at once. He'd done this for her and Eve. He'd listened as she'd rambled on about her dream nursery. The wall color, changing table, stacks of diapers and clothes, the bumpers in the bed were from the colorful animal design she'd shown him. He'd even remembered the lavender blanket draped over the bed rail and the purple stuffed elephant in the corner. "It's perfect."

He walked her through the adjoining bathroom into the room that would be hers. Decorated in soft grays and lavenders, this room was also exactly like the pictures they'd looked at together online. Her meager belongings made a sad pile in the corner.

She ran her hand over the dresser top where he'd laid the baby book. All of this was just a product of his innate kindness, she reminded herself. His protective nature. Not love or lust.

"You did this for us, didn't you? I remember this was the bed and comforter you showed me. Why?"

"I have strong feelings for you, Norma. I want to give us a chance as a couple. But a big part of what I need is for the two of you to be safe. I know there's been a lot of upheavals in your life and I've bungled this.

"I won't rush you or try to take advantage of you. We'll take life one step at a time. First, we'll create a healthy environment for you and Eve."

He kissed her forehead. "Take your time and get settled. I'll go make us lunch then you can nap a little before you have to be back to the hospital."

An hour later she lay in the middle of the perfect bed he'd bought for her. Over lunch he'd admitted all the furnishings were new. He'd actually only moved into the house four weeks before the water pipes had broken. Since meeting her, he'd purchased the spare bedroom furniture and furnished the baby's room.

When he'd stopped to fill the gas tank and needed her to hand him his wallet from the console, she'd seen the SUV purchase agreement dated the day she'd been attacked. All these things he'd done with her and Eve in mind.

Mitch was perfect in every way. Kind, thoughtful, smart, helpful and so sexy he filled her sleep with sensual dreams. But dating her wasn't a promise of a future.

What would it be like to be loved by him?

CHAPTER NINE

On Valentines' Day, Norma woke up with Eve in the early morning. Mitch's shift had started at midnight and he wouldn't be home until around one. He'd left her a message he was picking up food for a nice dinner and planned to cook for her.

She'd discovered two packages on the counter addressed to 'his girls'. One held a onesie sleeper for Eve with a baby elephant blowing red hearts, and a bow for her fuzzy hair. For herself, she'd unwrapped a red cashmere sweater and black pull-on slacks.

His thoughtfulness brought a tightness to her chest. This was so different from every other relationship she'd ever had. He gave and gave, where other boyfriends, and even family, had expected her to do for them, but had never returned the gestures.

Norma shook out the freshly-washed sheet and fitted it to Mitch's king bed. She had some money saved and wanted to do something nice for him, too. She'd think of something while she cleaned and then take Eve for a quick shopping trip.

Six weeks ago, he'd said he wanted to see if they could have a relationship. Since then, his touches had been pleasant, his friendly kisses tempting. But he hadn't taken her into his arms and given her a knock-your-socks off kiss or even pressed the length of his body to hers. Although a few times she'd thought she saw him adjusting his girth as he walked away. He'd been careful to hide any physical reaction from her. If he actually ever had one to her post-baby body.

She was so out of his league. He was classy, sophisticated, and high end— everything from the champagne he'd had for New Year's, down to his Armani suit she'd picked up at the cleaners. She was Goodwill clothes, cheap wine coolers, and pizza.

What did he really see in her? Didn't he want her sexually? Or was he being a gentleman and giving her more time?

If he wanted a relationship, when was it going to start? Last week at her doctor's appointment she'd been given the green light to resume normal activity. She'd expected Mitch to at least ask her how the visit had gone, but he hadn't. That night they'd followed their same evening pattern of sharing baby duties, then putting Eve to bed, followed by a couple hours of TV. As always, he'd walked her to her bedroom door, given her a chaste kiss and wished her a good night's rest.

He doted on Eve. Sometimes Norma was a little jealous of the snuggles and kisses her daughter received. He often held Eve for hours talking, singing and snuggling.

Norma finished making his bed and picked up the duster for the side table. Over the weeks she'd learned he had a penchant for personal tidiness, always putting things away when he was done with them. Yet he didn't get flustered by the chaos in the baby's room or the messes she made when cooking.

She opened the drawer to put away the book he'd left on top of the table. Two unopened boxes of condoms filled the space where he normally kept his reading materials. Her breath hitched. Maybe he'd paid more attention than she'd thought.

Mitch left work at two in the afternoon. Already running late, he had a lot to accomplish. His first stop was at the florist for red roses. Next the market for steaks, potatoes, asparagus and salad, then Spampinato's for a tiramisu cake, one of Norma's favorites.

Loading the Jeep after his last stop, he sat in the parking lot and gripped the steering wheel until his knuckles turned white. He had to tell her tonight. He couldn't keep this pretense of simple friendship up much longer. What had started out as a way to take care of Norma and Eve and keep them in his life had become torture.

He wanted her so badly, he was in a constant state of arousal. Everything about her drove him to lust-filled fantasies. Her scent, her laugh, her smile, her sexy body. When she cuddled Eve to her breast, he was in awe of her gentleness and innate motherly instincts.

Yet he longed to suckle her sweet flesh himself, to kiss and caress her perfect mounds, bringing both of them to ecstasy. He wanted her in his bed, under him, on top, any way he could have her. He feared her ex's attack may have caused lingering distress and fear. He had no idea how the asshole had treated her sexually. What if he'd always been aggressive? Hurtful and inconsiderate?

They needed to talk, but he was afraid of the answers. He was afraid to lose her, so he'd hidden his true feelings.

He leaned his forehead on his hands. Fuck. He was a doctor and dealt with tougher conversations every day. Straightening, he started the Jeep and threw it into gear. Tonight, he would discover if she wanted him as much as he wanted her.

Pulling into the driveway, he opened the garage door and parked. He grabbed the bouquet of flowers and the bag of groceries and headed toward the door into the kitchen. As he reached for the handle, the door opened. Norma stood before him with a huge smile on her lips, Eve cradled in one arm.

Standing on the step above him, she met him eye to eye. Instead of stepping aside, she placed her hand on his chest and slowly slid it over his pec and shoulder before cupping the back of his head. As she lowered her lips to his, she whispered, "Welcome home."

Her tongue teased his lips, then gently pressed forward to explore his mouth. He was instantly throbbing. When she finally pulled back, he cleared his throat and handed her the bouquet. "I got you roses."

"They're beautiful. Thank you, Mitch."

He kept the counter between them until he could convince his body to calm down. Once the groceries and dessert were put away, he reached for Eve. "How was our girl today?"

"An angel. She ate really well. I'm excited for next week's weigh in. I was going to bathe her early so she can wear her new outfit for you. If I do that now, would you mind watching her while I take a shower?"

"That'll be perfect. Then I'll shower and start dinner."

"Why don't I cook?" she asked. "You just came off a shift."

"No. I want to do it for you. You cook for both of us almost every night. I can sleep all day tomorrow. We may actually get a couple hours together today."

"Hush, you'll jinx us."

"Get started. I'll get the steaks marinating and join you to bathe Eve."

While Norma took her own shower, he dressed Eve then settled with her into the rocker. "How's my girl? I missed you today. I like that you're home with us now, but I kind of miss visiting you on my breaks. You look gorgeous in your heart onesie with this big red bow in your hair.

"Eve," he whispered. "I need you to do me a favor. I'd really like some adult time with momma tonight, so could you eat really big and maybe take a three-hour nap before you need to feast again? I promise I'll give you extra cuddles if you do."

"What are you two scheming?" Norma asked from the doorway.

She'd donned the new outfit and looked stunning. The soft sweater cupped the fullness of her breasts and the pants molded the curves of her hips and thighs. Images of the two of them on the floor, her legs wrapped around his hips as he claimed her filled his head. His heart raced and his breaths grew shallow. Damn, how he wanted this woman.

"It's a secret. I'll tell you later." He stood. "Will the two of you keep me company while I prep dinner? Then I'll take a fast shower."

Norma kept Eve awake until after she and Mitch had eaten. While he cleaned the kitchen, she nursed and put the baby down for what she hoped would be at least a couple hours. Quickly, she changed her clothes before she lost her nerve.

Mitch sat on the floor after starting a fire in the fireplace. When she walked into the living room, he glanced up. His eyes widened and quickly turned dark. His tongue darted out to lick his lips.

Please let me be reading this right.

"I hope you don't mind that I borrowed your robe. I wanted to get comfortable, but was a touch chilled."

"I like it better on you. I thought the night air warranted a fire and some hot apple cider. Come sit with me." He held out his hand.

She dropped to the floor next to him and reached for the steaming mug he offered. "Hmm, perfect."

He sighed. "Next week I work noon to midnight. I feel like I miss so much with Eve on that shift. I was thinking, maybe I take over her middle of the night feeding with a bottle. That way you'd get a little extra sleep and I'd still get to spend time with her."

"You're really attached to her, aren't you?" Norma asked.

Mitched studied his mug before shifting sideways and meeting her gaze. "I love her. I love you."

When she gasped, he took the mug from her trembling hand.

"I know with everything you've been through it's probably too soon for you. But I can't keep this in any longer. You're in my soul, Norma. I've known since the first time I met you. I won't push you. I'll give you time to see if you can grow feelings for me. If—if you don't, I'll understand. But I'd like a chance to see if you could come to care about me."

"You silly man." She reached out and stroked his cheek. "I've loved you since you brought me gouda sandwiches. I just didn't think I would ever be enough for you."

"Oh, Babe, I have no idea what you mean by that. You are my everything and more. You're honest, kind, gentle, sweet, beautiful. You make me smile and my blood pressure skyrocket."

She blushed and arched an eyebrow. "Really? You've hardly kissed me."

He dropped his gaze, then raised it with a self-deprecating expression on his face. "I spend more hours hard for you than not. I didn't want to force myself on you. I didn't know how your ex treated you, and when I found out that he'd hit you, I worried you'd be afraid. Then there was everything with the baby. I didn't want to rush you when you were dealing with the premature birth and all.

"I thought having you live here would be perfect. We'd get to know each other, build trust. Then one night, I barely stopped myself from putting my arms around you at the sink and rubbing against you. I freaked myself out worrying you'd think I was a pervert trying to take advantage of you."

She clasped his hand in hers. "And I thought I was only a charity case because you're a good man."

"I want to be a good man." He lifted her chin until their eyes met. "I want to be very good. I want to give you a dozen orgasms. Have you waiting at the door every night for a dozen more. I want to worship your beautiful body from head to toe. Once a night will never be enough. My fantasies include the kitchen counter, the shower, you over the back of the couch, you riding me on the bar stool. I have a fantasy for every room in this house, including the pool table scheduled to be delivered to the basement next week. I've just about worn out my hand in the shower over the last month." He gave his head a shake. "Yeah, I want to show you how very, very, good I can be. But I want you to know, I want the whole package. I'm in this for a lifetime."

Norma rose to her knees to face him. Slowly she untied the belt and let the robe she wore slide from her shoulders and fall to the floor. "What about in front of the fireplace? Is that one of your fantasies? Because it's one of mine."

"Hell, yeah." He took in the red satin, barely-there-baby doll lingerie she wore. "I don't know where you got that, but we're going to need some more."

She lifted her hand holding two condoms in her finger tips.

Mitch grinned. "Definitely more of those, too."

He leaned forward, easing her onto the rug beneath him. Her unrestrained laugh filled his heart. "I love you, Norma Brown."

"I love you, Mitch Smith."

With that, he kissed her sweet lips savoring her softness.

She slid her palms down his back and cupped his butt pulling him into the cradle of her hips. "I'm not very good at this. I'm a little nervous."

Mitch kissed her forehead and nose. "No need to be nervous. We already know we're perfect for each other." Leaning on one forearm, he slowly skimmed the strap off her shoulder and bared her breast. "So beautiful." He cupped her full globe before lowering his lips to suckle her hard nipple. "So sweet."

He kissed a slow trail down her body, easing the flimsy gown down with him. Raising to his knees he pulled the delicate fabric off, tossing it to the side. Then he shucked his own clothes. Stretching out on the floor between her legs, he dropped his attention to her bare mound. "So perfect."

He brought her to one climax with his tongue, then another with his fingers before ripping open a condom and sheathing himself. "Now. I need you now, love."

Notching the head of his penis at her entrance, he slowly entered her pulsing heat until he was buried deep inside her. Finally, he was where he belonged. In the arms of the woman he loved.

She hugged him closer and whispered in his ear. "I love you."

The certainty of his feelings was like sinking into a warm and welcoming bath, surrounding him in peace and love. Home.

Need took over and he began to move. Norma met him thrust for thrust. As he reached his breaking point, he slid his hand between them and trailed his thumb over her clit. Shout for shout they exploded together.

As they cuddled in the aftermath, she whispered, "That's never happened to me before."

He stroked the hair from her cheek. "What's never happened? Did I hurt you?"

"I've never orgasmed during intercourse before."

"I promise it won't be the last time. I take my professional status seriously."

Norma laughed. He stood and lifted her from the floor, swept her into his arms and headed to the master bedroom. "Time for fantasy number two. Our bed."

CHAPTER TEN

*M*itch lay in bed the following Saturday morning and studied the sleeping faces of his girls. Norma had brought Eve to their bed to nurse and both mother and child had dozed off after finishing.

Resting on his elbow, he basked in the sense of love and completeness filling his heart. He let his mind wander to all the experiences he planned to share with them. An image of him leading a hiking trip up the nearby mountain filled his imagination. A partially grown Eve followed him. She turned and laughed at something the smaller boy behind her said. Two more children followed, and Norma brought up the rear.

He grinned. He could see the future so clearly. The chime of the doorbell pulled him from his musing. He glanced at this phone, but there were no messages from the hospital.

Norma stirred and asked sleepily, "What's wrong? Who's here?"

"I don't know. I'll go check." Pulling on his sleep pants,

he padded to the entrance and glanced through the peep-hole. He jerked open the door.

"Mom, what are you doing here so early?"

"Mitchell Gabriel Smith, what do you think I'm doing here? This is the big weekend, and I wanted to see my new granddaughter. You've kept me away long enough."

Mitch glanced over his shoulder. "Shh, Mom. She doesn't know. It's tonight."

"Well good thing I'm here now. I can babysit, so you two can celebrate like adults. You did make special dinner arrangements, right?"

"Mitch, is something wrong?" Norma asked from the open foyer behind him.

As he turned, his mother blew past him, pulling a small travel suitcase.

"You must be Norma. I've been so excited to meet you. I couldn't wait any longer to come." Releasing the bag, she wrapped Norma and the baby in her arms. "You're even lovelier than all the pictures Mitch has been sending. Oh, and this little one is so precious. May I hold her?" she continued as she gently pried Eve from Norma's arms.

Norma's wide-eyed gaze met his and he chuckled. "This whirlwind is my mom, Ruth. Also known as the baby magnet."

Ruth looked up with a gleam in her eye. "Oh Mitch, she is every bit as adorable as you said."

Norma reached for his hand. "You've been talking to your mom about us?"

Ruth laughed. "Nonstop for almost three months. He forbade me from coming because he said you needed time to get used to him. Now, which way is the nursery?

Grandma is going to check diapers while the two of you talk. Mitch, put coffee on, please."

Norma followed him into the kitchen. "You really told your mom?"

He nodded as he started the extra strength brew his mother liked. "Yes. I—we, don't keep secrets. We couldn't even when we tried. Mom has some kind of mother radar and always seems to know when something is up with each of us. I think it was my second day at the motel when she called wanting to know what was up."

"She doesn't mind that—that I have a child?"

He raised an eyebrow. "You can ask that after the way she stole the baby from you and made an excuse to have her to herself? Listen, she's already singing to her."

Norma paused and listened to the baby monitor and smiled.

Taking her hand, he led her to the breakfast nook and sat next to her. He took both her hands in his. "Norma, do you believe me when I say I love you?"

Norma studied his face carefully before blowing out a breath. "Yes, I believe you."

"I love Eve, too. She is the child of my heart. If you'll marry me, I'll be the only father she ever knows. I want to adopt her. I will love her without reserve. I know these are only words, but I hope you can trust me to follow up with action."

"Are you asking me to marry you?" she whispered.

"Yes. Well actually, I was going to ask you tonight at dinner." He glanced over her shoulder. "But mom got here a little early."

"Traffic from Denver was lighter than I expected,"

Ruth explained as she walked in the room and handed him a small box.

Mitch dropped to his knee in front of Norma and opened a blue jeweler's box. "Norma, will you marry me? Will you share your love and life with me? Will you let me be the father to all the children we are blessed with? Will you wear this, my grandmother's wedding ring? The ring that united my grandparents for sixty-five years?"

Norma struggled to hold back tears. She couldn't remember ever feeling this certain about anything. Cocooned in a cloak of safety and belonging, she knew she'd found someone who wanted and cherished her and their child. Someone she loved with equal conviction. A home. "Yes, Mitch. Yes, I'll marry and love you for all my life."

EPILOGUE

Twelve years later

$\mathcal{M}$itch paused at the trail's passing zone and glanced down the mountain toward his family. Eve stopped beside him. He wrapped his arm around her shoulder and hugged her against his side, kissing the top of her head. Emerson came next, then Emma. Norma brought up the rear laughing at something Eddie, their youngest, said as he held her hand and guided her up the path.

The first time he'd envisioned this day so many years ago, he'd missed one notable piece.

Now he waited for the love of his life to look his way. Remembering the first day he met her, he smiled when her laughing glance met his. He let his gaze slide down her luscious body to her new sweet little baby bump.

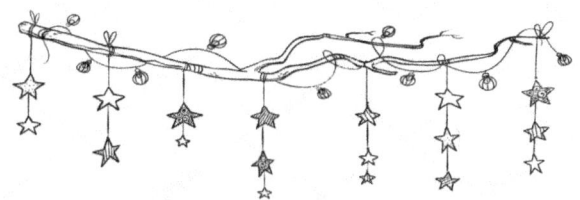

THE
PERFECT
SNOW GLOBE
CHRISTMAS

*lizzie starr

THE PERFECT SNOW GLOBE
CHRISTMAS-CHAPTER ONE

a rustle of bedding and a ten-month-old's chatter distracted Oakley Fifer from the blank page filling his laptop screen. He held his breath, stared at the baby monitor, and listened. The small girl fell quiet, and he grinned, thankful for the reprieve. If her antics woke her brothers from their naps, he would've had his hands full of cranky triplets. Since their parents would be gone until late that evening, he was hoping there'd be no other disruptions to their normal schedule.

He needed at least another half-hour of quiet to get his next project started. Although why he decided to write a short story about Christmas and have it posted online by Christmas Eve—. He'd promised his fans a story, and a story they'd get.

Somewhere in his brain he'd discover an interesting tale. He hoped.

He jotted a few notes on the pad next to his laptop. Gave one of his story people a name he didn't connect with. No. Wait. Why not use characters he'd already developed? There was enough Sci-Fi fan fiction written about the people in his books, obviously readers wanted to know more about them beyond the pages of his stories. He could write his own fan fic.

He scratched out his previous notes, then chuckled at himself, tore the sheet off the pad and wadded it into a ball. Of course, he missed the trash can. That's why he was a writer and not a sports star.

A cry erupted from the baby monitor.

He enjoyed being the nanny to a set of adorable triplets, but the kids seemed to have the worst sense of timing.

Oakley switched off his laptop, but his mind still sorted through which characters he would give a special Christmas. That would set ideas simmering on a back burner in his brain while he took care of the kids. Another cry joined the first. Seconds later the third child joined in the fray. He scrubbed his hands over his face. "On my way, kiddos," he mumbled and left his private rooms.

Oakley loved being a nanny and had lucked out when hired for this position. While the triplets were over-whelming at times, their parents, Ryder and Vianna Barlow, were much more involved than the adults at his last job. Instead of taking interest in their children when it was convenient for them, the Barlows were the primary caregivers. Even with their extremely busy lives, time with their children came first. Oakley didn't mind simply being back up at those times.

One of the benefits of being a nanny was that even with the daily care and enrichment of three almost-toddlers, he had plenty of time to work on his other, somewhat secret career. He'd told the Barlows he was a reasonably successful author during his interview and neither had seemed concerned. As an artist herself, Vianna encouraged his writing, often asking how his book was coming along, or offering to read pages. She made excellent suggestions when he got stuck.

Which had been a lot lately.

He stood in the doorway of the large nursery, shook his head, and grinned. All three babies were standing, clinging to their crib rails. Their crying faded when they noticed him and wide-eyed, they watched him enter the brightly decorated room.

"All right now. What's up with you guys? You should still be sleeping."

At his voice the two boys, identical twins, plopped down on their bottoms. But their sister bent her chubby knees and bounced until she fell over with a startled gasp. Oakley had already determined she was going to be the wild child of the three, leading her quieter brothers into all kinds of trouble. He'd had friends who'd grown up with overbearing older sisters and felt a little sorry for the boys. At least they had each other.

He checked diapers—no problems there—and tucked each child back into their bed. He sat in one of the three rockers and queued up naptime music. Soft tones filled the room. Oakley's mind wandered but never made it back to his writing as he set his rocker in motion and closed his eyes.

"Isn't that the cutest thing?"

Oakley woke with a jerk to find both Ryder and Vianna grinning at him.

"Kids wear you out today?" Ryder asked.

Oakley struggled to gather his thoughts and stood. Late afternoon sunshine created a pool of light in the center of the nursery. He glanced at the cribs where the three children were in various stages of waking up. Then he narrowed his eyes at his employer. "What are you doing here?"

Ryder nudged his wife with his elbow and his grin widened. "What are *we* doing here? It's our house."

Oakley gave a dismissive wave of his hand. "No. I mean now. Weren't you having date night?"

Ryder's grin faded. "Got cancelled. There's a heavy snow forecast, and we decided we'd be better off here than stuck in town." He strolled to the cribs and picked up his daughter. He lightly tapped her nose until she giggled and grabbed his finger. "Besides, now I get to spend time with my two best girls."

"She's such a daddy's girl," Vianna stage-whispered to Oakley as she passed him on her way to the cribs. "And here are my darlin' boys."

Both boys held out their arms and with ease of practice, she settled one child on her hip then reached for the second. She grimaced. "You guys are getting so big. And so wet. Oakley, before you settle into your weekend off, would you help me clean these two up?"

"Of course," Oakley replied and moved to take one of the boys. "Come on, Yohann, dry diaper first then you can snuggle with your mom."

The small boy held out one hand toward Vianna, then

wrapped both arms around Oakley's neck and sniffled. Oakley patted his back. "If you lay still, this won't take long, kiddo."

When he'd started caring for the Barlow babies, Oakley had thought having three changing tables was a bit much. But at moments like these, he was glad he didn't have to line up and wait his turn. With Vianna and Xadrian using the table next to him, Ryder lay Zaylah on the third. A rank odor wafted down the row of changing tables.

Both Oakley and Vianna turned toward Ryder who wore a pinched expression as he peeled back a loaded diaper. Vianna chuckled. "Yep, she's Daddy's girl all right."

After agreeing to join the family later for supper, Oakley retreated to his rooms and settled cross-legged on his sofa with note pad and pen in hand. He rested the yellow paper on his knee and tapped the pen against his teeth. For the life of him, he had no idea what to write. Staring around the room, he searched for inspiration.

When he'd moved in seven months ago, he'd been pleasantly surprised at the accommodations the Barlows had added to their already large home. He gave a soft snort. Everyone in town still called the spectacular home Ryder's cabin. The two-story addition housing Oakley's quarters merged seamlessly with the original building. Being accustomed to a private space of only a couple of rooms—if he was lucky, the full apartment had at first seemed like too much room.

A dedicated writing space and his bedroom were on the second floor to be close to the nursery. A small but well-equipped kitchen and living room filled the first floor. Other than the ability to enter the main house from either floor, the place was a self-contained apartment. Definitely more than any nanny expected.

Or needed. However, with his employers' insistence he have a life when he wasn't on duty, he'd come to appreciate being able to heat his frozen meals or crunch a milkless bowl of cereal without disturbing anyone. Ryder had even arched his eyebrows and given Oakley permission to have a 'guest' on his nights off.

Oakley shook his head. He hadn't thought of that embarrassing moment for a while. Nor had he taken advantage of the opportunity. Of all the beautiful women in Spencer, none had held his attention for more than the amount of time it took to notice them. As absorbed as he was in creating worlds in far off galaxies, most women were bored within minutes. He wrote love scenes when his characters demanded, but his own sex life had been dismal for years.

Pressing the tip of his pen to the pad he drew a spiral and began a list of his fans' favorite *Stars of Jirvanta* characters. His sales would be just as dismal if he didn't come up with the story he'd promised.

CHAPTER TWO

*P*riscilla Van sat at a tiny table near the front of Cookies' Cakes and nursed an espresso. She eyed her half-eaten butter brickle crunch cupcake and set down her cup to finish the treat.

She'd been lucky to find a parking spot along one side of the park in the center of town. Coming to Spencer a week before she was scheduled to start a new job was a good idea, or so she'd thought. With all the driving around she'd done, she had a fairly good idea of the town's layout and where every motel had hung out a no vacancy sign. She'd read about the town's Winter Festival online when she was applying to work at the new therapy camp but hadn't realized how huge the event really was.

Or how tourists would fill every available motel room. How was it possible there was absolutely no room at the inn? She chuckled at her thought and returned to sipping her cooling coffee. Denver wasn't that far. She could find a place there to stay. But the snowflakes that had started as tiny flurries when she'd driven into town had turned huge and wet and were accumulating rapidly.

She hadn't wanted to bother her new boss, but she was edging toward desperation. As a Tucson native, she hadn't had much experience driving in snowy conditions and tackling the miles to Denver was a foreboding thought. She reached for her phone and checked the weather report. Again.

More snow was expected. She had to make her decision now. If Mr. Barlow would allow her to settle into her new apartment at the camp early, she could grab supplies from the big box store and be okay, and safe from the snow. That would also give her extra time to become familiar with her brand-new kitchen.

Priss drew in a deep breath, then sighed. This would be the first time in her career she'd have all new equipment, down to the spatulas and mixing bowls. A dream come true. But she also wanted this extra time to test out the stove, ovens, and other appliances in case there were adjustments required. Discovering items that hadn't been provided was also on her to-do list. There was always something...

Decision made, she took another deep breath and made her phone call.

Fifteen minutes later, she drove down a smooth, gravel-covered road to her boss's home. The building she parked beside was far from the simple structure she'd imagined when he'd said, 'his cabin', boasting two stories and a fascinating combination of roofline angles. This was a mansion of a cabin, and despite Ryder Barlow's friendly invitation, she wasn't sure how she should act. The man was part owner of a huge tract of land where the soon to be fully opened Stick Pony Therapy Riding Camp was located.

Maybe she should turn around and take her chances on the road to Denver.

Before she could return the key to the ignition, a door opened, and a tall figure waved then descended the deck stairs. She wasn't going anywhere now.

She tucked the key into her purse, opened the door and slid from her car. The man rubbed his palms together when he stopped in front of her then held out his hand.

"Ryder Barlow. Surprised you're in Spencer early, but happy to finally meet you in person."

"It's nice to meet you, too. I'm so sorry about all this. I had no idea there wouldn't be any motel rooms available."

He shrugged one shoulder. "The festival gets bigger every year. You'll have to go explore it this weekend. Now, come on in. It's freakin' cold out here. Can I help carry anything?"

"I only need one bag. I didn't bring much since you said the apartment was furnished. Luckily, my folks have a second garage where they let me store some of my extra stuff."

Ryder peeked into the vehicle. "Which bag?"

"The purple flowery one." Priss closed her eyes. Hopefully her ragged college suitcase didn't make her look less professional.

He tugged the large, heavy bag from the back seat and hefted it easily. "Follow me." Speaking over his shoulder, he moved toward the house. "We're on first name basis here, and at the camp unless you want to be known some other way. My wife's anxious to welcome you to our home. And you'll meet my three wonderful kids."

She couldn't hold back a grin at the pride and love in his voice when he mentioned his children. If that gentleness extended to those who came to his camp for therapy, they would be the lucky ones. She sensed this man loved life, people, and helping others, her thoughts supported by what she'd learned about him and the camp online. Priss had always made rapid assessments of people, gauging their inherent goodness and in matters of business was rarely wrong. With matters of the heart? Not a great track record there.

At the cabin door he stomped snow off his boots and held the door wide for her to enter first. She matched his stomps then stepped inside, moving away from the door so he didn't have to crowd in after her.

"There's a mat to the right for your shoes," he said. "Easiest way to keep the floors clean is to leave 'em at the door. If you need thick socks or slippers, Vianna can loan you some."

"No, I'm good. Thanks."

She slipped gratefully out of her damp canvas shoes then turned to study the cabin's great room while Ryder removed his boots. "Wow."

He stood beside her and nodded. "It is impressive when it looks like this. But Vianna will be bringing down the triplets in a few minutes and there will be an immediate explosion of toys." He chuckled. "Guest room's on the other side of the fireplace. You'll be far enough away from the nursery, you shouldn't be disturbed if the kids are up at night."

She drew a breath.

Ryder shook his head. "Nope. Don't apologize. Shit happens. Plans get derailed. You're in Spencer now, and part of the Stick Pony family. Family takes care of family."

"Thank you, Mr. Bar—Ryder," she finished at his arched eyebrows. "I'll move out to the camp tomorrow morning or as soon as I'm able."

"Uh, about that," he said. "When I said the apartment was furnished, I'd intended it would be. Should have been done last week, but there were shipping delays and other problems. Nothing to worry about, but you won't be able to move in for about a week. As long as nothing else goes sideways."

"A week?" She'd planned on the possibility of only a night or two in a motel before moving to the camp. Once the festival was over, she'd still have to use her savings to cover five or six nights lodging. Arriving in Spencer early was turning out to be a horrible idea. "I don't know. Where will I find a place to stay?"

"Here of course," Ryder stated. "Plenty of room. It'll give us the opportunity to get to know each other, and work on our expectations and hopes for the food service component of the campers' experience."

"I don't want to be in the way."

Toting her suitcase, Ryder started across the room. "Won't be. After the weekend, I'll take you over to the camp. Show you the kitchen and dining areas. And you can arrange your apartment as deliveries come in. Here's your room."

He moved the suitcase to the end of a queen-sized bed and pointed to a closed door. "Bathroom's there. Should be plenty of towels and such. If you need anything, just let us know."

"I can't stay here for a week."

Ryder planted one hand on his hip. "Why not?"

"I'm imposing. You don't know me."

"And you don't know me either, or you'd know an invitation in this house is simply that. An invitation. No strings. No expectations." His grin widened and his eyes twinkled. "Although..."

"Although?" Hopefully he wouldn't notice how her voice shook.

"I'm fairly sure none of us would be opposed to turning over kitchen duty to a professional for a few days."

Relief chased away another rise of panic. Cooking would be an easy way to repay her new boss for his kindness. "I can do that. Just point me toward the kitchen."

He chuckled. "Not tonight, Priscilla. Vianna and I have supper handled. And Oakley, our nanny, will be joining us as well. I know today's been stressful for you. Take some time to relax before supper."

The bed did look comfortable, and the afghan tossed over the back of an armchair begged to be wrapped around her shoulders. "That does sound good."

"Excellent. We'll try and keep the kids quiet."

"Don't worry, they won't bother me."

His expression told her he didn't believe her assurances, but he only nodded. "Later."

The door had almost closed behind him when she remembered. "Wait," she called.

Ryder stuck his head back through the doorway. "What?"

"I brought dessert from town."

His grin returned. "Trying to soften me up with a sweet bribe?"

Oh no, he didn't think that did he? "No. Just because you opened your home to me on this snowy day. A thank you. I was at the cupcake store anyway."

"You brought Cookie's cupcakes?" His eyes and smile widened. "What kind? Nope, doesn't matter. I love 'em all."

"But I left the box in the car."

"Want me to go get them? I promise to try not to eat any until supper."

"You don't mind going out in the snow again?" When he shook his head she dug through her purse, finally extracting the keys. Surprised at how quickly she'd come to trust this man, she held the fob out to him.

Ryder closed his fist around the keys. "I'll leave these on the mantle for you. And no, I don't mind. I'd do just about anything for a cupcake from Cookie's.

A sharp rap on the door woke Priss from a deep sleep. She blinked and took a few seconds to remember where she was. A second knock had her springing from the armchair. "Just a moment, please."

After fighting her way from the cocoon she'd created with the crocheted throw, she ran her fingers through her hair. Hoping she didn't look too rumpled she spared a glance in the mirror over the dresser and opened the door.

A grinning, bearded man with a toddler perched on his hip greeted her. "Hi. Supper's about ready. Come meet the baby Barlows."

Unable to form a reply, she stared at him. He was the embodiment of every wish she'd made since her first crush. His beard was trimmed close to his chiseled jawline, merging with wavy hair just a shade lighter. His eyes, a deep ocean blue, twinkled when his grin widened. Priss nearly pressed her palm against her heart to contain the rapid beating. Thank goodness she had some control.

When the vision before her cleared his throat, she blinked and tilted her head to one side. *Say something.* "And you are...?"

He held out his free hand. "Oakley Fifer. I'm the nanny."

He was the nanny? She'd imagined someone far different when Ryder had said the name Oakley. Priss had fallen asleep wondering if the nanny would become her friend. A *girl* friend. This was... he was... Mentally shaking herself out of a daze, she took his hand. She hadn't been staring too long, had she? "And I'm Priscilla Van. I'll be the cook over at the camp."

"Don't sell yourself short. She's the chef," Ryder shouted from across the room. "Come on over to the kitchen. About time to eat."

The child Oakley held reached for her. Priss took a tiny step back then worried the action might taint the man's opinion of her. She lifted her gaze to him.

Oakley chuckled. "Looks like Zade has taken a liking to you. He's usually shy around new people. Go ahead, take him." He paused and gave her an assessing look. "Only if you want to."

She didn't have any experience with babies. She wanted a child someday. Maybe. She wasn't sure she'd make a good parent. "Maybe later?"

Oakley's grin softened. "No rush. Whenever you're ready. Let's go eat. This big guy is hungry."

He turned and started across the large open room. She followed slowly, trying to keep her focus on the child wearing a tiny pair of blue jeans, a western designed tee shirt and crocheted cowboy boots. But her gaze kept slipping to the fine, firm shape of the nanny's ass. By the time they reached the dining table, she'd worked enough moisture back into her dry mouth to speak.

"I really could have helped with the meal."

A dark-haired woman shook her head, tossing her short curls. "At least for tonight, you're our guest. I'm Vianna. You've met Zade." She pointed toward a trio of highchairs where Ryder was attempting to seat a squirming child. Vianna continued, "Daddy's trying to get Zaylah settled. Lala is a handful. Sitting quietly like the good boy he can be is Yohann. Han for short."

Han wore an outfit matching his brother's while the girl was dressed in a flowery shirt and crocheted Mary Janes. Priss sighed. "They're so adorable."

Oakley gave a soft snort and secured Zade in his highchair.

"Oakley," Vianna admonished with a laugh. "Don't disparage my perfect children."

"No, ma'am." He ruffled the boy's hair. "Never. I'm just glad they're on their best behavior this once."

Lala tossed a plastic spoon to the floor. Vianna rolled her eyes as Ryder retrieved the utensil. "Yeah, they are."

Watching the friendly interplay between the adults and children, Priss worried her bottom lip. She'd grown up in a family who easily expressed love and laughter. Who accepted each person for who they were rather than forcing expectations on each other. But once she'd moved out and started searching for that comfort and security in new relationships, she'd discovered how rare those people were in her life.

Experience should have taught her to be wary of first impressions.

Yet she sensed this family was exactly as they seemed. Even with the inclusion of an outsider, a nanny. And now her.

Oakley took a bowl from Vianna and dished out a spoonful of small food items onto Zade's tray. He held up a piece of bowtie pasta and encouraged the child to wrap his fingers around the morsel, grinning when the food finally made it to the boy's mouth. He caught her staring, again, and arched an eyebrow.

Vianna set a large bowl of pasta on the table. "Ah, adult food. Sit down, Priscilla, and dig in. We don't stand on formality here, especially when we have this trio of messy eaters. They're little, but they're learning."

Priss sat in the indicated empty chair next to Oakley and watched how the three adults managed the triplets, interesting the children in the food before turning to their own plates and conversation. It was like a well-choreographed and rehearsed dance. She didn't have experience with small children and tried to absorb any knowledge she could through observation. Awkward and feeling completely out of her element, Priss answered the questions meant to draw her out but mostly just watched the others.

Once the meal was done Priss rose and began stacking the dishes. "At least let me clean up. The meal was great, so it's the least I can do."

Vianna leaned back in her chair. "I'll take you up on that. But later. Sit down. We've still got cupcakes for dessert."

Ryder nodded. "My kids and I can't function without dessert."

When the others laughed, Priss relaxed her shoulders. "Want me to go get them?"

"The plate's on the back counter," Vianna said. "Have to keep them hidden so everyone eats real food first." She narrowed one eye and pretend-glared at her husband.

"Cupcakes are real food, honey." Ryder rubbed his belly. "Right kids?"

Once Priss retrieved the sweets, and tiny portions had been placed in front of the triplets, her new boss rolled his shoulders and rested both forearms on the table. "Oakley, Priscilla, I need to ask you both something."

A knot tightened around Priss's heart, and she searched her scrambled thoughts for anything she might have done wrong.

Ryder waved a dismissive gesture in her direction. "It's nothing terrible. Relax."

Oh no. She'd allowed her expression to...

After removing the wrapper, Ryder tore a cupcake in half then stuck it back together with the icing in the middle and took a bite. After swallowing he continued. "I got a call this afternoon from some folks I know from my days in Hollywood. They'd agreed to invest in the camp even before we got the land. They're going to be in Denver for a few days, but obligations don't allow for them to come to Spencer."

Hollywood investors? Priss tamped down her curiosity. A part of the contract she'd signed for her work at

Stick Pony included a non-disclosure privacy clause to protect campers' identities. She assumed the same would hold true for investors. And Ryder had also told her while the town of Spencer catered to celebrities, disturbing visitors, or making a scene was discouraged. Still, she couldn't help but wonder.

"After the delays in the full opening of the camp last year, they want to meet with Jack and me. So we'll be heading there day after tomorrow to reassure them we're back on schedule now. And taking our ladies with us." He smiled softly at Vianna before turning a grin to Priss and Oakley and arching one eyebrow. "We plan to be gone four days. A little alone time without our kids. If you know what I mean."

Oakley returned the grin and shrugged. "Not a problem."

"You had a couple days off scheduled..."

"Nothing planned though, boss. You go and enjoy some quiet time."

Lala squealed and Priss winced at the piercing sound. If the girl did that often, her folks definitely needed some quiet time. Then her brothers joined in the chorus and Ryder clapped his hands over his ears, turning toward his children. He must have made a funny face because the shrieks turned into giggles.

Priss smiled. Who could resist baby giggles?

Vianna said, "Thing is, Zoe, Ryder's mom is out of town, too. So our usual back up isn't available. Oakley, I know you can handle the kids, but twenty-four-seven with the three of them for four days? We don't want to chase you away."

"It's not—"

Ryder interrupted, "It is a lot. That's why I was hoping we could talk Priscilla into staying here during that time. Yeah, I know the apartment we promised isn't furnished yet, but you could move to a hotel once the festival is over. Priscilla, it would mean a lot to us if you could stay here and help Oakley out for those few days."

Her gaze danced between the two men before she studied the now quiet children. All three watched her as expectantly as their father. Were they old enough to understand what was going on around them? She'd have to do some research. Then Zade giggled and reached sicky, cupcake covered hands toward her, and she lost her heart to the tiny boy.

"I can do that."

Stockinged feet propped on the coffee table, Oakley slouched against the armrest of his couch and stared at the drapery covered window. He'd decided on the characters so now an open plotting notebook rested on his thighs. Unable to focus on the story he needed to write, he gave up, stuck his pen behind one ear and allowed his thoughts to wander.

To the most appealing woman he'd met in a long time.

Oakley chuckled softly. Ryder hadn't told Priscilla their nanny was male. Probably on purpose. But she'd recovered from her surprise quickly and handled an awkward situation with a calm grace Oakley admired. She'd been reluctant to even hold Zade so he assumed she hadn't had much interaction with toddlers. They did take some getting used to. He was surprised she'd agreed to help while the Barlows were away.

She'd watched him throughout the meal. At least as much as he'd surreptitiously glanced toward her. Her simple beauty tempted him. A lot. His fingers curled and he imagined releasing her hair from the messy bun and discovering the length and softness of the golden-brown strands. He would stare into the depths of her dark brown eyes, then lean closer and experience the wonder of her full lips.

With a groan, he tossed the notebook to the end of the couch and plopped his feet to the floor. He crossed the small room and drew the drapes to one side to stare out at the dark, winter night. Yes, he found Priscilla attractive. Beautiful. But he'd met a wealth of attractive women. What was it about her? Why couldn't he shake thoughts of her from his mind?

As a writer, he watched and studied people. He'd even taken a few psychology classes in college with thoughts of becoming a social worker if his writing didn't pan out. He grinned at his reflection in the window. Even with the continued success of his sci-fi series, he'd decided to become a nanny instead. His smile faded. One who still used those learned observation skills.

That made him wonder about the fear tempered by longing in Priscilla's expression when he'd offered to hand Zade to her. Why she skillfully turned conversations away from herself. Why she rounded her shoulders to hunch forward when she noticed him looking at her.

They had four days alone—except for the triplets. Maybe he could draw her out and discover the answers to some of his questions. Or not. When he wanted to know something, he tended to prod, so needed to be careful. Pushing her away would be the worst thing he could do. Unacceptable for so many reasons beyond the fact they had committed to work together.

A sharp cry sounded from the baby monitor, startling him from his vivid imaginings of other experiences they might enjoy together. He dropped the drapes back in place. Guess it was a good thing he'd forgotten to turn off the monitor for the night. He listened until he heard the low rumble of Ryder's voice in the nursery then switched off the device and returned to the couch and his inability to come up with a workable story idea.

CHAPTER THREE

*P*riscilla dug through the trunk of her car for her hiking boots. Her new boss was sending her along with Oakley to check out Spencer's Winter Festival and pick up groceries and other needed items for the days the two of them would be watching over the triplets. She hardly thought she needed to go along, but understood Ryder was giving her and Oakley a chance to become acquainted before being left alone.

Where the hell were the boots? The heavy things might be better suited to hiking the desert mountains, but still should keep her feet warmer than her canvas shoes— she curled her toes—which were still damp. And, since she was staying here for a few days, she might as well take in a second suitcase.

"Give you a hand?"

"Yikes." Priss jerked and bumped her head on the trunk lid. "Ow!"

"Shit, I didn't mean to scare you." Oakley took her elbow to steady her.

She waved away his concern then carefully touched her head. "It's not bad. And not the first time I've done that." She chuckled. "I once had a friend who gave me a bicycle helmet because I bump my head so often."

"You're sure? Least I can do to make up for the bump is to carry something for you."

Once she'd directed him to carry two suitcases—why not take advantage of the willing labor—she sat on the wide stairway to change into the suede boots. Conscious of Oakley's eyes on her, she carefully double knotted the laces. She stood. "I'm ready."

"Those things waterproof?"

"Uh, not really."

"They should do for today. Ryder said plows were out all night, including the one he sent into town from the camp. So there shouldn't be too many places where we'll have to walk through snow. But you probably should consider getting better boots. We can check in the big box store if you'd like."

"I wasn't as well prepared for winter in Colorado as I thought." She shrugged one shoulder. "More concerned about the job itself rather than where I was going to be living."

"I moved here from the northern midwest, so I'm accustomed to heavy snowfalls."

"We had snow. Sometimes." She didn't know why she felt so defensive about snow. Time to move on. "How long is our shopping list?"

He waited an extended moment before answering and she tried guessing his thoughts. She didn't know him well enough to gauge his reactions to her or her questions, so needed to tread lightly.

Finally, he blinked and shook his head. "Not too bad. We're supposed to add on whatever we want for groceries. Do you want to drive? Get to know the area a bit?"

Driving would give her some control over the day. But even plowed, there would probably be icy spots. Eventually she would need to learn Colorado winter driving. But not today. "Not really."

The deep rumble of his chuckle sent goosebumps dancing over her arms. She forced herself to ignore the sensation and kept her arms at her sides.

"Let's go then."

During the short ride into town they decided to visit the festival first. It was still early enough the parking lot at the fairgrounds was mostly empty although a good number of people were walking toward the entrance from other directions. After the previous day's snowfall, Priss was delighted with the clear, blue sky and how sunlight sparkled off the piles of freshly plowed snow. She slipped on her sunglasses. Sun she could handle.

After a quick stop at the food pavilion, they each carried large coffees and munched on cinnamon sugar donut holes as they toured the exhibits. Standing in front of a glistening ice sculpture of a twelve-foot tall wishing well, she asked, "Do you prefer manny?""

"Dear god, no. That's a pretentious term someone came up with probably to protect their manhood. Nope, what I do falls under the description of a nanny, and I am proud to be of assistance to my families."

"Families? This isn't your first job?"

He shook his head and took a sip from his cup. "Nope. I had three clients before the Barlows. Chicago area. Only two kids each time. Different ages. The triplets are quite an experience."

"I'm sure. Did you always plan to be in childcare?"

"Nah. Kinda fell into it in college. Took my first position to help out a professor."

"So, you don't have a degree in kids or anything like that?"

"A degree in kids? That's one way to put it. Just practical experience for that one. I have a degree in English. I, uh, do a little writing on the side."

"Are you published?" She loved to read when she allowed herself the time. Which she hadn't since her ex had called reading frivolous and ripped one of her favorite paperbacks to shreds. No. She would *not* think about him. Never again. She lifted her gaze to Oakley's.

He held hers a moment then angled to step away, reaching into his jeans pocket. "I've had a little success in publishing. I want to leave a donation here for the Dream Weavers then how about we take a spin through the craft tents?"

"Oh, okay." His body language rang loud and clear. He didn't want to talk about his writing. She took his empty donut bag and wadded it with hers before tossing them into a trash container. "I'm not crafty, but I enjoy looking at how creative others are."

The tight set of his shoulders relaxed. Good. Until she learned what might trigger his anger, she needed to tread lightly. She clasped her hands and lowered her head to wait for him to drop his donation into an opening on one side of the ice sculpture.

When he returned to her, he bent to look up into her face with a grin. "Ready?"

Nodding, Priss released a long breath and filed away her observation. Oakley seemed to easily let go of minor issues. Although this one time didn't really mean much. Her ex had been pleasant enough. At first. She'd met Oakley less than twenty-four hours ago, so she needed to remain on alert.

Because damn it, she was attracted to him. A lot. Falling into another hurtful relationship was not in her plans. For the immediate future, with starting a new job in a new town, a relationship might not be the best idea anyway. Unfortunately, her wishful, longing heart didn't agree with her logical, 'keep me safe' brain.

The four days of being alone with him should tell her a lot about what kind of a man Oakley Fifer was and the best way to act around him. The Barlows trusted him with their babies, so that was a huge mark in the plus column. Great. Now she had a list started. Enough already.

Another deep breath and she lifted her head with a smile. "Ready."

After supper, Vianna had shooed Oakley back to his rooms for another night off before leaving him alone with the kids. Not really alone, but despite how Priscilla had tried to help out during the meal, he knew he'd be the main caregiver. As it should be. It was his job after all. He'd been about to ask Priscilla if she wanted to join him for the evening when she'd scooted back her chair and made excuses about needing to work on menus or some such thing to do with her job.

Honestly, he'd been captivated watching her throughout the meal and hadn't paid attention to her words until she was halfway across the room. He blew out a breath and stared out the wide floor to ceiling windows of the living area. The mystery of Priscilla Van intrigued him almost as much as her physical beauty.

Behind him, Vianna chuckled. "You're going to have to try a little harder, Oakley."

Giving himself a mental shake, Oakley turned in his chair to stare at her. "Huh?"

Vianna waited until Ryder carried the third triplet to their play area. She sat next to Oakley. "You like her."

He shrugged one shoulder. "Yeah. So? Isn't that a good thing?"

Rolling her gaze to the ceiling, Vianna grinned. "Yes it's a good thing, but your like goes deeper and wants more than just a co-worker friendship."

"Are you reading me?" He straightened and focused on Vianna's face. When her guides or other spirits spoke to her, there was an unfocused dullness in her eyes, a slight tilt of her head as though she was listening to a distant voice. Which he supposed she was. Normally he found her spiritual insights interesting—because they were about other people. He wasn't sure he wanted ghosts butting into his business.

Tonight her eyes were clear, and she waved one hand indicating the air above her head. "Just my own observations. And this is what I see. You're both hiding something. I've had experience with that and it's not a good thing."

Oakley started to deny her statement, but bit back his words at the knowing arch of her eyebrow. "Yeah. I know. Now that my books are bestsellers, I probably should come clean. Not just with her, but with my fans. After eighteen books, the anonymity still suits me, but my publisher is pushing."

"There's that, and it's important. A strong part of who you are. You also need to start showing her how you feel. I don't know for sure, but it feels like she's closed off part of her life. You'll need to go slow. But don't take too long or I'm afraid you'll lose your chance."

"Gee, that's helpful. Thanks."

"Everything is a balance, Oakley. You need to balance the life you want with how much you show to the fans who love your books. They'll love you as you, too. Getting to know Priscilla will be a give and take until you both find the balance in your relationship."

He couldn't argue with Vianna's words, even with a new layer of confusion settling over him. From what he'd witnessed, even when the spirit world didn't speak through her, Vianna's own thoughts could circle in ways that gave him ideas to examine and ponder. "Thanks, Mom," he said with a laugh.

"You know what I mean." She rose. "Now, get going. After I've done the dishes, I'm joining my darling babies for some play before bedtime."

"I can—"

She held up one hand. "Nope. You'll have enough to do for the next few days. Go write some of your wonderful words."

When he glanced toward the guest room door, Vianna's hand landed on his shoulder. "Tomorrow is soon enough to start. She needs time to figure things out, too."

Once in his apartment, Oakley avoided opening his laptop by deciding it had been too long since he'd last done a deep cleaning. He wasn't normally a messy person, but a layer of dust had accumulated on the shelves, and he didn't recognize what was in a couple of containers in his refrigerator. So he turned on music, tried to turn off his brain, and settled into cleaning mode.

Well after midnight and exhausted, he set out a fresh set of sheets for remaking the bed in the morning then fell onto the mattress with a groan.

He'd be worthless if he didn't pull himself together. But trying to shove his attraction to Priscilla to the back of his brain wasn't working. Maybe he just needed to run with it. Slowly though, so he didn't scare her off. Subtle enough to easily back away if she rejected his attempts. A tender seduction to bring back the interest and unconscious invitation he'd seen in her eyes and the soft parting of her lips.

Thinking about those soft lips renewed the pleasurable, heavy throb low in his body. He shifted, moaned at the slide of his flannel lounge pants over his groin then rose and stumbled to the shower. If he didn't take matters in hand, he'd never get to sleep.

CHAPTER FOUR

*P*riss spent the evening pretending to make lists and planning for her new job at the camp. Each of the many lists she'd started only had a couple of bullet points. Her family had thought her starting a job in winter was odd for a camp. She'd explained how once the operation was fully up and running, Ryder planned to have the facilities open year-round. And there were already events planned for early spring that needed her skills.

Moving from her pillow supported perch on the bed to the chair, Priss frowned. She couldn't focus. Not on her job. Not even on how much she'd enjoyed the time in town with Oakley and how being with him made her feel safe and appreciated. As though he really liked her without expecting something in return. That lack of expectation frightened her. She didn't know how to react, how to judge what might happen, or what to say.

Oakley didn't make everything about *himself*. Not like her ex had. But then, Ted had been different in the beginning, full of compliments, gifts, and sweet words. All the attention had snared her quickly, and he'd drawn her into his web so subtly she hadn't realized how narcissistic he was. Or how much he'd controlled her and her actions—just to make everything about him.

Priss shuddered and ran her hands up and down her arms trying to chase the chill. She'd never considered herself stupid and was still amazed at how quickly she'd believed Ted when he told her they were in love. He'd never once said he loved her. Only that they were in love and belonged together. After the initial wooing and she'd moved in with him, Ted had changed.

His demands became unreasonable. If she didn't perform to his standard, he'd punished her verbally. Or he'd destroy something she cared about. Over and over, she'd forgiven him and believed his 'look what you made me do' was truth.

Until the day she used cilantro instead of parsley in a dish and he ripped up the notebook containing some of her grandmother's handwritten recipes and tossed the pages into the fireplace. Thankfully most of the pages missed the hottest part of the fire and while he screamed obscenities at her, she'd scrambled to pull them from the ashes.

After he'd slammed the front door and squealed his tires backing from the drive, she'd gathered her few belongings and escaped. Ted hadn't tried very hard to get her back and only a couple weeks later she'd seen him with someone new on his arm, the woman's face turned toward him in adoration.

Priss sighed. She should have warned the woman not

to listen to Ted's pretty words and promises. Hopefully the woman realized his true nature sooner than Priss had.

Digging through a bag, Priss found her journal. She hadn't felt the need to unpack that old relationship baggage for a couple months. But the wishes her heart made whenever she thought of Oakley were stirring up her memories. At times she didn't know which were memories and which were her own fears and self-doubts. Everything was so mixed up and confusing, she had to straighten out her own thoughts before continuing to move forward. She picked a favorite pen from her stuffed pencil pouch and sat cross-legged on the bed.

Pen hovering over a blank page, she closed her eyes. Took a deep breath. And began to write.

The adult Barlows left after the babies' morning snack time and Priss attempted to keep out of Oakley's way by puttering around in the kitchen. But once she'd completed prep for the rest of the day's meals, she heard interesting noises through the baby monitor and couldn't put off joining Oakley and the kids in the nursery.

Oakley sat on a rug decorated with large numbers surrounded by the triplets and a scattering of toys. He glanced up when she entered the room and smiled. "Welcome to the funhouse. Pull up a piece of carpet and join us."

She chose a spot opposite him and sat, curling her legs to one side. As soon as she'd settled, Zade noticed her and scooted toward her on his diaper-clad bottom. Using her legs for balance, he pulled himself to his feet.

"Wow, great job, Zade," Oakley said.

The boy turned his head toward him and fell back onto his bottom. Oakley chuckled. "Good start anyway, Zade."

"What's that all about?" Priss asked as the boy struggled to climb to his feet again.

"He's trying to keep up with his younger sister. Lala has been standing for a couple weeks now. The way she's going, it won't be long until she tries walking."

"They're so little."

He shrugged one shoulder. "They're all right where they should be according to the developmental experts. Lala is the youngest, but she's usually been the first to move from stage to stage. The boys try to keep up with her. I have a feeling it's gonna be like that for them all their lives. Here, offer him this."

With Priss's pantleg tight in one small fist, Zade made it to his feet and laughed. She took the soft block from Oakley and held it out to the baby. His quick reach for the toy nearly toppled him but Priss's hand at his back kept him upright.

Oakley nodded approval. "Good job, both of you." He sighed and rose to follow the third triplet's rapid escape across the room. "Okay, Han. We know you're the best crawler. You don't need to show off for Priscilla. Now, it's time to play on the rug."

Plopped onto the center of the play area, Han's lower lip pouted out and quivered. Priss held her breath.

But Oakley shook his finger at the boy then placed a toy xylophone in front of him before handing over a plastic mallet and grimacing at her. "It's going to get noisy in here."

Once Han started pounding on the metal keys, Oakley set an easel in front of Lala and she pushed at large buttons making an assortment of bell sounds. Zade dropped his block, sat, and scooted toward his siblings. Oakley set a third musical toy in front of the boy and handed him a mallet.

Holding his hand toward her, Oakley used his chin to gesture toward the rocking chairs. "Let's sit over there where it's marginally quieter. The kid's will be fine. They love—uh—music."

After he tugged her to her feet, he kept her hand in his as they crossed the room. Priss's palm tingled from the contact. Okay, more than just her hand. As much as it frightened her, the attraction also brought with it a sense of comfort. Of something more that she dared not consider. Dull, cool disappointment filled her when he released her hand. Using the tip of her toe, she set her rocker in motion. The smooth back and forth relaxed some of the tension from her shoulders.

"So," Oakley began. "I've been wondering why you came to Spencer early. I didn't think your job was supposed to start until the first of the year. Didn't you want to spend the holidays with your family?"

A partial answer was easy. "My sister and her family are in Hawaii. They invited our folks and me over for Christmas on the islands. My folks left last week."

"Why didn't you go? I'm pretty sure the weather will be more pleasant there."

"Oh, no. Despite not knowing how to drive in it, I like

the snow. I would have enjoyed palm trees and a sandy beach, but…"

He matched the motion of his rocker to hers. "But?"

"I freak out if I have to get on a plane. Really freak out. I'd have to be totally unconscious just to fly from Phoenix to Tucson. I can't. I just can't."

Eyebrows arched in surprise, Oakley stopped rocking to stare at her. "You're that afraid? Have you tried—"

She held up her hand. "Everything. Drugs. Hypnosis. Exposure therapy."

"Hmm. Have you tried cognitive behavioral therapy?"

"Now you sound like the therapist my parents hired."

"Sorry. I took a lot of psychology classes in college. At one time I thought about being a social worker."

Priss gnawed on her lower lip. Psychology? And if he asked about CBT, he probably had a pretty good grasp of the subject. He watched her now, and she imagined the thoughts running through his mind. She really did need to be careful.

At a loud crash, he glanced toward the babies who continued to pound on their musical toys despite how Lala's easel had fallen on its side. He shrugged. "They're okay. And so are you. Sometimes therapy doesn't work out. It's a shame you have to miss a family Christmas though."

"It's fine. My folks will come to Spencer when they get back. We'll celebrate then. We'll probably have a video call sometime. I'd like to see my niece and nephew open their presents. What about you?"

He shrugged again. "I have parents. No siblings. No grandparents, aunts, or uncles. We never really did holidays. Whenever I could, I spent them with friends. Or in my room. I never had a computer, so I never got into gaming. I read and filled notebook after notebook with words. Those stories were my company, my best friends, my confidants."

"That sounds lonely."

"At times. But since I don't really know anything different, I don't have a true sense of what I might have missed out on. I've always been the one to volunteer to work on the holidays so those with families could be with them."

Priss's heart ached for Oakley's past. An idea blossomed and she spoke before she fully thought through the implications. "Since we're both going to be alone, maybe we could spend the day together out at the camp. I'd be happy to fix a Christmas meal for us."

His smile widened but he shook his head. "That would be great, except Vianna and Ryder have already decided I'm spending the holiday with the Barlow family."

"Oh. That sounds nice." It did, except it meant she would be alone. A couple days ago, that was what she wanted. Now, after meeting Oakley, alone sounded so… lonely.

"Even with Ryder's mom, sister, and their men here, they'll appreciate having another adult around when it's time to deal with excited, overtired triplets." He stopped rocking and covered her hand with his. "Vianna will insist you join us. I think I can guarantee that. Like Ryder said your first night here, family is family."

"But no one knows me. I don't want to be an imposition."

"What's your favorite thing to cook for a holiday dinner?"

She blinked at his change of subject then thought for a moment. "I love the cooking part. Preparing a whole meal isn't a big deal. Wait. I could offer to do that if they invite me."

Oakley shook his head and her growing excitement faded. Of course they wouldn't really want to have her around for a family celebration. Why had she let that tiny bit of hope spark? She knew better.

"I'm sure your offer will be appreciated, but not necessary. Everyone is supposed to bring something different. We'll check with Vianna to see what else is needed. I'm bringing vegetables." He ducked his head, but his eyes sparkled. "Because I can't cook worth a damn."

His fake, self-deprecating remark stole the misgivings from her, and she leaned back to set her chair rocking again. "Maybe if you ask nicely, I'll help you out. I've got an excellent brussels sprout au gratin recipe."

When he lifted his head, she couldn't look away. The depths of his dark eyes held a promise she dared not believe. He spoke softly. "I'll ask very nicely."

Then in one smooth movement he rose and started toward the triplets. He stopped and looked back over his shoulder with a wink. "And I'm not above begging."

CHAPTER FIVE

*P*riscilla moved around the spacious laundry room pulling the triplets' clothing from the dryer, folding, and sorting the pieces into neat piles. The satisfying task gave her quiet time to think. And send a thank you to the universe for the local diaper service. Someone would need to be on almost constant laundry duty to keep up with the demand of three little ones.

She chuckled and held up a small pair of jeans. These tiny clothes were adorable. Her heart thumped hard, and she shook her head as she folded and stacked the denim. She had no right to be thinking about how she would dress her own children. Oakley's kids, she admitted. She wanted Oakley for her children's father. She was so messed up.

The past four days alone with him and the kids had been frightening, educational, a whirlwind, and fun. Ryder and Vianna would be home later this morning and Priss's imaginary life would return to reality. She'd move out to the camp as soon as the apartment was ready. Life would continue according to her plan.

She'd run a successful kitchen. Alone.

She'd have time to rediscover her grandmother's recipes and write a cookbook. Alone.

She'd have a good life. Alone.

Leaning her hip against the dryer, she scrubbed her hands over her face. When she'd taken the job and set out for Spencer, alone had sounded wonderful. No one watching her twenty-four-seven, making snide comments on every move she made. No one trying to wipe her past and her individuality from her. No one to destroy everything she cared about.

Her ex had sucked her in with pretty words and promises. He'd nearly broken her. She straightened and lifted her chin.

But he hadn't. The past few months had been difficult, but she'd rediscovered who she was. Mostly anyway.

Only now that 'alone' she'd struggled to define, discover, and pledge herself to no longer felt right.

Because she'd met Oakley. In the past few days her priorities had shifted. Her outlook on life and her future had brightened and she didn't know how to deal with the sudden change.

Or the fact she'd fallen in love with Oakley Fifer.

She moved back to the counter, planted her elbows against the smooth surface and rested her face in her hands. In love? What did that even mean?

Her ex had told her she was in love with him, and she'd believed him. But he'd never said he loved her. That should have given her a clue. She snorted softly and returned to folding the tiny outfits. He'd taken, but never given.

Unlike Oakley, who gave of himself with his whole heart, expecting nothing in return. At least out loud. At times his dark eyes held an interesting swirl of desire and question. The prospect of answering that question and giving in to the desire beginning to simmer between them… no, she didn't know his feelings. She needed to remember her past and not make more out of a few glances or touches than was there.

Priss forced her thoughts back to reality. Once the Barlows were home, there would be no reason for her to spend so much time with Oakley. That was it. They'd been forced together so she'd imagined possibilities. Okay. She could deal with this. When she moved to the camp and created some distance between them, she'd be able to put her emotions into the proper boxes and get on with her life.

Struggling to find the appeal in moving on, she loaded the folded clothing into a basket and returned to the nursery.

Oakley stood at one of the dressers holding a sniffling Lala in one arm while he dug through one of the drawers. He tossed three shirts on the dresser and turned the girl to face the pile. "Okay then. Which shirt do you want to wear?"

Silently, Priss moved closer and began transferring the basket contents to the second dresser. Oakley glanced at her and rolled his gaze to the ceiling before hefting the baby girl closer to the shirts. "Which one, Lala?"

After a long moment, Lala reached toward a bright

yellow shirt with a ruffled bottom. Oakley separated it from the pile. "This one? Okay. Now what about shoes?"

He set three pairs of shoes in front of the girl who immediately slapped her palm against neon pink Mary Janes.

"Really? Okay then. A bow for your hair?" Oakley asked, placing a choice of three in front of her.

Once Lala made her choice, Oakley sighed. "Alrighty then. Let's see how all this goes together."

Priss joined the pair and glanced at the mismatched pile of clothing. Oakley answered before she asked. "Lala didn't like what I tried dressing her in. Fought me like a tiny wildcat." He bent until he was nose to nose with the girl. "Didn't you, little diva?"

"Isn't she a little young to choose her own clothes?"

Oakley shrugged one shoulder. "I only set three choices in front of her at a time. Maybe it's accidental, maybe she chose. But if it gets her dressed, that's what counts. Although, I will try and get her into something that is more presentable before her folks get home. Don't want it to look like I'm a slacker."

"They'd never think that."

After getting Lala into her green leggings and yellow shirt, he glanced at Priss and winked. The simple gesture drew a rise of butterflies in her stomach. And lower. Inhale on a six count. Exhale on eight. Nope, that didn't help. Strangely enough, she was glad. The sensation of wanting someone without an undercurrent of fear was new. Delightful.

"Here we go, pretty girl," Oakley said as he lifted Lala until she stood on the dresser. "What do you think, Priscilla?"

She gave the bright outfit a long look while the girl tangled her fingers in Oakley's hair. A rise of jealousy surprised Priss. She wanted, needed to run her fingers through Oakley's dark hair to gauge the softness. "She certainly is a ray of sunshine."

Oakley straightened the yellow shirt emblazoned with an orange *daddy's little sunshine* then lifted her from the dresser and deposited her in the crib next to her brothers. "Yep, her daddy's gonna love it."

Lala smacked her lips then after a burst of unintelligible babble, began chanting, "Da da da da da."

Seconds later Han joined her. When the boy frowned at his brother, Zade added his soft "da da" to the chorus. Lala waved her arms as though directing a chorus and Priss bit back a chuckle. They were so stinkin' cute.

A noise from the doorway halted the trio for a moment then squeals irrupted from all three.

Ryder stepped into the room. "Now that's what I call a welcome home."

"After the past four days, it feels weird to be doing something without the babies," Priss said as she and Oakley found a parking space just outside Pearl's.

Oakley stretched and grinned. "Love my job, but it is good to get away occasionally. That's one piece of advice I always give when anyone asks about hiring a nanny. Adults deserve and need private time. So, lunch then shopping?"

The Barlows had kicked the two of them out of the

house for the rest of the day and evening, claiming the need for baby time. Ryder had also given her a list of what items were supposed to be delivered for her new apartment and told her to get whatever else she needed. She'd argued, but he insisted she use the company credit card.

"I am hungry. Let's eat and go over this list. If the truck arrives on time tomorrow, I'd like to be able to get set up and moved in."

The slight downward tilt of Oakley's lips made her catch her breath and rethink her last words. But then his easy smile returned. "Sounds like a plan."

While they enjoyed the day's special of chicken fried steaks and mashed potatoes slathered with creamy gravy, they made their plans. First a walk around the other businesses not located in Olde Town. She didn't expect to find things like bedding or towels there but hoped to discover something decorative to make her new home hers.

A wave of sadness washed over her, the memories of everything she'd lost when her ex grew angry and destroyed her belongings threatened to ruin the day. She refused to let that happen. She was done with him and his manipulations. The man across the table from her was kind and considerate. He even held the door open for her as they left the café.

She walked next to Oakley with her hands stuffed in her jacket pockets wishing her fingers were intwined with his instead. Their elbows brushed occasionally, sending longing deeper into her heart. They enjoyed how the high school art class's holiday windows decorated many of the storefronts, and peeked around the fresh, acrylic paint to check out the interiors before deciding which stores to enter. Even with the freezing temperature, they planned to stop at Curley's Cones on the way back to the car.

Needing to warm up before starting that return trip, Priss stepped into Aunt Cora's Attic, an antique store fully decorated and bursting with seasonal charm. "Oh," she said, stopping at a large glass case displaying an assortment of snow globes. "Look at all these."

Some of the globes were the cheap, touristy plastic toys displaying vacation locales. She'd fallen in love with the domed souvenirs on the first vacation she remembered her family taking to the Grand Canyon. The white snow had seemed out of place to her when the background photo had been of the sun-filled canyon. She hadn't cared.

Some of these on display were truly vintage. The water had partially evaporated from a few, and time had dulled some of the brightly colored bases, but each globe was clean and well displayed. This shop understood and cared for the treasures they sold. She clasped her hands at her chest and sighed.

Oakley leaned closer to study the pieces. "You like snow globes?"

"Oh, yes. I had a collection—once." She angled so he wouldn't see the tears stinging her eyes and pretended to look closer at a large globe on a low shelf.

"Like these little ones?"

"Some. When I was a little girl. Then when I was in high school, I started collecting nicer ones. Usually newer globes made by one of those companies that specialize in collectables. Occasionally I was able to afford an old one like these."

"What happened to your collection?"

Tempted to blow off his question with some glib statement, Priss drew a deep breath. Then released it slowly. If
she wanted to explore a relationship with Oakley, she
shouldn't sugarcoat her past. Hell, he already knew about
her fear of flying.

"I took the nicest ones with me when I moved in with
my ex-boyfriend. He even put up a special shelf for me.
But once he had me fully ensconced in his home, in his
life, he changed. He'd been so charming in the beginning.
Considerate. Loving.

"That quickly changed because of me. According to
him everything wrong in our relationship was my fault."

Oakley's mouth opened and she touched his lips with
her fingers to keep him from speaking.

"I know it wasn't. He's a narcissist. Everything had to
be about him. I didn't see it when he drew me in. Now I
constantly remind myself the blame he placed on me was
a lie. One day I didn't do something he wanted—I don't
even remember what silly thing it was—and he blew up.
Stomped around the house yelling. Finally, he ripped the
shelf of snow globes from the wall. The ones that didn't
break then, he crushed under his foot.

"Of course then he was sorry, and told me even though
I love him, I'd made him do that. I'd *made* him destroy my
things."

"Priss, I'm so sorry. It wasn't your fault. It wasn't your
fault you fell for his lies in the beginning."

She gave a sharp laugh. "I know that. Now. Thankfully
my family helped me stand up to him when I moved out.
Stood by me while I worked through everything in
therapy."

"Was that incident when you left him? No, you don't

have to answer that. Really not my business and I don't want to bring up messy pasts while we're having a good day."

"It's okay. I still have strong, inappropriate reactions occasionally. Kinda like PTSD, I guess. Talking about it, especially with you, is important." She held her breath. She was testing the waters, trying to evaluate Oakley's reactions.

"I'm a good listener, sweetheart. Anytime you want to talk."

"You're not just saying that because you took social work classes, are you?" Then the realization hit. He'd called her sweetheart.

He laughed and the woman at the counter lifted her gaze and smiled at them. "No psycho-babble from me."

He continued as though he didn't notice the catch in her breath. "Maybe you should start your collection fresh. Buy one of these. Unless that would constantly remind you of that rat-bastard."

"You're giving rat-bastards too much credit. I'll think about collecting again. But I don't want to start until I've moved to the camp and see what kind of space I have for personal items."

Oakley's bright expression faded, and his brows drew together. "That makes sense." His easy smile returned although the expression didn't reach his eyes. "Good plan. Sun's going down soon. What say we head back to the car then finish our shopping before it gets too much colder?"

*O*akley carried a heavy handful of grocery bags into his kitchen and made a show of huffing as he lifted them to the counter. Priscilla stood in the doorway shaking her head and chuckling. Mission accomplished.

She'd been quiet after they'd left Aunt Cora's and had made only a few decisions to complete her shopping list, returning to her excuse of needing to see the camp kitchen and apartment first. He honored her decision but missed her smile and their easy conversation. She'd drawn in on herself after telling him about her ex.

But after Ryder had called with plans for take out pizza that night, Priss had insisted she would cook instead and seemed to cheer up while shopping for her needed ingredients. And she'd needed everything because his cupboards held little but cereal and canned soup.

Oakley forced his fingers to uncurl from his painfully tight grip on the bags. When she was ready, she'd talk to him. "Do you need any help?"

She moved to the counter and pulled fresh vegetables from one bag. She cleared her throat. "You said you weren't so good in the kitchen, didn't you?"

She'd caught her lower lip between her teeth but struggled to contain a smile. Reaching into another tote, he lifted out a bag of flour. "Take a look in my fridge."

"Oh my gosh. Good thing Vianna has you eat with the family. How old is this?" she asked and wrinkling her nose, held up and opened an old whipped topping tub with indistinguishable contents.

Shit, he'd missed one on his recent cleaning binge. Reaching for the tub, he held it at arm's length and carried it to the garbage. "No clue. So I guess this means you don't want my help?"

"Not this time, okay? I haven't cooked for my new boss yet, so I want to make sure everything is perfect."

She was perfection, so how could she not make a perfect meal? Still, he knew his skills—or lack thereof—would just get in her way. "I can use the time to write. I'm behind on my self-imposed deadline. Promise you'll let me know if you need anything. Can't find something. Whatever."

"I promise." Drawing his attention, she sketched an 'x' over her chest.

He had to leave the kitchen. Now. Before he acted like an idiot and did something crazy. Like molding her body against his and kissing her until she forgot any other man ever existed. "Let me, uh, grab a bottle of water. I'll be just in there. In the living room. Writing. On my computer. A story."

Wrinkling her nose, she laughed. "Okay. I'll try not to bother you."

Bother him? Knowing she was only a few steps away in his kitchen got him hot and bothered. Wisely keeping his mouth shut, he saluted her with the bottle and escaped to the next room.

He settled into the comfort of his couch, laptop perched on his thighs. After reading through a few of the pages he'd written the previous day he nodded to himself. The story was finally coming together. One of his fans' favorite characters, a space pirate named Danelle, and her mate, a tree-bound spirit she'd discovered on an abandoned space platform, were sharing and combining winter holiday traditions.

Easing back into the story, he easily picked up where he'd left off. The quiet sounds floating from the kitchen created a perfect background for the baking of Danelle's favorite Winter Lights treat. Well, what baking there was going on. This pair was one of his lustier couples who took him in often unexpected directions.

Maybe today though, he was writing what he wanted to be doing. He imagined himself in the distant spaceship's kitchen. With Priscilla at the ultra-modern cook station.

He chuckled and created a scene break. His fans were going to love this story. Stretching, he winced at the tightness of his jeans over his groin. The words on the screen hadn't caused the reaction. His awareness of Priscilla kept him on edge.

Stop. The scene was written. Now he was back in the real world, and he needed to remember his promise to go slow.

Priscilla moved into his peripheral vision, hovering in the kitchen doorway, drinking from a large mug.

When he turned his face to her, she lifted the mug. "Coffee?"

"Perfect."

"I don't want to disturb you, so just tell me to go away and I'll stay in the kitchen. Although watching bread rise is only slightly more exciting than drying paint."

He glanced at the clock. "We've been working longer than I thought. Come, have a seat." He patted the cushion next to him.

Holding up one finger she turned back to the kitchen then appeared with a second mug. After handing the coffee to him, she remained standing, looking around the room. "I'm a bit anxious about supper. Don't think I can sit still. Do you mind if I explore your bookshelves? It's always fascinating to me what people have displayed."

The disappointment of her warmth not sitting next to him warred with his curiosity. What would she think of him once she'd circled the room? Because he had a lot of bookshelves. And a lot of books. "My life is an open bookshelf. Enjoy."

Her smile made his heart thump heavily against his chest. The pressure created a welling of emotion such as he'd only written about when he'd imagined his characters being in love. Some readers scoffed at those bits and pieces—especially his macho-pretending fan boys—and claimed the emotions were unrealistic and sappy. A real man would never...

He held back a snort. If they believed that, those boys would never be 'real' men. Whatever the hell that was. Oakley didn't care. He was who he was. And he was in love. Nothing else mattered.

Definitely not the fan boys' fragile feelings.

He watched Priss over the rim of his mug as she wandered the room. She ran her fingertips over book spines and Oakley shivered. She leaned closer and he wondered what had drawn her interest. When she paused at the shelves holding his published works, his breath stalled.

Exposing the alter ego he fiercely kept hidden was taking a huge chance. Could he trust her with the knowledge? If he pursued the relationship he wanted with her, this couldn't be kept a secret. Her reaction would drive his next decisions. Why did love have to be so flippin' complicated?

Priss turned to set her mug on a coaster on the coffee table and paused at the wary expression on Oakley's face. Fear nearly kept her from making the comment hovering on her lips, but she reminded herself she didn't need to be afraid with Oakley. Or fear him. She straightened and waved her hand at the shelves. "You have a huge collection of H.M. Murdoc's books."

Oakley nodded slowly and remained silent.

Priss turned back to the shelves and touched each volume. "Murdoc is one of my favorite authors. I've read almost every book, had most of them in paperback, too." Her fingers lingered on one of the most recent releases. The one her ex had… "My ex didn't approve of my taste in reading material. He destroyed one book by tearing out each page in front of me. Then he dumped the rest of my library."

Unable to face Oakley after another painful admission, she shrugged. "I guess mass market paperbacks aren't necessarily a precious thing, but it still hurt like hell."

The sounds of Oakley shifting preceded his warm

presence at her side. She continued scanning the books, stopped, and pulled one from its place. "Oh, my. Is this one in German?"

"I have a few foreign editions."

"That is so cool. You really must like the author."

His lips twisted and she couldn't tell if he grimaced or attempted to hide a grin. "I guess."

"And here's the last two. I haven't had a chance to read them yet. Do you... could I borrow them? I'll be careful. I don't dogear or break spines or anything like that. Not if I can help it anyway."

He took her hand and tugged her toward the couch. "I'm sure you're a very careful reader. Priss, have you ever wondered why there's no photos of Murdoc?"

"I suppose whoever the writer is wants to maintain their privacy. Or some secret. I've always wondered, but a person's life is theirs to do with as they wish. It's got to be extremely difficult to keep someone this popular hidden, though. Especially with all the social media and cell phones."

"You think Murdoc's popular?"

She gave him her best incredulous look. "Yes. I do. I imagine an author would need to sell a lot of books to make a bestseller list. And he's on those lists all the time. And I like the books."

"There is that. Hey, would you like to read what I've been working on?"

"Are you as good as H. M. Murdoc?" Teasing him was taking a chance.

Oakley's lips tilted to a smirk. "I'd like to think so."

"Then yes, of course, are you kidding? I've wanted to read something ever since you said you wrote."

Lifting his laptop from the coffee table, he held her gaze for a long moment while he made his final decision. When she was about ready to give up hope, he gave a sharp nod, clicked on the screen, and handed her the computer.

If he felt the nerves and painful anticipation like she did when someone tasted a recipe she'd prepared for the first time, he was hiding it well. She wouldn't waste the trust he placed in her, or the opportunity to discover something new about Oakley the writer. Offering him a smile, she began reading.

Only a few paragraphs into the excellent story she stopped, closed the laptop, and studied him. His attempt at a relaxed posture was ruined by the stiff set of his shoulders and the tense flat line of his lips. "Are you writing Murdoc fan fiction?"

"Yes. And no."

Priss arched her eyebrows. That was no answer. "What do you mean? No, wait. I only read half a page, and this is good. Really good. Good enough you should be using your own characters, not someone else's."

"Yes, this is for the fan fic community. I promised a holiday story."

Grinning, Priss fanned herself with her hand. "You chose two of my favorite characters."

Oakley returned the grin. "I'm glad." Then he leaned forward and after taking the laptop from her, gathered her hands in his. "They aren't anyone else's characters."

She stared at him. What was he talking about?

He tightened his hold as if he feared she would run away. "Priscilla, I write under the fiercely guarded pen name of H.M. Murdoc."

CHAPTER SEVEN

*S*tunned, Priss sat frozen staring at Oakley's hope filled face. Like so many fans, she'd imagined meeting her favorite author. And here she was. H.M. Murdoc. She squealed then pulled one hand from his to cover her mouth in embarrassment.

"Priss?"

Attempting to center herself so she wasn't any more of a fool, she took a deep breath and gave herself a shake. "Really? You're really him?"

With a wry grin, he waved to the laptop. "I could show you my last royalty statement for proof."

"No. No, I believe you. I just can't believe you're him. Sorry. I'm acting silly. I'm an idiot. Oakley, I won't tell anyone. I promise. But if I buy a book, will you sign it for me? I won't even show it to anyone."

His dark eyes sparkled and widened like she'd surprised him. "You don't need to buy any books. I have boxes in the closet. I'll sign any you want."

She returned both hands to his and scooted closer.

"Thank you. I mean what I said. Your identity is safe with me."

"I wouldn't have told you if I thought otherwise. Maybe it's time. My publisher is ready to force the issue. I just can't have the exposure affect any family I work for. I'm not ready to give up being a nanny. At least until the Barlow three are older. Then I'll decide what to do going forward."

This new facet of the man she loved settled like flower petals in her soul. This single act of trust erased the final, tattered shreds of the weak woman her ex had tried to create. There would always be moments of doubt, but now she could deal with those times strengthened by Oakley's trust. And with her own growing belief in herself.

Cautious hope filled Oakley's expression and he held himself still as though waiting for her to make the next decision. She touched his cheek. He pressed against her fingers, his soft, short beard tickling her palm. The sensation traveled over her skin in tantalizing waves. "Oakley? I want to kiss you."

The sparkle returned to his eyes as they darkened. "Oakley or Murdoc?"

She shook her head and leaned closer until her lips nearly brushed his. "Aren't they one in the same?"

He groaned and their lips came together, soft and tentative. When he cupped her face with his palms and tilted her head to a perfect angle, Priss touched her tongue to the slight parting of his lips. Delighted with her own boldness, she explored and tasted. He matched her exploration, but never pressed beyond where she'd already taken the kiss.

Long before she wanted the sensuous moment to end, Oakley gently twisted his lips from her, grazing her jawline with his tongue until he reached her ear. "We need to stop."

The warmth of his breath over her ear and neck tickled delightfully. "Why?"

"The timer's going off."

"Timer?" Priss straightened and frowned. The insistent chirp of a timer echoed from the kitchen. "Oh. Time to finish supper. Damn."

"If I help, prep might not take so long." He drew her back and kissed her neck.

"I'm sure you can pat out pizza dough."

His lips moved to the base of her throat. "Probably." He lifted his head to look into her eyes and stroked one finger over her cheek. "As long as you don't want it round."

Priss burst into laughter.

"Not the reaction I expected," Oakley complained before pressing his lips to her temple.

"I—" Priss bit her lip to hold back her secret. Despite his obvious interest in getting physical, now wasn't time for her to admit her love.

Speaking against her mouth, Oakley said, "Just another minute, sweetheart. Another kiss. Or twelve. Then I'll roll out the best pizzas ever. Trust me?"

Her answer was to slip onto his lap, wrap her arms around his shoulders and get a good start on those twelve kisses.

The pizza turned out great, much to Oakley's surprise. But the dough she'd made was soft and stretchy and a joy to shape into individual pizzas and the specially formed sticks for the kid's tiny hands. Her sauce had tasted of fresh tomato and basil. He didn't miss the overabundance of cheese he normally ordered on a delivery pizza. He'd discovered he didn't mind working in the kitchen—when the cook at his side was beautiful and smiled at him with luscious lips he'd taken his time getting to know.

Now they stood side by side in the main kitchen, filling the dishwasher and clearing the counters while Vianna played with her children and Ryder paced the large room, his phone pressed to one ear. When Oakley accidentally-on purpose brushed against Priss's hand, she gave him a smile with a coy twinkle in her eye. Then returned the gesture.

If he'd known telling her his pen name would allow the sensual woman to escape, he might have spilled his secret sooner. He paused with a towel in one hand and a pan half-way to its home in the cupboard. Too soon, and she might have thought he was attempting to push her toward a relationship that wasn't to her benefit. Like her ex had.

Today had been the right time. Thank god he'd taken the chance.

Ryder pocketed his phone and after touching Vianna's shoulder moved toward the kitchen. Leaving the triplets babbling to each other on a blanket, Vianna joined him. He planted both palms against the counter. "Good news is the trucks are on schedule for tomorrow. The first with kitchen items should be at the camp by nine. The apartment furniture is expected at noon."

Priscilla folded her towel and placed it on the counter. Excitement sparked the air around her. "Oh, that's great. I'm anxious to get started."

Ryder sighed. "Yeah, well. I just spoke to Deke—head of security at the Aspen Gold Lodge. Seems there's been numerous occasions the past couple weeks where people have crossed camp land to try to sneak onto Lodge property. There's been a few guests with huge paparazzi followings."

"That's horrible," Priss said, turning to glance wide-eyed at Oakley.

He gave a slight shake of his head. Before the evening was through, he'd bet she would ask if he feared that kind of notoriety. What he feared was that it would chase her away.

"Here's the thing," Ryder continued. "Jack and I didn't consider more than minimal security in our plans. Then when we came up against regulations and staffing concerns last year, just keeping the camp in minimal operation took our energy.

"Right now the camp has one groundskeeper who's doubled for what little security we thought we needed, along with routine drive throughs from the sheriff's department." His head dropped forward, and he stared at the counter. "I should have expected this. I'm amazed Granddad or Deke didn't. At least not that they mentioned.

"Priscilla, I can't allow you to move out to the camp until we have more security in place. And I really don't want you out there alone even during the day."

He and Vianna shared a look filled with silent communication. A wish blossomed in Oakley's chest. He wanted that closeness, that understanding with Priscilla. He closed his eyes. He'd give her the time she needed. To catch up to his feelings. *Go slow*, he vowed. *I will go slow.*

Priscilla crossed her arms and leaned back against the counter. "That sucks."

Startled, Ryder chuckled. "That it does."

"Oh no. I mean, I understand. And I appreciate your concern for my safety. Is there some way to arrange for someone else to be there?"

With a nod, Ryder straightened. "Now that we really are back on track, there's plenty of camp business one or any combination of the partners can complete in the office. There's a few tradesmen I trust finally doing finishing work on the main building. I'll get a schedule of when they plan to be there."

"Ryder's mom is back in town, and ready for some grandbaby time," Vianna added, giving Oakley a wicked grin. "That will free up Oakley to accompany you."

Priss turned to him. "But… don't you have… you know…"

Her attempt to remind him of his writing without mentioning it warmed his heart. She was a treasure. His treasure. He jerked his head toward the grinning Barlows. "They know. I'd never take a position where the family didn't know there was a possibility of media exposure."

"So, you told her," Vianna stated.

"She figured it out."

"I did. I'm a huge Murdoc fan. Then Oakley let me see the story he's working on and… he doesn't have time to babysit me at the camp. He's got anxious fans to placate."

"Sweetheart, I can write anywhere." The tips of

Oakley's ears burned. Shit. He hadn't meant to call her sweetheart out loud in front of the Barlows.

Ryder slapped his hand on the counter. "Settled then. Tomorrow the two of you can meet the deliveries. We'll figure out a schedule for the rest of the year over the next couple of days." He glanced at them expectantly.

Thankful his boss had ignored his verbal slip, Oakley nodded. But at the twitch of Ryder's lips, Oakley knew he wasn't free of the danger of a few teasing comments.

"Now," Ryder continued, "We're planning on a super-hero movie, with popcorn later. Would the two of you like to join us?" He glanced over at the triplets. "I can't promise an uninterrupted viewing though."

After putting the final baking sheet away, Priss shook her head. "I've just gotten access to books I haven't read yet from one of my favorite authors. I'd love to just curl up with a book tonight."

Wishing she'd want to curl up with the author instead, Oakley pointed to the large television close to the guestroom door and said, "It'll be quieter if you want to read in my apartment."

The smile she gave him shot desire straight to his groin. Not good with Ryder intensely watching their interaction. Oakley shifted.

Vianna cleared her throat. "I think some quiet reading sounds great. Maybe you can encourage Oakley to work on his story tonight, too."

"I'm planning on it. He let me read the first part and I can't wait to read the rest."

"You and the rest of the fan-fic group," Oakley grumbled. Once again he regretted promising a Christmas story. But he wouldn't disappoint his fans. Or Priscilla. "Let's go. I feel some inspiration coming on."

He took a chance and held out his hand. Priss chuckled and wove her fingers through his. "I can't wait."

Ryder's booming laugh followed them until Oakley shut the apartment door behind them and leaned back against the polished wood.

Priss tugged him through the kitchen and pressed on his shoulders until he sat on the couch. She chose the book she wanted from the shelf, turned, and stared meaningfully at his laptop. With an exaggerated sigh, he reached for the computer and settled into a comfortable writing position. When he glanced at her, Priss nodded her approval.

This would be an interesting experiment. He seldom wrote with others in the same room. Never with a woman who had so captured his heart. She inspired more in him than simple creativity. He wanted, no, he physically ached to be better for her. A better writer. A better person. A better lover.

Her lover.

Good thing he'd chosen the characters he had for this story. There was no way now he could pull back the sexual tension from his words. From his own body.

Priss moved to his side, knelt, and captured his face with one hand. She held his gaze for a long moment then her eyelids lowered, and she kissed him. Too soon she eased back, patted his cheek, and rose to sit and curl her legs to the side at the other end of the couch. So close. So far.

She opened the hardcover book and glanced sideways at him. "That was for inspiration."

CHAPTER EIGHT

*T*he day dawned bright and sunny although the forecast on Priss's phone said there was a possibility of snow that afternoon. Even after the late night reading—she'd read nearly half of the long space fantasy—and lengthy kisses rewarding Oakley for the progress he'd made on his latest story, she'd been up early, excited to explore her new domain.

After returning to her room, she hadn't been able to sleep much. She'd lingered in sensual memories of Oakley's touch, of how his kisses had showed how much he wanted her, but with no demands. Her ex had been all demand and lust. There'd been few moments to cherish and remember.

She wanted Oakley in ways she had never experienced with another man. Her needs weren't about sex. Well, not just sex. And she somehow knew Oakley was the man who held the answers. Who held her heart. Who she loved.

Stuffing the notebook with her lists into her purse, she

studied her reflection in the mirror. She didn't look different on the outside. Then she tilted her head to one side and wondered what Oakley saw when he looked at her so intensely. Or with soft, dark eyes shimmering with what she hoped was desire.

Enough. Today was about her job and her new home. Even if she wouldn't live there for a while, she'd be able to start making the place her own.

She had her own kitchen to manage now, too. Even with that excitement churning through her, she was unsure whether her life had really changed so much in the past weeks, or if it was how she felt about herself and her internal changes that made life seem so different.

Oakley drove her car to the camp, and she leaned forward against the safety belt to peer at the world around her. Snow covered Rocky Mountains edged the wide valley. Buttes and tree covered rises rose to tower in the distance. Different than the mountains near where she was raised, but the familiar sense of home was the same.

The drive to the camp wasn't that far, yet the changes from the busy tourist town to pastures and widely spaced homes made it seem a different world. They passed under a tall arch displaying the Stick Pony logo. Oakley pointed out the road leading to the equine rehabilitation hospital. "That's where Jackson Spencer and his family live. The center has had a more successful opening than the riding camp did."

"What exactly happened?"

Oakley shrugged. "From what I understand, they had some early success with private therapy before the first round of major construction was completed. But when they thought they were ready to begin accepting campers, turns out there were still a few governmental hoops to jump through. Staffing became an issue. People they thought were on board weren't."

"Like the kitchen manager?"

"Yeah. Showed up but couldn't handle the operation. And at that time, whenever there was someone at camp, they were bringing in food from off-site. Left after a month."

A twinge of fearful concern prompted her next words. "The camp is ready to go this time, isn't it? I know I'm not planning on going anywhere, but…"

Oakley chuckled. "Understand that what I'm telling you is strictly from an observational viewpoint."

Trusting his observations, she nodded.

"I think Ryder and his cousins jumped into this without much planning. They had ideas, great ideas, and the need for such a facility is huge. While the top layer of regulations, management, building, et cetera were all handled well, they didn't dig deep enough through the layers. Adding three babies—well, four since Jack's boy is just over eighteen months now—and with Ryder discovering he had a sister, their lives went crazy. Things turned around once they started listening to Mr. Spencer, Ryder's grandfather. He's recognized as a brilliant businessman. Got the guys back on track."

"I worked a few years in a nursing home kitchen. There were regulations stacked on regulations. All for the benefit of the residents, but sometimes the paperwork load made the actual food prep feel like it came second. One of the reasons I wanted to start early was to try to get a handle on regs and record keeping for the demographics of campers."

"Sounds like you've got the official jargon down. Here we are."

He stopped at the front of a large, log building with clear signage indicating it contained offices and the dining hall. "Wow," Priss whispered.

"The offices are to the right. Dining hall on the left. Kitchen's in the back."

She nodded. "And my new apartment is above the kitchen."

"First truck's early."

She angled in her seat to watch the large truck lumber up the drive and clapped her hands. "I can't wait to see everything."

Nearly six hours later Oakley shut down his laptop and stretched. He'd been ensconced in the kitchen office writing while Priscilla greeted both trucks and directed the unloading. He stood and glanced around the dimly lit kitchen. The raised office had glass walls allowing the occupant to survey the entire operation.

He'd taken advantage of the opportunity to watch while Priscilla explored her new kitchen, put part of the delivery away, crossed things off the list in her notebook and added new items. The ease and surety with which she moved inspired him and words fell from his fingertips onto the page.

When the second truck arrived, she'd insisted he continue working. Without her distraction, he'd completed his short story and made notes while the computer read his words back to him. A few more edits and *A Holiday on Jirvanta* would be ready to post on the fan-fic site.

The second truck had left about an hour ago, and Oakley could no longer contain his need to see Priscilla. Telling himself he was only curious about the furniture he'd seen carried to a huge freight elevator and wondering if she needed assistance moving any of the heavy pieces, he took the stairs to the apartment level two at a time.

The door opened before he knocked and Priss took a quick step back with a gasp.

"Sorry, didn't mean to startle you."

Patting her chest, she grinned. "No worries. I was just coming down. Want a tour?"

Strands of her hair had escaped from her messy bun and curled against her cheeks and forehead. What he wanted was to capture the softness between his fingers and bury his nose against the fresh herbal scent that drove him mad. He wanted to touch, taste, discover. He wanted his body against hers, in hers.

"Oakley?"

Dear god, how long had he been standing there staring at her, imagining them together? If the tightness in his jeans was any indication, too long. Or not long enough. With Priscilla, he was off kilter. Didn't know up from down. "Yeah." He cleared the roughness from his throat. "A tour would be great."

She turned before he had time to understand the shimmer in her dark eyes or the tilt of her lips. He stepped into the apartment and closed the door.

In the center of the living space, Priss stopped and

faced him. "I'm pleasantly surprised at how large the apartment is."

Keep the discussion on the room, the furnishings. Calm, boring stuff. "The Barlows are kind, generous people. When they showed me where I'd be living I thought they had to be kidding. At my other positions, I considered myself lucky to have anything more than just a bedroom. Even an en suite was a rare luxury."

Her grin widened. "Wait until you see the bathroom here. It's like a luxury hotel. Not that I've been to that many. And the kitchen? Wow. You know those recycled glass counters in Vianna's kitchen? They're here, too."

"Sounds like they wanted to spoil the camp chef."

"I wish everyone would quit calling me that. I'm not a chef. Just a good cook. With excellent management skills. So, what do you think of the furniture?"

It was damn difficult pulling his focus from her to look around the room. Huge logs formed the outer wall and framed large windows. He wandered closer. The view of the camp and mountain background was spectacular. Returning his focus to the interior, he didn't know if the heavy furniture was Priscilla's style, but it fit the lodge vibe of the apartment.

She joined him at the window and took his hand. "Bedroom's this way."

Low in his body, desire settled hot and heavy. All he'd be able to do was take a quick peek at the room. He couldn't allow himself more. Not now. Not yet.

But she didn't allow him to hover in the doorway and tugged him close to the huge, tall bed. The bedroom was in a corner of the building, so the bed was centered between two windows while a slider led to a small, snow-covered deck. Priscilla waved one hand toward the deck. "Won't that be a great place for coffee in the morning? Or maybe some wine after a long day?"

She flopped on the bed and grinned up at him. "Check out this fabulous bed."

"Uh…"

She scooted until she was leaning against the headboard and patted the mattress next to her. "You've been hunched over a hot computer all day. Stretch out and relax."

He searched for an excuse. "I, uh, don't want my shoes to get your new sheets dirty."

Arching one eyebrow at his flimsy attempt, Priss patted the bed again. "Then take them off. Now, scoot around to your side of the bed and give it a try."

His side of the bed? The leaping of his heart at those words matched a stiff twitch at his groin. Thankful he'd worn his shirt untucked, he circled the bed, toed off his shoes and sat carefully at the very edge of the mattress, tugging at the shirttail that felt way too short.

Priss cupped his shoulder and pressed until he gave in and angled to lift his feet onto the bed. She fluffed a pillow and placed it under his head. When she returned to her position against the headboard, Oakley was able to breathe.

"I'm glad I decided to wait to get a comforter," she said. "What I'd thought I'd like just wouldn't fit here."

"So another shopping trip is in order?" If he kept the conversation neutral, maybe he could get his insistent body under at least minimal control.

"Yeah. And I want to get some Christmas presents for the Barlows. Especially the babies. So I need ideas."

"I can probably help with that." Hoping she wouldn't notice his discomfort, Oakley released a series of long breaths.

After a quiet moment, Priss broke his attempts at calm with a sensual sigh. "See, isn't the bed comfortable?"

Knowing he'd find comfort in any bed he shared with her, Oakley nodded. "Very nice."

Priss fell silent. This was the moment she'd been thinking about most of the afternoon. Ever since the delivery guys set up the bed and she'd covered the plush mattress with fresh, new sheets.

She was done being afraid to ask for what she wanted. Her ex had nearly broken her spirit and it had taken her move to Spencer to realize how to finally set aside the old, useless patterns and be herself.

She hadn't liked the woman her ex had forced her to become. The her now? This woman she was coming to like. She was strong and mostly confident. There was always room to grow but she wasn't so afraid. Proud of her skills and talents, she had what she needed to be successful and happy.

Almost everything she needed. What—who—she needed most right now, lay next to her. She studied the square, tense set of his shoulders and how he'd tightly clasped his hands over his stomach. She'd noticed the bulge he tried to keep hidden. Felt the heat of his gaze when he didn't know she was hyper aware of him. Of every move, every smile, every gesture.

Oakley. She needed him with desperate longing. Taking a deep breath, she steeled her resolve and said, "I never went off birth control."

Oakley's jerk shook the bed. "Uh…"

"After my ex. I'm still protected. And I had a physical before coming here, so I'm healthy."

"What are you saying?"

She grinned at the rise of hope in his words. "What about you?"

Oakley remained quiet for so long, Priss feared she'd misread his interest. Then he turned to his side and propped his head on his hand. He held her gaze captive. "I haven't been with anyone in a couple of years. Never met a woman I wanted. Until you."

He wanted her. Priss's heart sang, and she moved until they lay facing each other. She traced his features until he caught her fingers gently between his teeth and touched the tips with his tongue. Flurries of sensation danced over her skin. "I never knew how wanting a man really felt. Until you."

"Until you," he repeated.

"Oakley?"

"Yes, sweetheart?"

"I… I want you. Today. This moment. Now. Make love to me?"

His slow, sensual grin tightened the ache low in her body. His dark eyes grew serious. "How about we make love together?"

Her heart understood the significance of his question. Neither of them would simply take their own pleasure from the other. She would find joy in him and he in her. Together. She nodded.

With a low groan, Oakley gathered her closer, molding her body to his, taking her mouth in a slow, tantalizing kiss. There was no need to hurry. They had all the time in the world, and to her delight, Oakley proved to be a master of time.

As if by magic, their clothing was tossed to the floor. Their whispered words, soft moans of pleasure, gasps and sighs filled the room. His hands, his mouth were everywhere on her skin, teasing, soothing, delving deep to take her beyond thought again and again.

When finally he rose over her, ready for his own release, his harsh breaths burst past her ear. "Look at me. I need to see what you feel when I'm in you."

"Hurry, Oakley. Please."

He shook his head. "Look at me."

The command in his voice was undeniable, yet in that tiny place where she could still think and reason, she knew if she refused, he would accept her choice. She opened her eyes and fell into the desire-hazed darkness of his gaze.

Resting her hands on his shoulders, she stroked her fingers over the tense muscles in his neck. Her mouth opened in a silent exclamation of joy. Oakley smiled as he slowly joined their bodies and whispered, "I love you."

CHAPTER NINE

*P*riscilla enjoyed the days before Christmas more than any other year she could remember, except when she was little and excited for Santa's visit. She spent hours at the camp organizing and reorganizing the commercial kitchen, making lists, and studying requirements both for record keeping and specific dietary needs campers might have. It was heaven.

Especially those days when Oakley was her safety companion and they found moments to sneak away and discover more about each other.

A week later, drawing on some reserve of courage, Priss had asked Vianna a difficult question. After a long hard look, and a couple of eyebrow waggles, the two giggling women had moved Priss's few belongings from the guest room to Oakley's apartment then Vianna insisted he take the evening off.

He'd enjoyed the surprise. They both had.

But he'd never again said 'I love you'. Nor had she

admitted her love for him. The lack was an invisible wall between them. One she was planning to break through.

All she needed to do was expose her feelings. And that frightened her. Not as much as she thought it might, but she still wasn't comfortable with accepting that aspect of her personal power.

On the afternoon of Christmas Eve, Priss double checked the ingredients for Oakley's vegetable contribution and the special dessert she planned as a surprise. Everything she needed was there and in place. She turned her back on Oakley's kitchen and returned to the living area and the book she was reading.

Oakley was on duty, watching the triplets while their parents were busy running final errands and adding to the piles of gifts already stacked behind the bars of a portable kennel surrounding the tree. The adults all agreed the kids didn't need any more presents, but that hadn't stopped the shopping trips. The triplets would be well supplied with toys and educational fun. To make room for the new toys, Vianna had already begun filling boxes with outgrown toys and clothing to be donated.

Priss turned her gaze to the small pile of packages ready to be carried to the party the next day. Not impressive in size or numbers but filled with love.

The most important part of the season. Of any season.

Oakley knocked softly on the door before entering his apartment then stopped just inside the door. Priss had curled up on the couch and fallen asleep. It was later than he'd expected to join her, but the kids sensed the holiday excitement in the adults, and it had taken all three of them to get the babies to sleep.

He was officially off duty until the day after Christmas, even though he and Priscilla would be joining the family for Christmas dinner. Secretly, after the day he'd experienced with the over-stimulated triplets, he was glad to not have to be involved in early morning stockings.

Instead he planned an early morning sensual Santa wake-up call with the woman he loved. Easing onto the couch, he cradled Priscilla's head and carefully lifted her shoulders until he was able to position her head on his thigh. She blinked and smiled up at him. "What time is it?"

"After nine."

Her eyes drifted closed. "Don't let me sleep past ten."

Stroking soft curls from her forehead, he nodded, realized she couldn't see him, and said, "I'll make sure you're ready for your call."

"You can talk, too," she mumbled.

"I'll meet your family later. This time is for you."

"Mmm, okay."

They'd set up a video call with her folks and sister in Hawaii, trying to split the four hour time difference so she could watch her sister's kids open the gifts she'd sent along with her parents. He regretted she couldn't spend the day with the family she loved but hoped his love would be enough to fill the gap.

He'd chosen gifts for her with care. Especially the one that wasn't piled on the bookshelf. The gift he planned to give her in private.

The warmth of the room, the comfort and rightness of

Priscilla curled at his side relaxed him and his eyes drifted closed.

A timer rang. He grumbled then opened his eyes to Priss's smile. She held up the kitchen timer and shook it in front of his nose. "Good thing I didn't depend on you waking me up." She chuckled. "It's about time for my call."

He grabbed the hand holding the timer and drew her closer for a kiss. Before he deepened the contact, she twisted away. "Oh, no you don't. I'm not going to talk to my family with swollen lips. Not when you're not ready to meet them. No." She angled her face. "Here, you can kiss my cheek."

He lingered there, his lips barely brushing her smooth skin. Sitting back, he grumbled.

"Oh hush, you big baby," she said through her laughter. "If you're not going to be on the call, get out of here."

He stood. "I'm going. To bed. Alone."

She touched his arm. "I'm not going to cut my visit short, but it won't be forever. There's a tray on the kitchen counter. Would you take it to the bedroom with you?"

He managed a swift kiss to her luscious mouth then nodded and retreated to the kitchen where he found a wooden tray holding homemade festive cookies and candies, strawberries, and a small bottle of sparkling wine. A pair of stainless steel wine glasses were each wrapped with a strip of ribbon and tied with a huge bow.

Passing back through the living room, he lifted the tray in appreciation. Priss blew him a kiss and returned her attention to his laptop where the call was connecting.

He placed the tray on the dresser, changed into lounge pants and a tee shirt, and stole a piece of fudge, rearranging the rest of the candy to cover the empty space. From the back of his closet, he pulled out a small package and placed it on Priss's pillow. A special something he hoped would please and delight her.

Without knowing how long her call might last, he set a few candles around the room but placed the lighter beside the tray rather than igniting the flames. With only a dim glow from behind the cracked bathroom door to chase the darkness, he turned off the lights and sat on an over-stuffed chair to wait.

Soft lips brushed his forehead. "Come to bed, Oakley."

Blindly, he reached out and caught Priscilla's hand. "Sweetheart?"

"My family and I talked a long time. It's late and I need to be up early. Come to bed."

His mind was fuzzy. He hadn't meant to fall asleep. "The wine?"

Her low chuckle vibrated through him. "I put every-thing away. I need to sleep."

Silent, he followed her to the bed. Before lowering the sheets, she retrieved the small package. "What's this?"

"Merry Christmas. Open it."

"Can't I wait until morning? When I can appreciate it more?"

Unable to refuse her anything, and yawning widely, he took the small present and set it on the dresser.

Once in bed, he spooned her close and kissed her neck. "Good night, sweetheart."

CHAPTER TEN

"No. Oh, no. Let me up."

Oakley woke to Priscilla shoving at his arms and legs, her panicked cries piercing through his sleep addled brain. "What? What?"

"We didn't set the alarm. It's late. There's barely enough time to finish up my croquembouche."

"Croquem—what?"

She rolled from the bed and stood over him with her hands on her hips. Her wild, messy hair flowed around her head as she moved. "The special dessert I'm making for today. Oh, thank goodness I decided to make the puffs and pastry cream early."

He sat up then flopped back against the pillow. "Take a deep breath, sweetheart. It'll turn out fine."

Pausing, she gnawed on her lower lip. Oakley bit back a groan as his body responded with more than just morning interest. Blowing out a breath she seemed to collect her thoughts. "Okay. I can do this. No, *we* can do this. While I put the dessert together, you're going to have to make the brussels sprouts."

Covering his face with her pillow, he grumbled. "You know I don't cook."

The fragrance of her disappeared when she grabbed the pillow and tossed it to one side. "I'll be right there telling you what to do. It's easy. Please, I can't do this alone."

"I'll do my best."

She bent to kiss him. "Why don't you take a fast shower and I'll get started. Meet me in the kitchen as soon as you can."

When she turned, she was already counting things off on her fingers. Oakley sat on the edge of the bed. "Priscilla?"

"Yeah?" Her distracted response made him grin.

"Merry Christmas."

She froze then turned back to him with a soft smile. "Merry Christmas."

The kitchen was in more of a shambles than he'd ever seen when Priss cooked but she moved with sure grace and purpose. He was confident her fancy dessert would be a hit.

"What's behind your back?" she asked while she waved a towel over a rack of cooling, small, round pastries.

He set the gift he'd wanted to give her the previous evening on the counter. "Merry Christmas."

"I thought we were going to do personal gifts later."

"Then, too." He offered her an innocent expression.

"I don't have time."

"Please?"

The exasperation in her expression was forced as she

wiped her hands on the towel she'd tucked in the ties of her apron and with a smile, took the gift. "It's heavier than it looks."

Oakley perched on a barstool and bounced his heel against the floor. He hadn't realized how much her reaction meant to him. Of course, she had to be a person who unwrapped the ribbon and opened each taped seam of the package with precise care.

She glanced up at him. "Yeah, I know. Taking it slow increases the anticipation." Her lips twitched. "And drives the gift giver crazy."

Finally she folded the gilt paper, opened the box, pushed the tissue aside, and gasped.

Lips parted, she stared at Oakley for a long moment before gently pulling an antique snow globe from its tissue nest. Oakley studied her reactions as she slowly turned the globe upside down then righted it. Tiny bits of white snow swirled and floated through the globe before settling to the bottom.

"It's the most beautiful globe I've ever seen," she whispered.

Priss rounded the island to hold the globe so they could watch the snow dance through tiny pine trees and cover the roof of a log cabin. Painted light shown from the cabin windows and if he squinted just right, two small figures danced near a decorated Christmas tree. As if the detailed interior wasn't enough, the base was a tangle of dark metal fir branches, dotted with flaking white paint.

"When I saw this at Aunt Cora's, I knew this had to be yours. The start of your new collection."

She beamed at him, and her eyes sparkled. She sniffed then wiped at a stray tear with the back of her hand. "I have no words. Thank you. For this. For thinking of me. A new start. Yes. This is for a new start."

He thought she wanted to say more. Felt a deeper meaning than just her surface words. But before he had the time to think, she'd set the globe on the island and wrapped her arms around his neck.

"Thank you, Oakley. I…" Her kiss was fierce. Determined. Erotic. Maybe they could skip dinner and…

She stepped back way too soon, one hand flat against the rise and fall of her erratic breathing. "Oh, I wish…"

With a rough cough, he cleared the thick emotion from his throat. "Me, too."

She held his gaze a long moment then gave herself a shake and straightened. "All righty then. Get back to work. Ready, Oakley?"

He was more than ready, willing, and able for anything she'd suggest. Even… cooking. He nodded, stood, and moved the snow globe to a side counter.

Priss rubbed her palms together. "Okay, the first thing you need to do is…"

As nervous as she was to meet more of her employer's family and provide a labor intensive showpiece dessert, dinner had been relaxed and enjoyable. Oakley's first au gratin casserole was a success and a perfect complement to the potluck meal.

And her croquembouche—was perfect. The cream puffs still crispy, the spun caramel full of snap. The compliments had embarrassed her, but also confirmed her career decisions.

Now mid-afternoon, the adults lounged in front of the fireplace with cups of mulled cider. Oakley sat next to her, his legs stretched toward the fire. Ryder's pregnant sister, Bonnie and her red-haired husband, Konnor, had brought along their two miniature doxies, and the tired dogs had joined the triplets for a nap, curled together in a portable playpen. Lulled by the peaceful moment, Priss imagined this could be her life. She could easily become accustomed to the warmth and acceptance. No, she didn't have to imagine or dream. She already had. More than just an employee, she belonged here as a friend.

The realization startled her, and sensing her mood, Oakley rested their joined hands against his thigh and drew his thumb back and forth along her wrist. Deep in how the distraction sent tingles along her skin, she nearly missed when Vianna stood and said, "Time for some adult gift opening now."

Chet, Ryder's mom's partner joined Vianna at the tree. "I've had lots of Santa experience this year. You sit. I'll deliver."

Priss leaned forward to watch Bonnie open a hand-made baby journal. Bonnie stroked the cover then turned the volume so everyone could see the painting of a pastel rainbow on the cover. "Vianna, it's so beautiful. I was hesitant to get a baby book after I lost… now I've got a beautiful book to record everything for this one. For my rainbow baby. Thank you."

Ryder leaned toward Priss and said, "My wife creates every bit of her journals by hand. Sometimes she allows me to help with the paper. But the covers and binding are all her."

Both the talent, and the fact Vianna had time for such creativity with three active babies amazed Priss. She wasn't sure she'd be able to keep up. This underscored how important Oakley's presence was to the household.

Oakley's package also contained a thick journal, the cover adorned with a swirl of stars and distant galaxies.

"For your next bestseller," Vianna said.

"Perfect. There's already ideas perking in my brain. I'll capture them with this."

Then Chet handed Priss a brightly wrapped gift.

"Before you open that," Vianna started. "I need to tell you something."

Nodding, Priss set the gift in her lap and focused on Vianna.

"Besides being an artist—"

"Don't forget fabulous wife and mother," Ryder interrupted.

She rolled her eyes and returned her attention to Priss. "Like I was saying, I'm also a psychic medium. That means spirits often speak to me. Especially when they want to pass a message on to someone. And many times when I receive such a message, I'm compelled to create a journal around that person or message."

Priss wrinkled her brow. "I don't understand."

"Open your gift. I'll answer your questions then."

Hesitant with everyone's eyes on her, Priss carefully unwrapped the journal. There was nothing on the cover. She glanced at Vianna who grinned.

"That's the back, Priscilla. Turn it over."

Curious, Priss flipped the journal. And gasped. It was

like looking into her grandmother's face, with her trademark smile and twinkling pale eyes. With one finger, she traced the edge of the painting and bent closer. Behind the portrait hazy images of recipe cards seemed to dance across the cover.

"It's Gran-gran."

"Sweetheart?" Oakley touched her shoulder.

Priss lifted her head and glanced at each person watching before settling her gaze on Vianna. She'd never given much thought to people who claimed to talk to ghosts but had no reason to not believe Vianna did. "It's my grandmother, but you knew that."

Vianna nodded.

Fully accepting this strange truth, Priss asked, "She had something she wants me to know?"

"You had a notebook of handwritten recipes from her."

"Yes."

"That was nearly destroyed."

"Yes. My ex threw it into the fireplace. I was able to save most of them. I've been trying to recreate those that were partially burned up." The tears that normally stung her eyes when she thought of Gran-gran and the missing recipes didn't come. Instead, a comforting sensation wrapped around her like a warm quilt.

A distant, vague expression softened Vianna's face. "She's here."

"I... I feel her."

"She says, use the journal for her recipes. Then fill the rest of the pages with the new delights you create. Uh, yes, I remember..." Her expression cleared and she blinked. "Your grandmother did something with me that I'd never experienced. It was like automatic writing. She controlled my hand and on some of the pages in your journal, she wrote an ingredient, or technique, and even a specific pan. She say's you'll understand when you see them to help recreate what was taken from you."

Priss opened the journal to a random page. The word *juniper* was written in the corner. In her grandmother's distinctive handwriting. The word blurred as tears filled Priss's eyes. "Juniper berries. Of course. Vianna? Is she still here?"

With a gentle smile, Vianna nodded. "She's always with you, Priscilla. You can always talk to her, and she'll listen. Watch for signs that she's near. We can talk later if you want."

"Yes. I'd like that." Priss cradled the journal against her chest and lifted her gaze to a spot above the star topping the tall tree. "Thank you, Gran-gran. I love you."

Snapping from the fireplace drew her attention. A tiny bit of flame rose above the others and the faint whiff of juniper swirled through the room.

CHAPTER ELEVEN

*C*urled together on the couch in his living room, Oakley and Priss shared soft kisses and holiday memories. The day had been exhausting—just watching the triplets open and play with their gifts was enough to wear anyone out. And there'd been eight adults versus the three kids. He wished Grandma Zoe luck. She and Chet had taken the kids for an overnight.

Oakley had all he wanted right here in his arms. Their first Christmas together. But not really. The final gift of his admission of love was still to come. He was just waiting for the perfect moment.

They'd escaped to his rooms and opened their private gifts. They were still new together, so gifting hadn't been easy for him. He'd wanted everything perfect and doubted anything topped the snow globe. But she'd loved the antique spice tins and the modern cookbook she'd mentioned once in passing.

She'd given him a fountain pen, telling him all good writers needed a special pen for special words. She hadn't known about the journal, but the barrel of the pen swirled with matching colors to create an accidental set. If the pen was meant for special words, then he'd use it to write words of love to her.

He'd turned into a sappy fool in love. Didn't mind a bit.

"Be right back," he said and rose to take the empty cookie plate to the kitchen. He paused to peer out the window over the sink. The night was a dark velvet but falling snow glistened in the faint lights from the building.

He knew.

Grabbing their coats and boots from near the outside door, he strode back to the living room and tossed Priss's jacket over her head. "Let's go outside."

"It's night. Cold," she complained and shoved the jacket aside.

He sat and placed her boots next to her feet. After tugging his on and she hadn't moved, he glanced sideways at her. Questions danced in her eyes, but she couldn't hold a serious expression. "Why?"

He shrugged. "Because I want to. And it's Christmas."

"Not necessarily strong arguments, but okay."

At the door, he grabbed a scarf and twined it around her neck, tucking the ends under her jacket lapel. She arched one eyebrow but didn't say anything. Then he took her hand and led her outside.

They followed a shoveled path toward the back of the cabin and the building Vianna used as her art studio. He stopped and they turned to look back at the house. Light poured from the tall living room windows, and in the glow, Ryder and Vianna danced beside their Christmas tree.

Priss turned them away. "I'm not a voyeur. Why are we out here?"

Waving one hand through the air, Oakley said, "A cabin with lighted windows. Warmth and home and love radiating from inside. Snow falling and gathering on the trees and the already snowy ground."

Hoping she'd understand what he showed her, he paused. She reached out a mitten covered hand and caught a few snowflakes. After a quick glance back at the house, she drew in a sharp breath.

"This is just like in the snow globe. That perfect little winter scene is right here. Right now. Oh, thank you, Oakley. Thank you for insisting I see this."

She spun in a circle, and he caught her before she moved away, drawing her close and cupping her chin with his fingers.

"Ooh," she whispered breathlessly. "Your fingers are cold. Where are your gloves?"

This was his moment. He prayed it would become *their* moment. But nothing would happen unless he spoke the truth in his heart. "Priscilla Van, I love you."

"You said that once before. Then nothing. I thought, maybe…"

"I should have told you every day, every hour since. But I didn't take the risk—you never said anything. I could be just a companion for now. I didn't know. Don't know. I'm scared shitless you'll turn me away. Tonight, now, I need to know. I love you. Can you love me? If not today, then someday?"

He hated the weakness in his knees as he waited for her to say something. Anything. Wrapping her more tightly in his embrace he pressed his cheek to the top of her head. This was right. She belonged in his arms. She was his and his heart belonged to her.

Wiggling until she could press her hands against his chest, Priss shoved gently. She couldn't breathe. Not because he held her so tight. That was glorious. But because he loved her and now she could say the words she'd carried in her heart.

Finally able to lean back enough to see his face she studied the tight set of his lips and the hesitant questions in his eyes. Snowflakes landed on his dark lashes and beard. She used her teeth to pull off one of her mittens and held her palm against his cheek.

"I wanted to tell you that day, too. It was foolish to keep my mouth shut when I love you with every bit of my heart and soul. I love you, Oakley Fifer. Today." She kissed him. "Every someday we will ever have." Another kiss. "Forever."

After a long, searching look he brought their mouths together again. Time faded. The cold didn't matter. The snow could cover them, and she didn't care. She loved Oakley, and he returned that love a thousand times over.

Breathless, they drew apart. Oakley chuckled.

"What?"

Keeping his arm around her shoulder, he turned them toward the house. "We have an audience."

Shadowed by the lights behind them, Vianna and Ryder stood at the window. Ryder waved, gave what she assumed was a thumbs up, then gathered his wife close and danced away.

"That's a little embarrassing," Oakley said.

"Are you embarrassed by our love?" She forced away the painful possibility.

"Hell, no, sweetheart. I'll shout it from the highest mountain if you want. Uh, in the summer. After the snow melts. Although getting snowbound with you has definite possibilities. No, but you know Ryder. We're in for some teasing."

"I suppose. Oakley, I don't know how you did this."

"Did what?"

"Made this moment so perfect. First you gave me the snow globe. Then this experience, and now I feel like I'm inside the globe. And you love me."

"In this moment, and every single one to follow. Filled with snow, memories and holiday lights, this night is ours." He kissed the tip of her nose. "And you love me."

"In this moment. Forever." She brushed the snow from his hair. "Our first Christmas."

"Our first perfect snow globe Christmas."

DEAR READER

Thank you for reading. Telling stories is one of our greatest delights and we hope you enjoyed your time in Spencer. Readers like you spark the energy needed to tell these tales. Again, thank you.

The Aspen Gold books are independently published by the authors. We thank you for your support, and we take pride in giving you quality books and excellent stories. We're thankful you've chosen to follow us and be part of the AG community.

With today's world of vast reading choices, word of mouth is the best advertising. So please let others know about this book. Tell your friends, relatives, acquaintances, the book reading stranger on the bus. By sharing a good book, you may discover a new friend.

Reviews help readers discover and connect with new authors. Every review is important to us and is greatly appreciated. Please consider leaving an honest review of this book at your favorite review sites or at any or all of these places.

Amazon
Goodreads
Bookbub

THE ASPEN GOLD SERIES

Once upon a time a group of writer friends got the grandiose idea to create a continuity series. We threw ourselves into developing characters, fashioning families, dynamics and a setting, which evolved from one member's love of all things Colorado. We created character profiles, detailed maps, brainstormed titles and themes. We collected photos and researched. We proposed our idea to a few publishers and got no traction. So, after a time the contracted books came first, members came and went, and the project was set aside.

Years after the initial idea, we rallied again to write the stories, now hoping readers will feel the same intensity and appreciation for this project as we do. We welcome you to join these families, laugh in their good times and cry in their sad times, follow them as they solve mysteries, expose secrets, recover from their pasts, reach for their goals and, most importantly, as the residents of Spencer Colorado fall in love.

BE SURE TO FOLLOW ALL THE ASPEN GOLD
SERIES UPDATES AT:

Aspen Gold: The Series Website
https://www.aspengoldseries.com/

Aspen Gold Twitter
https://twitter.com/@gold_aspen

Aspen Gold: The Series on Facebook
https://www.facebook.com/AspenGoldSeries/

Never miss a release and all the news with our newsletter:
Rocky Mountain Rumors, the newsletter
https://www.subscribepage.com/n9n7p3

ASPEN GOLD BOOKS

Dancing In The Dark~Cheryl St.John
He had everything a man could want--except her forgiveness...

Call Me Mandy~Debra Hines
The last man she loved took everything from her...

Ryder's Heart~*lizzie starr
She can't allow secrets to steal love from her...

For Keeps~Barbara Gwen & *lizzie starr
Hiding the truth is like denying the sun...

Second Chances~Donna Kaye
She tried the fairy tale and the fairy tale didn't work...

Sleepin' Alone~Bernadette Jones
Every man is guilty of the good he did not do...

Stay A Little Longer~Bernadette Jones
Death wasn't frightening. Living scared the hell out of him...

Speechless~*lizzie starr
How many peonies does it take to get married?

Close to the Heart~Debra Hines
He'd raised her child as his own...

Finding Hope~Donna Kaye
Is the peace he's found too good to be true?

Fortunate Cookie~*lizzie starr
This woman... wearing frosting... and nothing else...

Lonely Eyes~Bernadette Jones
She'd come to the right place. He was the monster hunter.

Whisper My Name~Cheryl St.John
She was the girl behind the headlines

Gorgeous Scars~M.A. Jewell
The rodeo never prepared this cowboy for bodyguard duty.

Another Night Alone~Bernadette Jones
She'd had the courage to save her child. Can she do the same for herself?

Yesterday's Promise
Romantic short stories from the Aspen Gold Authors

Maybe I'm the One~Cheryl St.John
While adored by millions, her world has become very small

Just My Imagination~*lizzie starr
Will his magic heal her reality?

A Better Man~Bernadette Jones
Stripped of everything, her life threatened, she's forced to trust a stranger.

I Sorta Do~Cheryl St.John
Her heart is under lock and key...his knock is irresistible

Christmas Promises
Holiday short stories from Aspen Gold

Coming Soon

Trust Me~Donna Kaye
Anything For Love~*lizzie starr
How To Be A Heartbreaker~Cheryl St.John
Serendipity~Debra Hines
Right Here Waiting~Bernadette Jones

CONNECT WITH THE AUTHORS

Cheryl St.John
email message sign up:
http://eepurl.com/bqCji9
Goodreads:
https://www.goodreads.com/author/show/24516.
Cheryl_St_John
Linktree:
https://linktr.ee/CherylStJ

Bernadette Jones
Website:
www.bernadettejones.com
Email messaging sign up:
https://www.bernadettejones.com/newsletters
Goodreads:
https://www.goodreads.com/author/show/19728724.
Bernadette_Jones

*lizzie starr
Website:
www.lizziestarr.com
Linktree:
https://linktr.ee/lizziestarr
Email Messaging sign up:
https://landing.mailerlite.com/webforms/landing/
o9q4q4